# SINGAPORE NOIR

### EDITED BY CHERYL LU-LIEN TAN

AKASHIC
BOOKS

This collection is comprised of works of fiction. All names, characters, places, and incidents are the product of the authors' imaginations. Any resemblance to real events or persons, living or dead, is entirely coincidental.

Series concept by Tim McLoughlin and Johnny Temple
Singapore map by Aaron Petrovich

Published by Akashic Books
©2014 Akashic Books

ISBN-13: 978-1-61775-235-3
Library of Congress Control Number: 2013956777

Akashic Books
PO Box 1456
New York, NY 10009
info@akashicbooks.com
www.akashicbooks.com

*For Cynthia Wong Mee Tin,*
*who taught me to love a good noir story*

# ALSO IN THE AKASHIC NOIR SERIES

**PHOENIX NOIR**, edited by PATRICK MILLIKIN
**PITTSBURGH NOIR**, edited by KATHLEEN GEORGE
**PORTLAND NOIR**, edited by KEVIN SAMPSELL
**QUEENS NOIR**, edited by ROBERT KNIGHTLY
**RICHMOND NOIR**, edited by ANDREW BLOSSOM, BRIAN CASTLEBERRY & TOM DE HAVEN
**ROME NOIR** (ITALY), edited by CHIARA STANGALINO & MAXIM JAKUBOWSKI
**SAN DIEGO NOIR**, edited by MARYELIZABETH HART
**SAN FRANCISCO NOIR**, edited by PETER MARAVELIS
**SAN FRANCISCO NOIR 2: THE CLASSICS**, edited by PETER MARAVELIS
**SEATTLE NOIR**, edited by CURT COLBERT
**STATEN ISLAND NOIR**, edited by PATRICIA SMITH
**ST. PETERSBURG NOIR** (RUSSIA), edited by NATALIA SMIRNOVA & JULIA GOUMEN
**TORONTO NOIR** (CANADA), edited by JANINE ARMIN & NATHANIEL G. MOORE
**TRINIDAD NOIR** (TRINIDAD & TOBAGO), edited by LISA ALLEN-AGOSTINI & JEANNE MASON
**TWIN CITIES NOIR**, edited by JULIE SCHAPER & STEVEN HORWITZ
**USA NOIR**, edited by JOHNNY TEMPLE
**VENICE NOIR** (ITALY), edited by MAXIM JAKUBOWSKI
**WALL STREET NOIR**, edited by PETER SPIEGELMAN

# FORTHCOMING

**ADDIS ABABA NOIR** (ETHIOPIA), edited by MAAZA MENGISTE
**BAGHDAD NOIR** (IRAQ), edited by SAMUEL SHIMON
**BEIRUT NOIR** (LEBANON), edited by IMAN HUMAYDAN
**BELFAST NOIR** (NORTHERN IRELAND), edited by ADRIAN McKINTY & STUART NEVILLE
**BOGOTÁ NOIR** (COLOMBIA), edited by ANDREA MONTEJO
**CHICAGO NOIR 2: THE CLASSICS**, edited by JOE MENO
**HELSINKI NOIR** (FINLAND), edited by JAMES THOMPSON
**JERUSALEM NOIR**, edited by DROR MISHANI
**LAGOS NOIR** (NIGERIA), edited by CHRIS ABANI
**MARSEILLE NOIR** (FRANCE), edited by CÉDRIC FABRE
**MEMPHIS NOIR**, edited by LAUREEN P. CANTWELL & LEONARD GILL
**MISSISSIPPI NOIR**, edited by TOM FRANKLIN
**NEW ORLEANS NOIR 2: THE CLASSICS**, edited by JULIE SMITH
**PRISON NOIR**, edited by JOYCE CAROL OATES
**PROVIDENCE NOIR**, edited by ANN HOOD
**RIO NOIR** (BRAZIL), edited by TONY BELLOTTO
**SAN JUAN NOIR** (PUERTO RICO), edited by MAYRA SANTOS-FEBRES
**SEOUL NOIR** (KOREA), edited by BS PUBLISHING CO.
**ST. LOUIS NOIR**, edited by SCOTT PHILLIPS
**STOCKHOLM NOIR** (SWEDEN), edited by NATHAN LARSON & CARL-MICHAEL EDENBORG
**TEHRAN NOIR** (IRAN), edited by SALAR ABDOH
**TEL AVIV NOIR** (ISRAEL), edited by ETGAR KERET & ASSAF GAVRON
**ZAGREB NOIR** (CROATIA), edited by IVAN SRŠEN

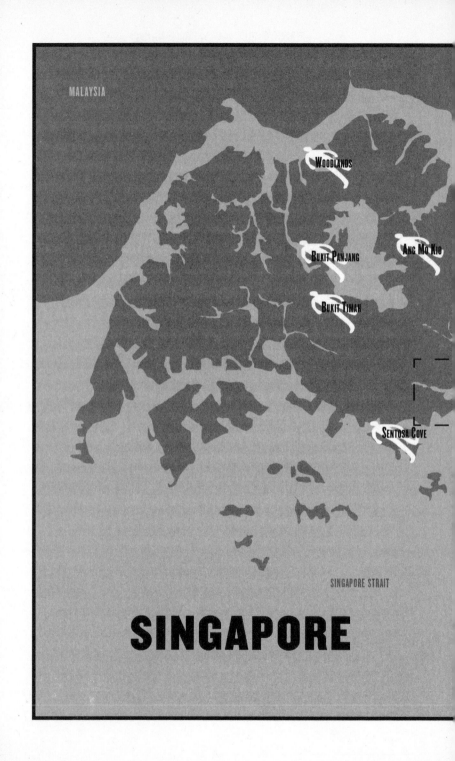

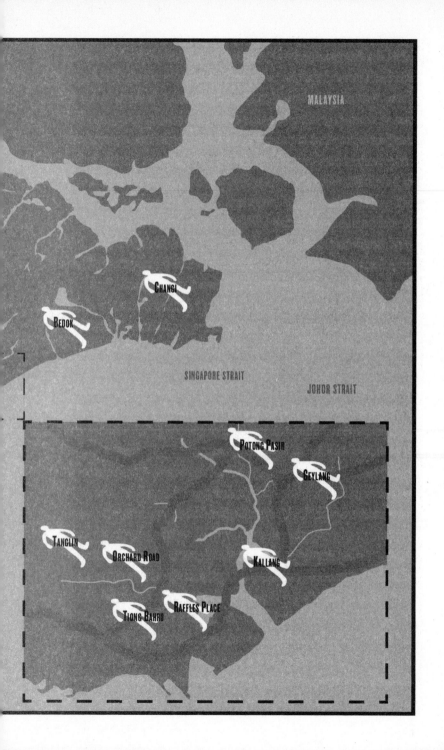

# TABLE OF CONTENTS

# INTRODUCTION
## The Sultry City-State

Say *Singapore* to anyone and you'll likely hear one of a few words: Caning. Fines. Chewing gum.

For much of the West, the narrative of Singapore—a modern Southeast Asian city-state perched on an island on the tip of the Malay Peninsula—has been marked largely by its government's strict laws and unwavering enforcement of them.

In 1994, American teenager Michael Fay was famously sentenced to six strokes of the cane after a series of car vandalisms in Singapore. Just the year before in a cover story for *Wired* magazine, William Gibson criticized the country, calling it constrained and humorless, saying "conformity here is the prime directive."

"Imagine an Asian version of Zurich operating as an offshore capsule at the foot of Malaysia," Gibson wrote, "an affluent microcosm whose citizens inhabit something that feels like, well, Disneyland. Disneyland with the death penalty."

As much as I understand these outside viewpoints, I have always lamented that the quirky and dark complexities of my native country's culture rarely seem to make it past its borders. The Singapore in which I was born and spent most of my first eighteen years was safe, yes—so safe that I could wander its city streets without fear at two in the morning as a teenage girl. And its general cleanliness is unrivaled—even now, I feel sometimes that one could, in fact, eat off the streets.

Beneath that sparkling veneer, however, is a country teeming with shadows. For starters, it has not just one but several red-light districts. There's the large designated area, Geylang, which is filled with dozens of narrow lanes and alleys where one can find prewar houses festooned with red lights and prostitutes pacing along blocks, clustered almost as you would find them in a department store—older Indian girls on this end, mainland Chinese sirens a few alleys over, and so forth.

And beyond Geylang, there are neighborhoods where one knows to go for Thai, Vietnamese, Filipina, and other girls. (Paul Theroux, in fact, set his 1973 novel *Saint Jack* amid the bordellos and triads of Singapore—a tale turned into a 1979 film directed by Peter Bogdanovich, which was banned in Singapore for its unsavory content.)

Gambling and its many fallouts have always been an issue in this country, one that was pockmarked with illegal gambling dens long before Las Vegas Sands poured about $6.5 billion into building a casino in the heart of Singapore in 2011.

And then there are the ghosts. Singaporeans love nothing better than to tell a good gory tale. And there are many. When I was a child, each time we passed a particular church along Orchard Road, Singapore's main shopping street, someone would always whisper: "Curry." In 1987, police arrested a woman and her three brothers, charging them with killing her husband, chopping him up, and turning his remains into curry, skull and all, in the church caretaker's kitchen. While the charges were later dropped due to insufficient evidence, the story remains widely enjoyed. (Though no one I know has dared to have Sunday supper at that church since.)

It could be said that of course noir is alive in a country built on the shoulders of entrepreneurs and rebels. My father likes to note that many of the ethnic Chinese in Singapore are descendents of fortune-seekers from the coast of Southeastern China, an area known, according to him, for "smugglers, pirates, and really good businessmen."

Singapore began humbly, as a knot of tropical Malay fishing villages located near the equator. Its name comes from Sang Nila Utama, a Sumatran prince who called it Singapura—*lion city* in Sanskrit—after spotting a frightening beast on its shores while hunting which his men told him was a lion. He officially founded Singapore in 1324, believing the lion sighting to be a good omen.

But it was only in 1819 that the island truly started growing—British statesman Sir Stamford Raffles sailed to its shores and established a military post and trading port there. Traders from India, China, and all over Southeast Asia began arriving, then settling. The country gained its independence in 1965 with Lee Kuan Yew, the founder of modern Singapore, serving as its prime minister until 1990.

Singapore in recent years has been in the spotlight once again—this time for its "tiger" economy, one that has made this 250-square-mile country one of the wealthiest in the world. (According to a 2013 *Wall Street Journal* story, the country had 188,000 millionaire households in 2011—which translates into one in six homes having disposable private wealth of at least one million dollars.) It has become one of the major safe havens for the rich to park their wealth; Facebook cofounder Eduardo Saverin made international headlines in 2012 when he renounced his US citizenship and became Singaporean. The country now boasts a bar that sells a $26,000 cocktail.

Despite recent changes, Singapore is still an Asian polyglot—its five million population is about 75 percent Chinese in ethnicity, 13 percent Malay, 8 percent Indian, among others, which is what accounts for its distinct patois, Singlish. You'll see some of it in the stories before you—this local pidgin is a combination of English, Malay, and a hodge-podge of Chinese dialects. Conversations may sound bizarre sometimes because although the words are in English, the sentence structure used may be Malay or Mandarin. The word *lah* is tacked onto most sentences for inflection—something like *okay* or *man* in American slang.

And its stories remain. The rich stories that attracted literary lions W. Somerset Maugham and Rudyard Kipling to hold court at the Raffles Hotel (where the Singapore Sling was created) are still sprinkled throughout its neighborhoods. And in the following pages, you'll get the chance to discover some of them.

British novelist Lawrence Osborne takes us along on a romantic, sinister romp in Geylang, while mystery writer extraordinaire S.J. Rozan explores the darkness that lurks in the cookie-cutter blandness of suburban expat Singapore. Hong Kong–based Nury Vittachi, creator of the Feng Shui Detective series, gives us a breathless fast-paced chase along glitzy Orchard Road, and American food writer Monica Bhide, in her fiction debut, weaves a heart-tugging tale of a boy and his mother.

You'll find stories from some of the best contemporary writers in Singapore—three of them winners of the Singapore Literature Prize, essentially the country's Pulitzer: Simon Tay, writing as Donald Tee Quee Ho, tells the story of a hardboiled detective who inadvertently wends his way into the underbelly of organized crime, Colin Cheong shows us a surprising side to the country's ubiquitous cheerful "taxi uncle," while Suchen Christine Lim spins a wistful tale of a Chinese temple medium whose past resurges to haunt her.

Colin Goh, a beloved Singaporean satirist, filmmaker, and cartoonist, delves into the seedy side of Raffles Place, the country's deep-pocketed financial district, while award-winning playwright Damon Chua gives us a tour of life after dark near the Malaysian border. Maids—who regularly make the news in Singapore due to reports of abominable maid abuse—are the protagonists in stories by Dave Chua and Johann S. Lee, one of Singapore's first openly gay writers.

Black magic is threaded through the yarn by Ovidia Yu, one of Singapore's leading and most prolific playwrights. And, of course, the enigmatic female figure, so alluring and so irresistible, is the key in Philip Jeyaretnam's elegant story. As for mine, I chose a setting close to my heart—the *kelongs*, or old fisheries on stilts, that once dotted the waters of Singapore but are gradually disappearing.

I have a deep sense of romance about these *kelongs*, along with the many other settings, characters, nuances, and quirks that you'll see in these stories. They're intense, inky, nebulous. There is evil, sadness, a foreboding. And liars, cheaters, the valiant abound.

This is a Singapore rarely explored in Western literature— until now. No Disneyland here; but there is a death penalty.

*Cheryl Lu-Lien Tan*
*March 2014*

# PART I

*Sirens*

# LAST TIME

BY COLIN GOH

*Raffles Place*

L ast time.

That's how Singaporeans say both "on a previous occasion" and "in the old days." As in, "Last time I saw her, she was wearing an emerald-green Moschino dress that accentuated her clavicle," as well as, "Last time, Singapore lawyers also used to wear wigs."

There's a photo of me wearing a wig on my desk at the firm. It's made of white horsehair, fringed with several rows of frizzy curls (the wig, not the photo). I'm also wearing a black robe with wide, open sleeves and a sort of flap over the left shoulder, the garb of an English barrister.

It's made by Ede & Ravenscroft, I said, handing her her tea. They're the queen's robe makers.

"You graduated in England?" She blew lightly on the tea before taking a sip. I'd left the door of my office open and could feel the eyes of the rest of the firm searing into the back of my neck.

No, I laughed. I had the picture taken during a holiday in England just before my final year at the National University of Singapore's law school. I'd been visiting friends who were graduating as barristers and thought it fun to get myself snapped in their ridiculous getup as well.

She raised an eyebrow.

It's ridiculous, I said, shaking my head. We stopped being

a colony over forty years ago, but Singaporeans who study law in Britain are still in thrall to the "tradition." (In hindsight, I am annoyed that I felt compelled to illustrate this observation by making quotation marks with my fingers.) I guess it's an understandable impulse, I continued, like visiting Disneyland and buying a souvenir T-shirt. But they soon learn we have to be who we are.

As she lowered her cup, my eyes followed the lipstick she'd left on the rim. The Singapore legal profession did away with wigs ages ago, I added. They're simply too hot for our tropical climate. In Singapore, pragmatism invariably trumps sentiment.

"But you still wear suits," she replied, picking up the photo frame and turning it over slowly. She ran a long, tapered finger over some lettering on the frame's back. "Made in China," she smiled, placing the photo back on my desk.

I remember my scalp tingling. It's funny the details that stick in your head.

"Last time, this all used to be the sea," our driver said, motioning with his hand as we headed down Marina Boulevard toward the Sands.

She didn't say a word, but her gaze was clearly fixed on the casino's dolmen-like silhouette.

I adjusted my tie and said, People say it looks like . . . and here I fumbled. I didn't know what Stonehenge was in Mandarin, so I just said it in English.

"What's that?" she asked, without looking away from the window.

A very ancient monument in England, I said. A group of stones that archaeologists think was a burial ground of some sort.

"You know too much about England." She leaned back in

her seat and reached over to pat my jaw. "You should get to know China more. You're Chinese, after all."

I'd like that, I said softly. Through the rearview mirror, I saw the driver waggle his eyebrows at me.

The last time I saw the Comrade was in the casino's main theater, on the night of her final performance. I was in the back row, tapping away absently at my iPad as she went through her routine of mic checks and lighting cues. A Facebook message came in with a photo of some of my fellow junior associates raising their middle fingers at me. *Bastard gets to bill for spending time with her,* ran a comment. *What does that make him?*

I smiled and looked up to see her waving at me. I waved back, and then realized she was actually waving to someone else behind me. Feebly lowering my hand, I turned around to see the Comrade lolloping down the stairs in a way that might have been comical except for the ashen look on his face.

I shot up and began shimmying toward the aisle, but was stopped by a grim-looking Mr. Chong, who'd appeared at the head of the row of seats. "Better stay here," he said. He was my boss, so I did.

Meanwhile, the Comrade had already stormed onto the stage, where he'd begun barking at her in his impenetrable Beifang accent. Clearly bewildered, she reached out to touch him, but he brushed her hand away and began stabbing an accusatory finger at her. From my vantage point, I couldn't make out their exchange, but she was now pleading with him. And when she tried to pull him closer, he struck her across the face.

I immediately bolted from Mr. Chong's side. By the time I reached the stage, two of her security detail had pinned the Comrade to the floor. He didn't put up a struggle; he seemed to know he had crossed a line. Her entourage was now swarming around her, but she waved them away with one hand, the other cradling her cheek. She wasn't crying. In fact, it was the Comrade who was whimpering, fat tears streaming down his Botoxed face.

Shall I call the police? I held up my phone as I drew closer to her.

She whipped her head around, a brief yet intense flicker in her eyes that jolted me. Then she fell into my arms with a shudder. "No," she whispered. As I held her close, I could see, past her perfect shoulder, Mr. Chong leaning over the orchestra pit, rubbing his jaw.

The first time I was in Beijing, I realized I wasn't truly Chinese after all.

Ethnically, perhaps. My family could trace its lineage to the Daoguang Emperor of the Qing Dynasty, and I spoke Mandarin fluently enough that I'd anchored my secondary school's Chinese debating team, a detail Mr. Chong felt necessary to invoke while explaining why he was dispatching me to the PRC to handle some matters for the Comrade.

Culturally, though, I had more in common with the American attorneys seated across from me at the conference table. Over dinner, we merrily shot the breeze over *Seinfeld*, *Star Wars*, and the byzantine narratives of *the X-Men* while the Comrade and his comrades downed their Château Lafite-Rothschild with Sprite.

But when she walked into the private dining room, I felt a ripple inside me, as if my ancestors had cast a plumb line into the well of my soul.

I'd heard the rumors about her and the Comrade, mostly from my secretary, who follows these things. But I never got the fuss, since I didn't know who she was. I loathe Mandopop, which I find either derivative or treacly or both, and a star-let canoodling with a businessman with party connections just wasn't news.

But seeing the Comrade drape his nicotine-stained fingers over her knee, a spider crouched atop a magnolia blossom, I was surprised to feel something akin to anger. I was just as sur-prised to find myself afterward at a music store in the Gulou district buying her entire back catalog.

Initially, I'd chalked it up to being starstruck, but the crush's load never ebbed. For some unfathomable reason, she attended almost every meeting I had with the Comrade. In fact, she asked almost all the questions while he mostly nodded as he puffed on one Double Happiness cigarette after another.

You should perform in Singapore, I said to her the first time we were alone together. Providentially, the Comrade had dashed out of the room, clutching his guts and cursing last night's lamb hotpot. She smiled and said she'd been planning a few dates, probably at one of the casinos. I told her that I'd like to take her to some of Singapore's best eating spots, but was afraid she'd be mobbed.

"Are Singaporeans like that?" She looked at me quizzically. "I thought you were all very restrained and law-abiding."

It depends on the subject, I replied. We've famously come to blows over Hello Kitty giveaways at McDonald's. And you sing much better than Hello Kitty, I grinned, since you have a mouth.

She laughed at this and said, "You must protect me, then." I willed myself not to blush.

Your first time in Singapore and even more people turned up to greet you than for Prince William and Kate Middleton, I felt proud to tell her.

"You mean you'd expect more Singaporeans would turn up for their former colonial masters?" She interlaced her fingers and stretched out her arms.

The bellboy patted her luggage and bowed. He didn't even look at me as he accepted my tip. His gaze was fixed firmly on her as she leaned against the glass window of her hotel suite, the evening sun glinting off her jewelry, transforming her into a literal star.

Mainland Chinese aren't exactly Singaporeans' favorite immigrants at the moment, I explained as I shut the door. They feel the working class are taking away the low-end jobs while the upper class are driving up prices. (I recalled the scene earlier that day of the Comrade in the conference room at my firm, signing purchase after purchase of property and stock, pausing every so often to spew a gob of phlegm into the wastepaper basket, and wondered into which class I would place him.)

But you're different, I added quickly. You have real talent. Most Singaporeans would consider it an honor if you became a citizen.

"Most?" she laughed, looking right into me. As she moved away from the window, she reached back to unclasp her diamond necklace. "A gift from the Comrade," she said. As was almost everything else she was wearing.

He must be very grateful to have you, I said.

"More grateful that I've denied our relationship to the press, the Party, everyone." She sat down at the dresser and laid the necklace in a velvet-lined metal box. "But most especially his wife." She let out a small girlish giggle.

You could have anyone, I blurted. What do you see in him?

Instantly, I wished I could have withdrawn my question. I'm sorry, I stammered. I had no right to ask.

She removed her watch, the gems encrusting its face sparkling at me, and placed it in the box along with the other baubles. "He needs me," she said. "And I need him."

I nodded, kicking myself. How could I think our encounters over the past year—on trips to attend to her lover, at that—had somehow earned me any degree of intimacy? I wondered if she would tell the Comrade. I could lose my job.

You should rest before your interview tomorrow, I said, backing toward the door. I'll be here at eight to take you to the TV station.

"Before you go," she said, "please help me put this in the safe." She held out the box of jewelry.

I moved toward her to take it, and she grabbed my wrist.

"Are you disappointed?" she asked.

I have no right, I replied, blood roaring in my ears.

"That's the second time you've brought up 'rights.' Rights have nothing to do with anything. Is that the lawyer in you talking? Or the Singaporean?" She pulled me down and whispered in my ear, "Sometimes we do things out of need, and sometimes just because we want to."

As she placed her lips on mine, I realized I couldn't remember the last time I'd made love. There were adolescent fumblings, but love . . . This. This might have been the first time.

The last time I'd seen a dead body was a drowning as well.

I was on holiday in Port Dickson with my family, and I'd scurried to the front of a crowd gathered at the beach, thinking they'd landed some fish, or maybe a turtle. Instead there was a drowned boy, his body sallow and stiff as a candle, save for his wrinkled hands and feet. It was the first thing that came to my mind when I saw the Comrade's pallid, distended corpse on the mortuary gurney.

She identified him to the police investigator with a single, solemn nod. There were no tears.

Outside in the hall, Mr. Chong told us he was confident the coroner would rule the death an accident. In the harsh fluorescent light, she shook her head and said, "No, he died of a broken heart." I put an arm around her shoulder, and told her she was very kind.

In the morning, I would brief her public relations firm to tell the press that she was "shocked and dismayed by the tragedy," but would not be canceling the upcoming dates of her Southeast Asian tour. In fact, she would dedicate a song to her "childhood friend."

I would go on to share with them only the facts: the Comrade's body was found floating on a stretch of the Singapore River not far from the bars on Boat Quay, where he had been witnessed drinking heavily. He had been under a lot of stress since the Commercial Affairs Department had begun investigating him for possible money-laundering offenses, allegations which he had strenuously denied.

I would not share with them, or her, or Mr. Chong, just how the CAD had come to build their case.

The last time I saw her perform in China, it was a multimedia extravaganza involving giant props, a multitude of costume changes, and an army of backup singers, dancers, and engineers.

Her premiere in Singapore was a pared-down affair, just a chamber orchestra and her voice—a velvety, almost husky instrument that occasionally swelled into a melismatic yodel to devastating effect. On that first night, I felt as if my senses had been fully activated for the first time. I started becoming aware of the smallest details.

The dust motes dancing in the spotlight above her.

The way her upper lip arched when she reached for the high notes.

The box that the Comrade bore away from her dressing room after the concert, and how it looked exactly like the one in which she had stashed his gifts of jewelry.

The fact that I never saw her wear a gift from him more than once.

The first time I'd actually taken a proper look at the paperwork was in the wee hours of the morning after her opening night.

As a lowly first-year associate, the main job Mr. Chong had given me was to ensure that the Comrade signed the correct documents in the correct places, the correct way, and by the correct time, and in a manner that caused him the least annoyance. It was more than a full-time occupation, but it involved relatively little legal analysis on my part, which was, frankly, fine by me. All along, I'd assumed the documents contained standard boilerplate culled from hoary precedents anyway. And they did.

But even after over a year of flying to and from Beijing, I didn't really know the extent or substance of the Comrade's business. There were various corporations with bizarre relationships, some of which had been in operation for years without any record of financial transactions. There were also multiple wire transfers between multiple accounts in multiple names in multiple countries, and subsidiaries purchasing everything from real estate to antiques to art to yachts to jewelry.

I'd just presumed it was all the usual rich-guy stuff. You know. Like keeping a mistress.

A mistress who could fly out of countries wearing expensive trinkets without attracting scrutiny from customs officials.

Trinkets that could then be resold or exchanged for amounts that might not reflect their true market value.

* * *

"Last time, money-laundering laws here covered just drugs," said Inspector Chia, almost apologetically. "Now we're more *neow*." I forced a smile at his use of the almost onomatopoeic Hokkien term for *finicky*.

The Comrade hadn't been seen for three days, since his outburst at the theater, and a warrant had been issued for his arrest.

I wasn't sure whether the authorities had been motivated by public relations considerations in calling her in for questioning only after her final performance in Singapore, but it was a lucky thing. Her voice was hoarse from continually breaking down in shocked response to revelation after revelation about the Comrade's true objectives.

Thinking back on it, it was probably her finest performance. The naïve waif, the convenient pawn of a savvy and callous mobster, the fairy gulled by a troll. A tale whose eternality could still resonate within the heart of the most hardened investigator.

Never mind a foolhardy young lawyer.

Tonight was the last time I would ever see her.

I thought that ratting out the Comrade would clear my path to her, but instead, my professional excuse for being with her had expired along with him. In fact, having to clear up the mess he'd left behind and the firm's possible abetment in his affairs necessitated my staying behind while she departed for the next stop on her tour. The CAD wouldn't let me leave with her even if I'd wanted to.

But I did.

But I also wanted to hear her say she'd like me to.

But she remained silent as we stood side by side, gazing at the computerized sculpture at Changi Airport.

I meant well, I said eventually.

"I know," she replied, her eyes hidden from me behind a large pair of sunglasses.

He was using you.

She said nothing, only turning to touch me on the cheek one final time.

And then she was gone, hustled off by her minders through to immigration and beyond.

Behind me, the sculpture's 1,216 silver raindrops flowed, languidly taking the shape of airplanes, kites, a flock of birds, a rondeau in mercury.

But all I could see were tears.

I wished I'd made the time last longer, especially since everything was now speeding by me in a blur.

But with the velocity came clarity.

Mr. Chong had entered my office brandishing a bottle. "It's been a rough few weeks," he said, closing the door, which should have struck me as odd, since we were the only two people working late.

"I thought you were from NUS Law?" he said, tipping his chin toward the photo of me in my wig and gown as he handed me a glass.

After the burn of the first sip had subsided, I repeated the same story I'd told her. I also pointed out the frame's *Made in China* label.

"They make everything now," he sighed as he poured me a refill. "Have you heard from her at all?"

I shook my head. He perched himself on the edge of my desk and told me he appreciated all my hard work. Then he raised a toast.

This time, I felt its sting between my eyes.

"I thought all that time in China would have trained you better!" he laughed.

I tried to give a thumbs-up, but felt a gurgle rise from my stomach to my throat. I lurched for the wastepaper basket, and emptied my guts into it.

Mr. Chong patted me on the back as I heaved. "Some fresh air will do you good." He opened a window, then led me toward it.

The warm night air blew in from across the marina. I could see the casino lights winking at me. For some reason, I felt compelled to ask aloud: What's *Stonehenge* in Chinese?

Mr. Chong gave me a puzzled look. Then he pushed my head further out the window. "Breathe deeper."

I closed my eyes and inhaled. There was an acrid mix of oil and something fermented in my nostrils. I could also feel Mr. Chong place one hand on my back, and another on my leg.

And then heave me up and push me out into the empty air.

As the wind rushed through me, my head began to clear. Narratives coalesced, and my fall became a journey of wonder.

I wondered what Mr. Chong would be doing now. Would he be placing the vodka bottle strategically on my desk? Perhaps nestled amongst some incriminating documents? Would he be telling the cops he had no idea that all this time I was in China, I was doing all this other secret stuff for the Comrade? Would he have drafted a suicide note saying I'd jumped for fear of the disgrace that would come with prosecution and disbarment? Or because of a broken heart?

Of course, I also began to wonder about the Comrade's accidental end. And whether she'd been his pawn, or he'd been hers. And who Mr. Chong's true client was.

I wondered what made me fall for her in the first place. I wondered about the cliché of the Singaporean beguiled by the China girl. I wondered if the fascination stemmed from blood, some dimly remembered or imagined bond. I wondered what my parents would think of their dutiful Chinese son who could never be Chinese enough.

I wondered if it really mattered in the end.

I wondered if I'd really mattered in the end.

I fought to keep my eyes open in those final moments, to catch the glass and steel, the glittering lights, the dolmen in the distance, the history and future, all whirring by like the reels on a slot machine.

One last time.

# DETECTIVE IN A CITY WITH NO CRIME

BY SIMON TAY WRITING AS DONALD TEE QUEE HO

*Tanglin*

### 1. DOISNEAU NOIR

This afternoon, I ride up the elevator of one of the most expensive and desired apartments in the country, a man in office clothes, my sharp jaw, the blue tie with brown stripes that you gave me hanging from my throat with my prominent Adam's apple. When the door opens, you are there in your work clothes—a severe gray suit with a white frilled blouse. Just back, taking off your black Ferragamo stilettos in the alcove before going into the living room, one stockinged leg off the ground, one slim arm pressed to the doorframe to steady yourself. You are surprised.

I reach for you, and you struggle to keep balance. I push you to your knees. I unzip. You peer up at me, wordless, your eyes large and bright.

There, at the alcove outside your apartment, one thin door—not fully shut—separates us from the corridor and the people walking past. When you hesitate, I put my hands at the back of your head and push your face forward. Your lips part.

We are lovers. We have done this before. But in bed, close and intimate as a kiss. Now you are on your knees, and I stand above you, commanding. Both of us fully clothed, just back from a world of mundane meetings and To-Do lists. And I am forcing myself into your mouth, deep, and thrusting, so my dangling belt jangles, slapping the side of your fine brow.

A couple kissing, for a moment lost to all but this passion even as passersby are rushing to and fro, are framed in Doisneau's famous photograph in the streets of Paris.

I look at your large clear eyes, your beautiful face, supplicant to this unseemly act, in this barely concealed space. I will remember this image as clearly as any photograph. I think this. Then I come.

In spurts. Into your mouth, across your open lips and your fair cheeks, on your fine nose, and into the deep valley of your eyes that blink instinctively.

You smile and you put me back into your mouth, cleansing me completely with your tongue. I tremble and you smile again. Then you tilt your head back and swallow. Your hand comes up as if to ask a question in a seminar, and your elegant fingers trace and gather the sticky ribbons from your face and, like a sweet child messy with chocolate, you lick each finger.

I sigh, exhaling all the air of too many air-conditioned meeting rooms where nothing is really discussed or decided, of all the hours between the time we were last together and now. I reach into my pocket for my iPhone and snap a shot of you. Then I offer you a handkerchief with my embroidered initials to clean the remnants of the mess.

"Hullo, darling," you say, and smile pleasantly as if seeing me for the first time. "How was your day?"

## 2. GUILTY WITHOUT CRIME

I am a detective in a city that, they say, has no crime. I am a lover in a city that—let's not pretend—has no art. I am cleaning my gun. I can do this blindfolded while listening to Fauré but not Stravinsky. I find the latter too unsettling, jumpy.

I lay the gun parts on a white cloth, clean each bit, and

then put them back together with maximum speed and care, whir the chamber, squeeze back the trigger on the empty chamber: I need to be sure the weapon will work when I need it.

Then I do push-ups. Three batches of thirty, thirty and then a long forty. I take my time, and do them until my arms burn and tremble. Then I go to the bar installed in the doorway and do pull-ups until I can do no more, until my hands cannot even hold onto the bar. This is my routine.

I am forty-one now. I was strong when I was young and used to assume that I would always be fit. Now I make no assumptions.

After I cool down, I shower and eat dinner. A meal of rice, *tauhu* for protein, and vegetables. A bit of soya sauce and chili on the side, and a touch of garlic on the veg but otherwise plain, and clean. Eating alone, food is fuel to keep me going. I eat it slowly, munching deliberately, not to savor the taste but for better digestion; spoon after spoon, like other people swallow vitamin supplements.

I think back about what I have seen during the day. I let my mind still and find its focus, until I see the events so clearly that I can hear all of what anyone said, even the low growl of that Maserati leaving the gates of the condo and then that man in austere black and gray walking in leather soles, *click-clack*, in the corridor. And then I can smell the curbside grass, newly cut by the two Bangladeshi workers in orange overalls, and the whirling grass trimmers, and the scent of frying oil from the kitchen of the café near the entrance to the Botanic Gardens. Then I jot notes down in my black journal, with my Namiki fountain pen.

I have done this every evening since before I can remember—albeit until recently with a humbler pen and journal.

I do this because, even if others do not realize it as they go about their business, rushing, waiting, doing everyday things, these are stories of the many people in this city that, they say, has no crime and really is without art. There are tales of crime, of sex, and even—most disturbing—of a kind of love.

Mine—ours—is one such story.

Let me relieve us from the very start of a popular misconception about this city: it is not illegal here to think of sex, nor to have sex, or indeed to pay for it.

True, the state is a nanny and the bureaucracy does not know how to let a person live without rules, and so they reduce life to a schedule of permits and licenses to be applied and paid for. They have allowed the seediness and confined it to certain quarters. The upper class are garrisoned with their respectability in other areas, all with rising real estate values. The government assumes the soul is a street that can be swept clean, a garden where order can be established—especially here in the suburbs of the wealthy, next to the Botanic Gardens.

To the contrary.

Now we read the headline allegations and charges involving associations between high officials and people who are trying to sell things to their departments, and of so many men caught with girls who are legally too young to sell themselves. Now we recognize the by-the-hour hotels ensconced among the middle-class neighborhoods, and the young girls from all over the world offering themselves online. Some are shocked. I am not.

There is sin in Singapore, in the very word of it. And one of our sins is sex. Not lovemaking between couples—the government will quickly point to the lack of procreation, an aging population, and an inverted pyramid that spells a demographic half-life. I am talking about in brothels, in short-time hotels at a littered street corner nearby, in massage parlors with flimsy plywood walls separating one customer from another, in karaoke rooms where the lights are dimmed so you do not see the stains on the furniture or notice how ugly the girls are, in toilets at the end of a fluorescent-lit corridor. I am talking about fucking.

I learned this early, after my graduation from university, when I was posted to Vice. Once, an eternity ago, I used to date, and thought there was a girl who might be the one for me. Once I thought lovemaking was something which a man chased after, hunted, and won through charm and the promise of dedication, and that was given to him because of merit of some kind; because a woman thought he was a good man with a good career ahead of him, or liked the way he kissed, or danced, or his sense of humor, or the cologne he wore. There were things we men did to increase the odds, like buying them drinks in a bar. But that aside, it was merit.

I quickly learned otherwise. Money cannot buy you love, but bucks buy fucks.

Look at the working girls. They sing, drink, and smoke, drape an arm around you, let you pinch their legs, laugh at your jokes, act sympathetic when you tell them your silly stories and then try to make you laugh. These girls open their legs and do so many things to clients, strangers who walk in from the street, through a door: I assumed they would be different.

They do dress and wear makeup differently on the job. Short skirts. Hugging tops with steep necklines. High-heel stilettos. Glitter. Bright red lipstick and cheeks. Manicured long nails, in bright red or else black with sparkles. But that is like a uniform. Just as I used to wear a policeman's uniform, they have theirs.

I met some in other places, off the job, in everyday clothes—when they were in normal makeup, normal clothes, I realized these girls are ordinary. Some are prettier than average. Many are not. I heard them talk among themselves about shopping, eating, movies, father and mother, friends, and hopes for more money, a good life. Some were nice. Others were not. They are just normal. Normal women.

That is what most disturbs me.

Fucking and lovemaking, sin and sacred: what differs is the intention, the psychological element, the context. The dick is in the same place. The mind is what is in a different place. The difference between lovemaking and fucking is fundamentally a question of attitude, and these attitudes can be criminal. The working girls are divided from normal girls only by the mind. Money is just the trigger to move from one mental state to another.

With this knowledge, a world of domesticity closed for me. I cannot marry. I cannot believe in love. It is too much make-believe, a Disneyland world; everything is pretty up front, but artificial, unreal. There is a man in the Mickey Mouse suit. Playing Snow White is a girl, just a girl. A girl who can be bought, for a price. A man who can be corrupted and indeed will corrupt others. I recognize that not just in the working women but also in so many others that I meet, in the city offices, in the fine restaurants and stylish clubs, and, yes, even in the areas where the rich and respectable live.

What I no longer recognize is myself. I think back to the time before I joined the force and I can remember what clothes and spectacles I wore, even the scent my T-shirt had when I put it on, fresh from the laundry and just after my mother ironed it. Yet, while I remember all this so clearly, I cannot recognize the world that I would see through those now out-of-fashion horn-rimmed spectacles.

What I do see now when I look around is this: We are guilty. The germ of a terrible crime is already in your mind.

### 3. STOLEN UNDER A THIEF'S MOON

I work at the DSI—the Directorate of Surveillance and Inspection. We are an agency no one has ever heard about but that has been around since the founding of the state, reporting directly to the leader. There are other departments that do so, including those that look at internal and external threats and the bureau to investigate corruption; in the early years, even the pollution-monitoring department.

At the beginning of our country's history, our leader gave much attention to details, and the DSI's mandate—surveillance and inspection—was to assist in that oversight of all things, to provide the many eyes that could quickly and shrewdly scan so that when the alarm bells rang and the red lights flashed, the leader and those he trusted could dive down into the muck and fix whatever was wrong.

These days—as the city has grown in pace and complexity—that may seem quaint and quite impossible. I don't know if anyone looks at the details anymore. Sometimes it seems like everything is too sophisticated, on auto-pilot. But in case anyone cares, we still do what we used to do.

We continue to watch and listen and survey and investigate. We continue to do so quite without attention—not just from the public but even within the state apparatus. If I meet you, and if I should give out my name card, it would simply say, *Deputy Assistant Director (Special Duties), Public Service Division, Prime Minister's Office.*

This is me, at least as much as I would like to say about myself. How about her?

When we first met, there was a thief's moon—what I learned as a child to call that night when the moon is at its ebb and things are darkest. It was in a Japanese restaurant, an *iza-*

*kaya* along the Robertson Quay stretch of the river—small eats, many drinks—and the lights allowed us to accept the darkness. Someone I somehow knew asked me along for the opening of the restaurant, hosted by the owners; I sat on a high stool at the end of the counter, with a person on my right more interested in the person on his other side, so I didn't have to talk too much.

I drank my super-dry Asahi. The beer was icy and the dishes were hot from the furnace, with a squeeze of lemon and a dusting of salt. *Okay*, I thought, *even if I don't talk to anyone, at least the food's good.*

Then she bumped into me. Literally. Turning the corner, the idiot waiter with the tray of cold beers gets too near her, and so she moves to one side and bumps into me as I'm putting the beer down. It spills a little on my black T-shirt but I respond quickly enough so no more than a bit hits the floor and counter. I don't get soaked and the glass does not empty or fall and break. No big deal.

But she turns, says "So sorry" more than a couple of times, and finds a napkin to dry me, dabbing the drops along my chest, while I just stand and look at her, and tell her, "No problem, it's okay, please don't worry."

Then she pauses, glances up at me, and realizes that we are standing close and she is touching my chest, the chest of someone she does not know and has not been introduced to, and she looks down, embarrassed, and takes a step back, bumping into her stool. She stumbles and I reach out and hold her so she steadies.

Our host comes over. He asks if everything is okay and I nod, while she says nothing. I withdraw my hand from the small of her back. He introduces us. I look her in the face.

Her features can be simply stated, drawn on an identi-kit in a police station: a long, straight, narrow nose; wide-set, rounded eyes; and a wide mouth, neither too full nor stretched and thin.

But the impact, the way it all adds up, cannot be mathematically or clinically summarized. This woman is immediately beautiful. Her skin glows, soft as the moon that was missing from the night sky that evening we met. Hers is a face no one can forget.

I thought that I would never see her again. She was seated next to the person beside me, and we spoke a little but she was nice to everyone there, neither too effusive nor aloof. She asked something about me and my work and said nothing about the usual lies I provided, but she also engaged others around the table. She was not loud or intrusive, and spoke modestly, with polite interest in what others did or thought. I only realized later that she asked about us much more than she talked about herself. I did not say too much about myself. I never do. But from her simple questions asked in a clear, mild voice, I learned more about the others around us than some officers I know could have from interrogating them for an hour under harsh lights in a cold room.

All I knew about her by the end of the evening was that she was half-Japanese, and part American and Chinese, and had lived in Singapore for some years as a child, and again for the past few months. Then the evening was over and the large group of people who sort of knew each other but didn't really have much to do with one another dispersed and I thought I would never see her again, even if I wanted to.

In the weeks after our meeting, the thief's moon grew to a crescent and then waxed full. There was a murder in Singapore, late at night, in an alley outside a karaoke lounge in Chinatown. The police traced it to two men who bumped into each other inside, earlier, when one—a Mr. Wong—was preoccupied with a hostess from Hangzhou, famous for its beautiful women, and accidentally walked into the other man, who was already tipsy. Mr. Wong was, for some reason the detectives could not find out, carrying his own tray of shot glasses to the table when the collision occured.

The spill was not so bad, the hostesses said. It splashed the other man later identified as Weng on his cheek and the collar and top part of his shirt. It splashed the woman too, a little across her bosom. She shrieked at first but saw the glare that Weng, her customer, gave to Wong, and so decided to try to cool things down by laughing and inviting Weng to lick her bosom dry.

She was, she later reported at the Central Investigation Bureau, scared when he continued to stare at Wong, while his buddies stood up and circled the hapless guy who was still holding the half-empty tray and stammering apologies, red-faced from both the alcohol and embarrassment. The man called Weng took up her wanton invitation, and happily licked away at the drops of whiskey that beaded in the cleft of her ample, enhanced bosom, but she reported that when she looked down, she could still see the hatred in his bloodshot eyes.

That face, she said, that was a face she would never forget.

As reported in the *New Paper*, just hours later, after Weng had paid a reported $1,500 for a quickie with a girl at the rear of the karaoke bar, he and his gang surrounded Wong once more and punched and kicked him to the ground, carrying on with their beating even after he was dead from the fall, having hit his head on the edge of the pavement at an odd angle.

A face you cannot forget can mean many things.

A chance collision and a spilled drink can mean many things.

The week after we met at the *izakaya*, I followed her.

I followed her to Bukit Timah, where the rich people of

the city live and so many others aspire to live. This is a quieter, greener sector of the city, sprung up around a river that has been concretized into a large canal, off a road that during World War II the Japanese took to get from the north directly into the city, like an artery carrying blood or poison to the heart. Except that this place where the rich people live is only an artery, and there is no heart.

Her area was privileged even in this context, at Nassim, nestled off the Bukit Timah canal, and right across from the Botanic Gardens, the green and ordered legacy from colonial times. Her apartment building was one of the newest and most prestigious, designed by some world-famous name, and developed by a company that targets only the uppermost elite. Its price could be matched by only a few other neighborhoods in the world. The rent is far beyond what she earns at the office, where I observed her at work, learned her job title and responsibilities.

She was either from a rich family or else a kept woman, I surmised—without judgment—but kept by whom? Possibilities and theories are useful, I have learned, but in the end can only be resolved by surveillance.

So it was late one night that I saw the black Mercedes S, accompanied by two Toyota Mark X's , all with heavily tinted windows, pull up to her apartment block. The heavyset men emerged in dark suits and white shirts, with hard eyes that peered around; it was apparent that they had been drinking, and I knew they were Japanese even before they spoke.

I was not surprised. Not wholly. The Japanese community is large in Singapore, and where their people go, these people will follow.

It did not surprise me to learn, as I did by the next day, that the man who goes up to her apartment is the gang boss for not just Singapore, but the whole region; he is on a list of people that we watch and monitor but allow in and out of the country so long as they do nothing here. It did not surprise me that he travels often for weeks or even months or that his returns too often coincide with her visits to the doctor for a bruise, a fall, a slip, a welt. What surprised me is how, just nights after we met under a thief's moon, and before I did any of this checking, we became lovers.

How did I steal you? Or is it that you—for whatever reason—stole me?

## 4. How Some Die, and Others Live

I begin to write this in bed, when you are still asleep, your dark hair spilling over the white pillow, your slim arm reaching out for something in a dream beyond this room. I move slightly, slowly, so as not to wake you, take the beautiful lacquered fountain pen and stern black notebook you gave me, and begin to write.

I look at you. Your leg peers out from under the white duvet. From the ankle to the back of the knee and the first curve of thigh is a path of delight. Along this path, we move from the simple pleasure of eye and mind seeing something of so much beauty to the awkward, heart-quickening, and limb-entwining physical act of possessing that beauty. To look upon you is to gaze and to desire. Then to possess.

We return to this path, repeatedly. Day after day, and night after night. In our repeated journeys, we find byways of desire, possession, and so much else, until we are covered in a fine sheen of perspiration, until we ache to stand, until we are uncertain whether what we do is acceptable to anyone other than us inside this room.

I have seen people die. What I have seen explains to me the uncertainty about a soul. One moment I see their eyes catch the light, move and flicker, fragile and also overflowing with life. Then the eyes glaze, turn gray and black, dull, dulled, blunt, opaque, oblique, closed, gone. Perhaps to another place none of us knows, that none can prove in a court with testimony. These are the eyes I have looked into when death came.

When we make love, I grasp your slender jaw in my thick palm and turn your eyes to mine when you are about to come, and do so again and again, until it is my turn. And what I see in your eyes becomes something to hold back the memories of what I have seen in the eyes of the dying.

When we are in bed, I know what it is to live. Every part of my body, every sense of being I have, is alive. And from this, I began to want to have that feeling in other parts of my day, to have you with me in more places beyond this bed, this room, this apartment. I investigate your days. I follow you, jotting down your routines in the black book you gave me to write my stories.

9:15 a.m. You get into your dark blue Maserati, and drive to the cold storage down the road from your apartment. You park in B3 and go to the elevators. A young Australian mother and child come out chattering in broad accents, and bump into you with their grocery cart laden with beef and wine. You do not complain.

9:30. You buy the bottled oolong tea that I like, the Ben & Jerry's Chocolate Fudge Brownie that we eat together some evenings, and then other basics for the apartment. You also buy a Japanese instant ramen with a sour-hot Korean kimchi flavor that I don't like, and I have never seen you eat. But I know immediately who the item is for—I remember thinking it strange that a Japanese person would like kimchi so much—and I feel my pulse rise at this inventory.

10:01. You push your trolley into the elevator, headed back to B3. I race down the stairs and catch you as you are unloading the bags into the trunk. I come up behind you, and hold you tight. You turn in shock but do not cry out before I have my hand clamped over your lips. Perhaps you recognize me, perhaps not. I push you over so you are halfway into the trunk, and your feet are off the ground. I hold your arms tight behind you, as you wriggle, quite helpless. I shush you. I reach under your quiet navy-blue skirt and pull your sheer blue panties to one side.

I finger you, slowly at first, and then, as your breathing grows heavy, I go faster. My fingers get slippery and I begin to slowly open up your other hole. One sharp gasp, and after that suspension of breath, you moan. I unzip and it is brief, and I do not look into your eyes.

10:19. You drive back to the apartment. I follow in my car. We head upstairs. We do not fuck. We lock the door securely behind us, we unload the groceries into the fridge and store-room, fold away the plastic bags. We shower and then we make love. Sweetly, tenderly, with the curtains drawn, like some newly married couple who were school sweethearts in a small town and have never known much of anything else.

Afterward we go out for lunch around the corner to the French place at the little row of shops along Bukit Timah that gentrified as the property values raced and richer people with richer tastes moved there. A Frenchman who married local and never left runs it; a small place with some comfy tables amidst racks of food and wine that they stock for sale and which feels like a warehouse.

We come here often because of convenience but also, I realize, perhaps because there is a sense of a couple here, making a home and comfort food amidst the commerce and bare floors.

Then we are back, in the big bed with the rumpled white cotton sheets and comfortable pillows, even as the city busies itself with commerce and common things. We nap, holding each other, and wake and make love again. Then evening comes.

Sometimes in this place and time, between us, there is nothing that can be said. Perhaps I feel silly for the pangs I felt when you stocked up things for him, what he and no one else likes, when I know it is his money that pays for not just whatever is in the fridge, but the fridge and the apartment, and that he is the reason that you are here in the first place and that we met. Perhaps I feel guilty for the way I have forced myself on you, in such a place and manner.

But you do not ask and I do not speak of these things. In bed together, there is no need for such things.

In my life, I have known sex and death. Now in this time, I have begun to know life—what that might truly mean. But I still know death better.

And in such moments, I know that no matter why this started between us, no matter how long this goes on, no matter how alive we are in bed, in our passion, when I am in you, this must end and it will end in death.

## 5. Coming to Endings

You haven't called or sent any messages all day. But that sometimes happens when he is in town, returning suddenly. I sent one text but then kept quiet when there was no reply. Instead of thinking about you, I have kept busy with all the scandals now in the political realm—not so immense and I am not directly involved. But our system has little experience handling such political scandals, and the agencies directly in charge must themselves be monitored for the ways they approach these issues. So it is dusk by the time I drive down that road to sit outside the gate that leads into your condominium.

There is a mover's truck outside with boxes of different sizes being loaded up. Nothing unusual, because your condominium, like so many others, always has people coming and going. But something in my gut stirs me out of the car. I speak to the movers and then the security guard. The boxes are coming from your apartment.

I ask the guard to buzz me up. He is used to me enough not to ask questions. But he tells me there is no one upstairs, that he has not seen you all day amidst the moving. I don't believe him and bully my way up, riding the elevator that has become so familiar in these months, and yet I arrive in a space that is unrecognizable.

It is the same apartment. But you are not there. Everything that you placed inside, and touched, has been emptied out until what remains is just a polished skeleton.

I head back down with questions. The movers—Bangladeshis paid by the hour—don't know what to say, but when I show the supervisor my credentials he brings out the manifest. What they are moving now is a second load of boxes, which are being sent on to Tokyo, while the first are in storage. The name on the invoice is not yours but that of a Japanese company. The destination address is also in the name of that company.

I snap a photo of the manifest on my phone, for follow-up. I order the supervisor to allow me to inspect the boxes here and in storage. He hesitates but relents when I bark. I open every one, not even knowing what I expect.

What I find horrifies me: there is the lamp that was by our bedside, the cushions that you held against your lap when we watched television, the television itself, and our bed, and the couch and other places where we lay together—all these and more things that marked our time with each other are bundled into boxes and wrapped up in cellophane, made inhuman, as if no one has ever used them, as if there has never been an us.

I stare at the boxes and hardly nod when the supervisor asks if they can seal them back up. Then I follow the truck to their office in an industrial park, just fifteen minutes away, up the road, in the part of upper Bukit Timah that still has some space for light industry and commercial buildings. Around them, more condos for millionaires are being built, and the construction crews are at work even at night. It is a different world from the quiet, upper-class, leafy neighborhood the boxes and their belongings have come from.

It is night as the supervisor and I stride across the cement floor between the office building and the storage area, where the first lot of boxes are kept. The sky is inky dark: a thief's moon. I sense something and it feels like fear.

When we approach the boxes, the lights come on and I see the stain on the floor that seeps from one box. Dark red. There is a strong, putrid smell.

The supervisor sees it too and is startled, not knowing what it is. Without a word I shove the other boxes out of the way and get to the one that is bleeding. I reach for my penknife and cut it open and then I kneel and with my hands tear apart the heavy cardboard, and move aside one item and then another to get to the source.

I breathe hard and deep as I work. I move urgently as if there are wounds that can still be staunched, crimes that may still somehow be prevented, and limbs that can yet be sewn back together to make a whole person.

And then, with an exhalation of breath, I find it. It is nothing more than a bottle that has been broken in the move, a bottle of liquid that has not been wrapped carefully and that indeed should never have been in the box without refrigeration.

I stare at the supervisor and he obeys when I insist we open every single box that remains. I find cutlery, crockery, cooking things, towels and linens, and all the heavy, bulky things that once allowed us to feel at home. Now they seem like props for a stage where nothing was ever real.

There is no other sign of you, no clue to where you are and why you left like this. In the days that are to come, I will search, with all the skill and all the contacts I have accumulated.

I cannot put to rest the question of whether he somehow found out because you or I were careless, or if he was simply reposted to another city. I will try to figure out where you are, and if the move is something you wanted, somehow to get away, and if you are alive. Without any resolution to these questions, I cannot know the answers that must apply to my life, my crime, and my death.

I have prepared myself for different possibilities. That you are with him in Tokyo, and have gone back to that life which you never really left. Or that I will find that you are dead, killed in anger or icy vengeance. Or even that you are alive, having run away not only from him but also from me, to begin anew in a small town where nothing really happens as we sometimes fantasized about.

As I look, I will also cover every track that you and I could have left between us, for even as I am looking for him and therefore for you, I am aware of the danger that he could in turn be looking for me.

At night now, I eat alone, the simple dishes of vegetables, rice, and *tauhu*. I clean my gun daily and do my push-ups and other exercises. Some mornings, I park the car and then run around the Botanic Gardens and down Bukit Timah Road to where we used to meet amongst the rich and respectable people, and sometimes—at all kinds of hours—I sit in my car on the street outside your gate as if expecting you to return to the scene.

I observe everything and write it down in my journal, with the pen that you gave me—which I fill with ink each day.

I am waiting for death, or life. I am waiting for something to happen, an ending that is to come.

I am a detective in a city they say has no crime. I am an artist in a city that—let's not pretend—no longer has a heart.

# STRANGLER FIG

BY PHILIP JEYARETNAM

*Bukit Panjang*

The strangler fig begins as an epiphyte, when a seed germinates in the crevice of another tree. Its roots grow downward, enveloping the other tree. At the same time, its branches grow upward toward the sunlight above the jungle canopy. In time, the host tree perishes, and the strangler fig comes to support its own weight. The ghostly remains of the original tree fall away, leaving a hollow core at the heart of the strangler. The strangler is doomed to this parasitic quest, drawn to engulf and overwhelm the other.

Bernard had observed one such tree over the course of his childhood. It grew in a remnant of old forest near the bus stop, where he took a bus each morning from Bukit Panjang to school in Bishan. In the early-morning darkness it looked especially sinister, its roots descending like the tangled beard of an ancient pirate. Bernard was a short but fierce boy—Chilli Padi was the nickname his schoolmates gave him—a boy who was afraid of nothing, who gladly fought kids twice his size, and won. Yet the sight of that tree would unsettle him. When he was in Secondary One, parts of the original tree still clung to life, occasionally green shoots would sprout. But by Secondary Four it had given up the fight.

He had grown up in Bukit Panjang. Wedged between the Mandai catchment area and the northern edge of the Bukit Timah Nature Reserve, it still had fragments of jungle, slowly drying out, and soon to be bulldozed no doubt, but for a while it was at least sanctuary for monkeys and birds. He compared trees by their reproductive strategies—particularly appreciating the Kapok trees for their seed pods bursting with fluffy fiber, the berries of the Tembusu that attracted bats at dusk, but perhaps most of all the Saga trees with their curling pods, twisting ever more tightly till they split open and discharged their jewel-red seeds. These were majestic trees, relying on their own strength and ingenuity.

The strangler fig offended him by its sneaky behavior. It depended on, made use of, and ultimately destroyed another.

The strangler fig is not the only possessor of this parasitic habit. Some women have it too. Chancing upon the right man, the more vibrant and sturdy the better, she draws him to her embrace. Her tendrils caress and soothe, tightening impercepti- bly yet irresistibly. The victim, unsuspecting at first, is charmed to be the object of such obsessive attention, until, too late, he is trussed up, his breath squeezed out. The gently deepening deprivation of oxygen lulls him into unconsciousness, as she takes from him the keys to his condo and his car, and of course all of his credit cards.

Bernard felt that he had spent his life struggling free from the embrace of women. Perhaps it was too dramatic to call them strangler figs, but certainly there were times when all his energy was being sucked from him. First there was his mother. After his father's death when he was just a boy of seven, she had identified his potential and driven him on, through the Gifted Education Programme at Raffles and onward to an army scholarship to study engineering at Cambridge.

Her constant refrain was the need to make the most of his time. Every spare moment should be spent reading or doing homework. Even meals were a distraction—she cared much less about how anything tasted than about whether it would provide the right energy boost at the right time for his studies. When he was in primary school she had warned him about his habit of loitering along the way to and from school. Once, exasperated by the fact that he had not taken her warning to heart, she told him that at dawn and dusk he must be especially careful, for in the shadows of the trees there would lurk female spirits, with long black hair, in long white gowns, and they watched for little boys who lacked purpose, who idly kicked stones at a street corner or missed their bus because of some foolish daydream or other.

When Bernard got married he thought he had found an equal, a partner in life, but his wife, who had pretended disdain for material things all through their courtship, was soon complaining about how low his army pay was compared to friends of theirs who worked for banks or in the legal profession. Even after he left the army and became chief executive of the energy regulator, as well as a member of Parliament for the ruling party, she was unsatisfied, and urged him to push to become a minister. Great pay, great status, she said. When he explained that what he really enjoyed was meeting people, trying to find answers to their problems, she told him he was wasting his time— no one would really be grateful to him anyway—and he should focus on impressing the PM instead. Sometimes she made him angry, and he would feel like striking out, but he kept himself in check. One can strike a man, but never a woman. The same boy who had without hesitation fought schoolmates upon any slight or insult had been unfailingly polite to his mother, to teachers, and in time to the women he dated. No matter how much his wife provoked him, Bernard kept quiet, carried on.

Whatever one does with the time one has, it passes. This morning Bernard had looked up from his phone and was startled by his own reflection in the mirror—how little hair he had was the first thought. But then, before self-pity overtook him, the second followed, the uplifting sight of his flashing white teeth, the crocodile smile that had proved so useful to his rise, first in the army and later in politics. People were disarmed by it. Charmed by him. And he had led a charmed life, in most respects.

The message on his phone was unexpected, a shock, but he would survive. Perhaps it was the chance of a lifetime, to change the pattern of others taking advantage of him. Today he would act from love. And he would find his reward in that one true love.

Perhaps because his father had died when he was young, Bernard had taken to heart the advice Polonius gave to his son Laertes: accept censure while not judging others; listen more and speak less; and above all, be true to himself. This had served him well. It even gave him the patience to endure his wife.

When Bernard first became an MP, the ruling party had a viselike grip on power. Promotion to minister was mostly about one's academic credentials and connections—being a minister was mostly about making decisions that were sound in economic theory that could then be implemented by an efficient, well-paid civil service. But it had all become so much harder when the people suddenly, unexpectedly, discovered that they could in fact vote against the ruling party without the social order collapsing, and that just maybe speaking up might not be met with a knock on the head but an apology and an offer to do more and better—to keep bus fares low, to provide more hospital beds, to limit the entry of foreigners.

Everyone and anyone wanted things done for them, and done for them *now*. They complained about anything and everything. To make matters worse, there was an apparent conspiracy of the heavens over the past three years—flash floods, MRT breakdowns, sex scandals—all conspired to make it seem as if there was nothing the ruling party could do right.

Many of his parliamentary colleagues resented the new situation. It was not the premise on which they had entered politics, which was meant to be a simple career progression—more pay, more status, as his wife had put it. They did not like the new orders to be on time for functions, not to keep people waiting, to be more approachable.

But the new national mood suited Bernard. He started a Facebook page. It quickly generated more "likes" than those of any of the ministers. He had taken to Tweeting too, and soon had many followers. He spoke his heart. He was true to himself. In the real world, he started to meet with citizen groups that had previously been ignored. Of course, it was not easy. Everyone wanted change in how things were done: Conservationists wanted a block on development. Hotels wanted more leeway to hire foreign staff. Gays wanted whatever it was they did behind closed doors to be allowed, to be legal. And if change did not happen—then the ruling party was to blame. But at least as an ordinary member of parliament, he had more freedom than a minister—to convince people of the merits of government policy, while not being entirely bound by it either. And people liked him, they truly did—his lack of ostentation, his modesty, his simple, open manner. He lived by the words of Polonius.

His wife, though, still nagged him. She felt that now was his chance to become a minister, given that it was precisely his EQ, his people skills, his popularity, that the party needed in these challenging times. For her, whatever strength he had was an opportunity for her to ascend. He was the tree she had found to be her scaffold. She badgered him to attend the right functions, and accompanied him so she could smile and flirt with the right people, who might support a promotion to the Cabinet for him. But he had long since come to feel that she did not love or care for him beyond the status he conferred on her, the network he gave her access to. At times, he felt as if she was truly intent on strangling him, choking him, her thumbs firmly against his windpipe as he gasped for air, although of course the pressure would never be enough to kill him, at least not until she had used him to get exactly where she wanted.

The message on his phone was from Evelyn, the woman he had let into his life six months before.

Evelyn was different from all the other women he had known. She loved him, of that he was sure. Loved him for himself. Not only did she love him, she did not depend on him. At last he had found his match, but in the best possible way. For the first time in a long while, he felt excited and purposeful about his life, and about the possibility of a new life with Evelyn, a new beginning.

He had met her unexpectedly, at a meet-the-people session with his constituency. She was not a supplicant, of course, but a fresh volunteer—something that had become rarer after the debacle of the last elections. Her blunt, offhand manner captivated him, as did her long black hair and tanned athleticism. When he offered her Lipton's tea or instant coffee from the pantry, she had made a face, leaving him speechless for a moment before her laughter told him she was teasing.

Afterward, he pulled out her file. One child, husband a doctor. Her eyes, gazing steadily back at him, were the last thing he saw before sleep overcame him that night. The next morning he had a plan, and his secretary telephoned her to ask her to call him. She did, and once he had her mobile phone number, he started WhatsApping her. Restrained questions, seeking her views on constituency and national matters.

He had prepared himself for a rebuff, but she was more than responsive. He was surprised how quickly she seemed to open up to him. They started with policy questions and political challenges, but were soon turning to more personal topics. It was not long before she was attending all of his constituency meetings. In between consultations they laughed and chatted together. Their WhatsApping grew more frequent, more direct and intense. Conspiratorially, she warned him of the perils of monitored communications, and he knew she was as interested in him as he was in her.

At last they had lunch, at a little French restaurant. Three hours of flirting disguised by earnest discussions of what the government should or should not be doing to win back popular support. He lost count of the number of times her hand had lightly rested on his forearm, drawing him toward her, how often she had used the index finger of the other to make a little tapping motion in midair, both emphasizing a point and quickening his heartbeat.

Lunch was soon followed by late-night drinks. They gazed into each other's eyes. This, he knew, was a relationship that was truly special.

The sex was good. Perhaps he had missed it for so long that he did not know any better, but he felt both fulfilled and truly triumphant. He had an apartment in River Valley that was between tenancies, and this became their sanctuary.

She asked for nothing from him, although along the way he occasionally sought to impress her, to offer her snippets of information or gossip that would keep her captivated. He realized that he probably needed to be more careful. Possibly, something he had let slip about measures the government was considering to cool the property market had tipped her to sell an investment property sooner than she had planned, but surely what he had done was not strictly illegal, and even if illegal was hardly likely to be detected. His tips were unsolicited, of that he had no doubt. He felt so comforted by her, so loved by her, that this was surely small recompense, no different from the necklaces from Tiffany & Co. that he bought for her, necklaces that she appreciated so much and never once asked for.

The risks were worth it. This was his one true chance at love, and for once he did not care about work, or being sensible, or what the world might think. Evelyn was the love of his life. Mostly it was light and luminosity, but at times the hunger for her burned so strongly that he could think of nothing else.

He became determined to possess her completely, for them to become one.

Her WhatsApp today had not been her usual Monday-morning chirp. It had been different, and simple. *Pregnant. Really sorry. Don't know what to do. Had to tell hubby. Mad as hell but wants to see you. Will you meet him?*

The first word thrilled him. He had indeed possessed her. They had indeed become one. But why was she sorry? Did she doubt him? Doubt his strength or resolve?

It was excitement that gripped him. Not fear or anxiety. Elation even. Bernard was never afraid of a confrontation, or a fight, with another man. He would talk to the husband. Explain that he had not meant to act dishonorably. But now that he and Evelyn were so very much in love, it was too late for niceties of honor. The husband must give way. Bernard would take responsibility for Evelyn and their baby. It was a sign that his life must change. He would resign, get a job in the private sector. Perhaps they could even move elsewhere—Hong Kong? Shanghai?

*Yes,* he WhatsApped back without hesitation, *I love you.* Then a moment later, *Don't worry.* And then finally, *I'll take care of it.* After another minute he called, to tell her he loved her and they would find their way. He wanted to meet immediately. He was surprised when she asked him to meet her husband first, but decided she must have a reason. He must do as she asked.

Mark was the husband's name. He suggested the visitor's center at the dairy farm entrance to the Bukit Timah Nature Reserve. *We can walk together,* he said. *Green is very soothing, and I think we both need to keep calm.*

Bernard had seen pictures of him, but Mark was still surprisingly big. They shook hands and then started to walk. Mark turned off the open path, up the slope toward Bukit Timah Hill, and soon they were alone together, Bernard following Mark. It was cool beneath the forest canopy. Even the light had turned green, filtered as it was by the dense leafy layers. Mark was right, it was peaceful, calming. Then Mark stopped, turned, and looked down at Bernard. The disparity in their height suddenly felt menacing. Bernard glanced around, wondering if he had made a mistake to venture up this trail.

As if reading his mind, Mark smiled and said, "Don't worry, Bernard, I'm not going to hit you. Not that I don't feel like doing so. There's nothing I'd like better than to bruise your pretty face. What would your constituents say to that, eh?"

Bernard looked off to the side. Let the man rant for a while. He was obviously hurt. But he couldn't possibly think that Bernard had been the first, could he? Evelyn had told him there was another before him, though she had not loved that man in the way she loved him. And certainly she did not love Mark, whom she had married too young, when she wanted above all else to leave home, to escape her father, a domineering man who had bullied her mother and alternately spoiled and disparaged young Evelyn, until she lost confidence in herself, only regaining it when she finished university, started working at a private bank, met Mark, and left home.

After a while, Bernard spoke. "I'm sorry," he said, "I had not realized . . . I thought you were more . . ." he searched for the right word, ". . . relaxed. I would not have, you know, pressed my suit, but now, now that we are where we are, well, you must understand, we love each other, I mean, she loves me, not you . . ."

To his surprise, Mark was laughing. "Oh, you are a funny fellow. She loves you, not me. Oh yes. Poor me, lucky you." Mark grabbed his shoulders. He brought his face close to Bernard's. "Look, man, love isn't real. All that's real is power and money. Don't you of all people know that?"

Bernard could see the sweat on Mark's stubbled chin. But his eyes were not so much angry as cold, as if this was a situation he was familiar with, and this a routine he had practiced before. For once Bernard was unsure, and it made him uneasy. He had expected anger, hurt, shame, the stock reactions of the cuckold. But this was something else.

Mark released him and turned away. On the uneven ground, Bernard almost stumbled, but then recovered. With his back to Bernard, Mark was talking quietly. "I do have photos. Much better than those of Anwar. Really quite professional, I'd say. But it won't come to that, will it, Bernard? You like your life, how everyone has to speak politely to you, pretend they agree with you. Big-shot MP, yes? You don't want to risk any of that, do you?"

Bernard could not bring himself to speak. He had to pacify the man, promise whatever he asked, and then find Evelyn. Evelyn could get divorced, he could get divorced too, they'd find happiness together, a new life with the new life growing within her. He would resign. His office meant nothing to him, not compared to love and happiness.

"How much are you worth, Bernard? Not much of a salary these days, I suppose, but how many sweet deals have you been cut into as an MP? Let's see—ten million, give or take? And I'll just take one million. Ten percent. Not a lot, I suppose, considering how expensive it is to raise a kid these days. You'll still have plenty. And then normal life can resume for you."

"How do I know you won't just come back for more?"

"You don't."

"Can I think about it?"

"I understand, you want time to talk to Evelyn. She's in love with you, she'll save you. But here, take this."

Bernard took the piece of paper. Details for an account at a bank in the Cayman Islands.

"You can talk to anyone you want, just make sure that one million dollars goes to this account by Friday. Otherwise, you'll see yourself online by Saturday." Mark pushed past him and headed down the slope. "I hope we don't have to meet again, so have a good life, Bernard. Have a wonderful life."

Bernard had not known what to do until that moment. And perhaps he still did not know the right thing to do. But he was a chilli padi by nature, and Mark's words were fighting words. One thing about the Bukit Timah Nature Reserve is that there is plenty of loose granite lying around, it having been a site for multiple quarries, now disused. Another thing is that in the midafternoon on a weekday it is deathly quiet. And the quarries are deep and filled with water. There'd be at least a week before the body was found, and in the meantime, Bernard would have liquidated what he could and he and Evelyn would be thousands of miles away. How happy she would be to get free from that monster! And he too would be happy—it was escape for both of them. Fulfillment too.

\* \* \*

He met her that evening at his apartment in River Valley. They held each other for a long while and then pulled apart. She looked uncertainly at him.

"I'm so sorry, Bernard. How did your meeting with Mark go?"

"Don't be sorry, dearest. We'll find our way."

"Of course, darling. But how did it go?"

"It was unexpected, I have to say."

"What do you mean? Is the amount too much?"

"No, it's not that . . ." His voice trailed off. She had known he was going to ask for money. "He told you?"

"I was surprised too. What are you going to do?"

"What do you think I should do?"

"What choice do we have? Perhaps if we pay him off, he'll leave us alone. Oh, Bernard, we could be so happy together. I know it's terrible but will you pay him for me, for our life together?"

"Do I need to pay him? We'll bring up our child together. I don't care if he goes to the press."

Evelyn looked alarmed. "Bernard, my love, pay him. Pay him quickly. It's the only way we can be together."

Happiness, Bernard thought, is about the little things—being with the person you love and who loves you, wherever in the world you might be. Waking up to her in the morning, or watching her sleep at night. Walking hand-in-hand along the beach. Shopping together. Sharing a hot chocolate. A million little things. But love is about the big things—moments of choice, moments of sacrifice. And he had done what he had done for love, for Evelyn, to protect their life together.

He loved her. And she had played him. He would have faced anything with her by his side. But that was not how it was going to be, he understood this now. For a moment, hopelessness gripped him. What was the point of a life without Evelyn? Then from the darkness it was as if his mother were speaking to him, telling him not to waste time, and warning him of the long-haired woman in the shadows. He knew then that he would not succumb, would not die in Evelyn's embrace, would not watch her grow strong as his life ebbed from him. She'd had the whole damn forest to choose from and she'd picked the wrong tree.

"Yes," he said, "I'll pay him. I told you not to worry, I told you I'd take care of it."

"Oh, Bernard, I feel so safe and secure when I'm with you, when I hold you."

He cupped her head in his arms and lifted her face so he could kiss her. His thumbs were at her windpipe, and he kissed her half a dozen, no, a dozen times. To his surprise, it was no harder with a woman. Or perhaps, he thought as her eyes closed, it's true what they say—the second time is always easier.

# SMILE, SINGAPORE

BY COLIN CHEONG

*Ang Mo Kio*

He had never been in an interrogation room. Where was the two-way mirror? The TV shows had those, but it was absent here. Where were the air conditioners? He had heard so much about those. Six, they said, at full blast, and they would wet you first. There was only one humming here. Perhaps the rooms with the many air conditioners were reserved for political prisoners. There were no cameras either. Wouldn't it be better to have those? To record everything a suspect said? And then he smiled. They could say whatever they wanted. A video camera couldn't lie.

He looked down at his hands. They had not handcuffed him and had let him rest them on the cold edge of the table. Perhaps they felt sorry for him. He was an old man, after all. The faceless officers who found him had been young, a sergeant and a corporal, barely adult. He had done everything they asked, resisted them in nothing. He had held his hands out to be cuffed—not meekly, but as a man who knew he had broken the law, though did not believe he had done wrong.

That was an hour ago. Perhaps more. He did not know. They had taken his wallet, his belt, his phone, his door keys, the keys to his cab. He let his eyelids droop—not closing them completely, but enough to shut out the fluorescent light and leave a slit for him to see the dull gray of the tabletop before him and his own elbows, jutting thinly beyond the fraying short sleeves of his shirt. He was not cold, he was not hungry, he did not need to piss. There was nothing to distract him. He put his hands together, left fingers over right, the tips of his thumbs touching, hands forming a circle, as he had been taught at the meditation center. He could meditate.

The door swung open. The old man looked up. There was a guy in the standard civil service attire—white long-sleeved shirt, sleeves rolled up, dark pressed trousers, formal shoes that made no noise when he entered the room. He had a clipboard. Another man dressed just like him followed, and a uniformed officer closed the door behind them.

"Mr. Tan," he heard the first man saying as he sat down. He nodded. He looked at the clipboard. There was some kind of form on it and they had already filled in his particulars, recorded probably soon after his arrest. They went through the items and he nodded or murmured yes to all their questions.

His name, Tan Seng Hock, his national registration identity card number, the particulars of his taxi driver's license. His address at Block 533, Avenue 5 in Ang Mo Kio. Not his home, just a room he rented. His landlady was probably in another room just like this one with another pair of officers. He hoped she was all right. She was probably not taking this well at all. She had teenagers, two boys, one thirteen, the other fifteen. Still too young to be left on their own without a mother—or a father. He had tried, in a way, to be a good role model for them, to take them out like a father or uncle would have, helping them with their math homework. He had slept with their mother, but only once. She had asked him for money after that. Not money for sex, she was quick to add. But pocket money. The kind due to a girlfriend, a woman you fucked, over and above the rent. He said he could not afford a relationship like that. He knew where the money went. There was a Singapore

Turf Club betting shop not far from their block, across the MRT train tracks, close to the Courts furniture place. She had left it at that and never brought it up again. Or mentioned sex again. He did not think so well of himself to ask. Besides, the rental was cheap and there were the boys to think about. He did not need a quarrel. Peace, that was all he asked for.

"Mr. Tan," the first officer began again. The old man looked up. He already knew what the question would be. "Where did you get the gun?"

"It was in my taxi. I was cleaning the taxi. My last passenger vomited in the back."

"Can you remember when?"

He nodded. How could he ever forget the night he found his gun? Half a year ago, on Christmas Eve. He had been driving at night, something he did not like doing, but he knew it would be busy. Besides, the boys didn't want to do any more math homework. His last passenger was a white man he picked up at Clarke Quay; he had driven him to the man's condominium on the East Coast, the Bayshore.

"Can you describe him?"

The old man shook his head. The passenger was tall, had brown hair in a short, stylish cut, and was dressed in a tight shirt and jeans. But he could not put a face to that memory. All white men looked the same to him. They only varied in height and body fat—and how much hair they still had left. He looked like any drunk white man, although he seemed quite steady when he got into the taxi. And it was six months ago. All he remembered was the man telling him he needed to puke, but there was no place to stop on the expressway and he had vomited shortly before the turnoff to his condo. The passenger had been apologetic and had given him a fifty-dollar bill and told him to keep the change to get the cab cleaned. The old man could still remember driving all the way home to Ang Mo Kio after that, his windows down, the sour stink of the puke still fresh in his mind. Tequila probably. He had found parts of a worm when he took out the mats. And the gun under the front passenger seat. The old man had dropped the revolver and it made a loud thud on the floor of the cab. He did not remember how long he spent just staring at it, listening to the wind rustling like spirits through the leaves above him. With the puke on it, it looked like a stillborn child and he did not dare to touch it at first. Then, without thinking, he dropped a wet cloth on it and picked it up. He realized his mistake as he wiped the muck off it. Any prints would have been wiped off too. And sitting there in his hand, with his prints, the gun had made itself his.

"I wrapped the gun in the wet cloth," he told the officers. "I put it on the front seat and I cleaned the cab."

"Why didn't you call the police immediately?"

Why didn't he? After the initial shock, the initial fear, he continued furiously cleaning the cab, trying to get the damned stink out and knowing it would be days before the smell completely left. But he was also suddenly alert, completely aware of the thing that now sat in the passenger seat. And the longer he waited, the less willing he became to make that 999 call, even though he knew it was the only sane thing to do. What if its owner came looking for it? Would they kill him for it? But how would they find him? Every fare had been a roadside pickup. There had been so many—and many had been short trips. Anyone could have left it in any cab. And he realized after a while that he was looking for a reason not to call the police.

After cleaning the cab, he had sat down in the driver's seat and cleaned the gun very, very gently, wiped off all the puke, then carefully felt around it until something gave a little, then unlatched the cylinder and let it fall open. He still had not put his finger on the trigger or his hand around the grip. There were five chambers and four were filled. He tilted the gun slowly and the bullets slid out, clicking against each other as they dropped into his open palm. Four of them. He lay them on the passenger seat and continued cleaning the revolver.

With the bullets out, he felt safer with his gun. He spun the cylinder then snapped his wrist sideways to close it—just as he remembered from the movies. He put his hand around the grip, touching lightly on the trigger, pointing it at the floor, and a little red spot of light appeared between his feet, between the accelerator and the brake. He jumped—then realized it was just a laser spot, just like the laser pointers he had once used at training sessions when he still had his old job as maintenance supervisor. Before he had been replaced by a foreign talent from China willing to do the same job for less money.

"Did you know it was a police gun?"

No, he had not thought about it. His gun was all black and he vaguely remembered police guns having some sort of wood grip. His had black rubber. He shook his head. He had not even known that police guns had laser sights. All he had been thinking about was how he was going to keep it concealed at home and when he was out. There was nothing in his room that could be locked—not the drawers, not the cupboard. Until that moment, he'd had nothing worth securing. He dropped his takings into a cash deposit machine every morning before he began to pick up fares. He did not even own a watch. There was a clock on the dashboard. He had a cheap Nokia phone, the kind sold at petrol stations, and an M1 plan that cost just ten dollars without caller ID. He had three shirts, two pairs of trousers, four pairs of boxers, three pairs of socks, his money pouch, and a flight bag from a long time ago, when he and his former wife had gone on a Chan Brothers tour to Malaysia.

But his little gun changed all that. Now there was a secret to protect. Something to hide. Something that was truly only his, not shown to the rest of the world. The first week was difficult. He tried his best to act normally. His gun replaced the cash in his pouch. He began to carry the cash in his pockets, tied up in wads with rubber bands. Not that there was enough to make a large bulge in his pants, he said. The second cop smiled.

The first one nodded; he saw no humor in the statement. "The officer who was issued that gun is dead," he said. "He was a narcotics officer. When we found his body, we could not find his weapon. His killers must have taken it from him."

The old man felt the blood leaving his face. "You don't think I killed him, do you?"

The cops stared at him and said nothing. Their faces were blank, expressionless. There had only been four rounds in the cylinder. Had he managed to return fire only once? Or did they kill him with his own gun?

"No, I found the gun. In my taxi."

"You have no criminal record. You are not linked to any of the suspects," the first officer said.

"I wouldn't have hurt . . ." the old man began, then stopped.

"So why did you keep it?"

"Singapore isn't safe anymore," he said. Two cabbies dead already in the past year. Their killer or killers had asked them to drive out to some remote place in the night, and there, had cut one's throat, stabbed the other, before making off with their money. Two lives for the meager sums that the drivers had struggled all day to collect. He shook his head. "We're just not safe anymore." His tone was accusing—he did not have to say the police were not doing their job. It was there, just in his tone, and the second officer looked away.

"So you kept it for protection?"

Protection? How else was he to defend himself? Against someone stronger—younger and fitter—and determined to kill him? Or if there were just more of them? With his gun, he had a chance. Four chances.

"Suntec City," he said. If these policemen were honest, they would blush, he thought. But they did not. "Suntec City," he said again.

Three drunk, young white men had beaten up an old cabbie at a taxi stand while white tourists in the line cheered them on as if they were in some underground fight club. Two Chinese men—local men—had gone to help the cabbie and wound up getting thrashed by the white men, to more cheering from the foreign white trash in the taxi line.

"Singapore is safe," he spat, "if you're white and rich."

"We caught them and one of them is in jail."

The old man shook his head. The fucking police had let them go. Let them go on bail. Two absconded. Was that the plan? Didn't they know the white cowards would run? They had not even bothered to investigate at first and the initial arrests had only been made after people on the Internet got involved, identified the men, and made a police report. And what had that fucking investigating officer said? Wah, *you guys very free. Can do better than the police.*

"We've dealt with that officer."

The old man sneered. His peace was gone and the original gentleness with which he had viewed these two men in front of him was also gone, replaced by the anger that had been slowly corroding his insides until he'd found his gun. So yes, he reckoned that he and other Singaporeans could damn well do better than the police.

"Do you know how serious your offense is?"

Offense? He had not killed any precious white "foreign talent," although he had considered it. There were only so many times he could drive by, refuse to stop to pick them up. There were only so many times he could stop, pick them up, take their condescending shit, take their scanning his cab for a NETS machine, and, seeing none, tell him they had no cash and ask if he had NETS. How many times had he driven to a cash machine—and have the fare never return to the cab? How many times had he been promised—*Hey, uncle, I'll pay you tomorrow. Just give me a call. Or pick me up again. I'll make it up to you.* White man's honor. So superior. And when he had called? A quick cut, no reply.

In the past, he had put up with it—it was an occupational hazard. People did that. Not just white expatriate types, but also local kids who never intended to pay their fares, making a game of leaving the cab quickly after he had stopped to drop them off. But over the years, the anger had grown and slowly eaten away at him. He had tried meditation. Since he did not like driving at night, he would go to a meditation center at Jalan Besar—a dingy place in a rundown prewar building at the corner of a traffic junction, above a bunch of dirty motorcycle repair shops. He had tried to find peace there. To find forgiveness for himself and others, to remember that all were one. But any peace he found would quickly disappear like incense smoke when he got into the cab and returned to the streets.

Until his gun came—and suddenly he was calm, knowing that if he really wanted to, he could kill every one of them. At first it was just the white trash. Then it was the Singaporean women—the sarong party girls—the unofficial prostitutes that made Singapore a kind of sexual Disneyland for these white bastards. He did not mind actual call girls—they were making an honest living, just like he was—it was legal in Singapore anyway. But not the local women who thought only the white foreign trash were good enough for them, who actually thought them superior to local men simply because they were white and had expatriate paychecks. His list grew—but as he included more stereotypes, from obnoxious mainland Chinese to lecherous Indian nationals to bitchy Singaporean women to increasingly primped-and-preened local men as bitchy as their female counterparts, the greater his sense of calm grew too. They could behave as they wanted. Knowing he could kill them was consolation enough. That sense of power, of control, was good enough reason to risk everything he had—not much—to keep the gun. It calmed him and it made him smile, which really was good for Singapore's tourist image. *And we want to keep attracting the white trash, right? Smile, Singapore.* He smiled—as a "taxi uncle" he was Uniquely Singapore too. His gun had made him a better man. Love all, serve all.

And he had never threatened a fare with the gun. Or killed a fare. His gun had never come out of that pouch. He had never brandished it in a threatening manner, never made a show of it to a passenger. No one had ever known he had it.

He thought of Ah Huat, who did not mind showing off a little, to those in the know. Ah Huat had a tiny wooden coffin in his cab. About four inches long, carved in a Chinese style, with the graceful sweeps and arcs that differentiated it from modern Western caskets. He had it in the glove compartment most of the time. But at night it rode on the dashboard, his silent passenger, the thing that watched his back because so much can go wrong at night. The thing that watched his back, and any passenger who understood would be fairly warned.

Those who understood would know that in that little scaled-down coffin was the bone of a dead child—somewhat difficult to come by now because of cremation, but more common in the days of burials and when child mortality was still high. That bone, in its coffin, kept the child's spirit with the owner. Both were bound to each other. Both were master and servant. Ah Huat had inherited that coffin from his father, and so now the child spirit that once followed his father, followed him to do his bidding—on the condition that Ah Huat took care of it. Ah Huat sometimes made a show of it, in the way that Christians sometimes liked to say grace loudly in public.

When he ate, he would order two meals. Or two cups of coffee. He would pay for both, but consume only one. Those who did not understand would simply think he had been stood up, probably by an inconsiderate child or an unfaithful mainland Chinese girlfriend only interested in him as a meal ticket or for his Central Provident Fund savings. Those who understood knew he was feeding his child spirit—and the waiters who knew would keep their distance from the apparently uneaten meal, to clear it later when it was safe.

And that was why Ah Huat never let a fare sit in the front passenger seat: it was already occupied.

The old man thought about his gun in the pouch, tucked in the side pocket of his door, the zipper facing up, ready to be opened quickly. Always there for him. He reckoned it gave him the same kind of comfort the child spirit gave Ah Huat. Both were dangerous, but Ah Huat and he were steady men, not prone to violence, not reckless, with no vices. When they met for the occasional meal, all three of them, Ah Huat sometimes talked about his child, about how it sometimes helped pick winning numbers or helped him get back at someone for some injustice. Better than any of his living kids, he said. The old man had heard these stories often enough and did not need to compare notes. He had his gun, and it made him feel safe. Security was good to have in old age. It was like a life insurance policy, though, a one-time-use thing. He would have to die on the road. He could not afford to survive a serious accident. While Ah Huat could call on his child spirit repeatedly, the old man knew his gun had only four shots, and if he ever had to use it, it would be all or nothing.

He knew the time had come when he got home late, after driving all day, to find the front door splashed with paint and the pale, bled-out face of a recently slaughtered pig hanging from the flimsy metal gate. His landlady had finally hit rock bottom. She had borrowed money from loan sharks—and defaulted on the payment. It was something she had said she would never do. There were enough neighbors with experience to serve as fair warning.

"I paid," she had insisted when he went in to find her and the two boys cowering in a corner of their room. She and the younger boy were crying and the older one was trying his best to comfort them. "I paid, I paid. They gave me a loan I did not ask for," she said.

He had eyed her dubiously. "Didn't ask for?"

"No, they just put it in the bank. I didn't even know."

This was new to him. An unasked-for loan, in the form of a bank deposit, followed by a demand for repayment—and interest, of course. "Didn't you even think about why you had so much money?" He found it hard to believe that, hard up as they were, she would not have noticed the extra cash.

"I thought you put it in," she had said. "I thought you put it in for the boys. I never used it."

"Then you can give it back. You give it back tomorrow." He had looked at the boys and nodded to them. "I will take care of you, don't worry." The older boy nodded back but the younger one was still terrified. He reached out to pat his head. "Uncle will protect you."

They came the following night.

They had announced their arrival with yelling and hammering at the door. He opened up to speak to them and pay them, and to his horror found that they had lifted the flimsy old gate from its hinges and now stood facing him with no barrier between them. It had been a simple matter of removing a few retaining pins—an old trick that contractors used when they wanted to convince people to "upgrade" their gates.

There were two of them, and in the narrow corridor already crowded with potted plants and now a dismantled gate, they had to stand one behind the other. They looked so ordinary. The one in front looked like anyone he could have met in the building, a man in his thirties or so, not so tall, but stocky. His face was pale and flabby, like the pig's head on their door the previous night. Pig Face.

The one behind was much younger, taller, and slimmer, like any teenage punk with dyed hair, piercings in his earlobes, and tattoos—pretty ones he probably thought made him look cool. The old man knew what actual Triad tattoos looked like. The boy was just a punk. It was strangely quiet, as if all the neighbors had gone into hiding.

"Pay," the first collector had said. "Don't waste my fucking time."

The old man had nodded and took out the wad of cash from his shirt pocket. The collector snatched it from him, removed the rubber band, and began counting. His beady eyes were angry when he looked up again.

"Fucker, you trying to waste my time, is it? This is not enough."

"That's everything you put in her account."

"I didn't put. My boss put. He tells me to collect how much, I collect. This is not enough. Interest?"

The old man had said nothing. He merely shook his head.

"That means you still owe my boss."

"She owes you nothing," he said. Then more deliberately: "Tell your boss to fuck off. And if he tries that again—"

"Try *what* again? What are you going to do? You fucking useless old man, what are you going to do?"

He had already known the outcome of this exchange. He had heard enough stories. Loan sharks, like every other Singaporean, really wanted permanent passive income. A dividend they could collect forever from a small initial investment.

"You think you can fucking protect this woman, those boys? You're a fucking old man, you got no fucking balls anymore, what are you going to do?"

He would have let an insult go, but not a threat to harm the woman and the boys. He was losing his calm, his peace. Then, to make his point, Pig Face slammed his palm into the old man's chest and he staggered back. Pig Face had stepped across the threshold into the flat and the woman screamed. The old man recovered his balance and reached behind his back for his gun, tucked into the waistband of his loose trousers, hidden under his shirt. Pig Face saw the movement and thought the old man was going for a knife.

"I also got," he spat, and drew out a knife from his back pocket, but even as he began to open the blade, he saw the tiny, glaring red light and quickly backed toward the door. "Run!" he yelled.

The teen with the dyed hair, piercings, and tattoos bolted down the corridor. Pig Face stumbled as he turned around. He tripped over the bars of the metal gate that they had so recently taken down and landed heavily on the ground. The old man loomed over him, the gun in both his hands, that wicked red eye glaring down at the guy.

"Please," the collector had whimpered. "They made me do this. I owe money also. I can't pay. They made me do this. I have a family." He slowly got up.

The old man watched him, following him with his gun, tracking the collector's face with the red laser dot. He knew it was the end. His gun was no longer a secret. And life as he knew it was over. One chance, and he had been forced to waste it on these punks. The collector turned around as he lowered his gun. The old man felt the anger and the heaviness return as the collector moved down the corridor as quickly as the pain would allow him.

Only one thing to do. He squeezed the trigger. He heard the bang and the echo as the sound ricocheted around the surrounding blocks, he heard the collector yell as the bullet hit him in the butt, he heard the woman and the boys shouting, the neighbors screaming in fear. The whole world had erupted in sound, but he heard only a calm silence in his own soul.

The collector struggled down the corridor, groaning from the pain and trailing blood, and the old man followed, the red laser spot on his back the whole time. He got to the stairs, fell down a flight, picked himself up, stumbled painfully down all three floors, the old man just behind him, as if seeing a guest out. It was a good feeling, to usher someone out this way, usher out all the bitterness, all the anger, all the frustration, all those feelings of helplessness. He had not felt so good, so strong, so powerful, in a very long time.

The collector reached the ground-floor lobby, right next door to the now empty and dark People's Action Party branch office. Downstairs neighbors had rushed toward the sound but screamed and ran when they saw the old man's gun.

The collector was weeping as he lay on his side, his face drenched in sweat and tears. "Please," he begged. "Please." It was a face the old man recognized. It was the face of everyone he had ever known—and everyone who had ever hurt him. It was a white man's face, an Indian national's face, a Chinese national's face, a sarong party girl's face, a new urban male's face, a teenage punk's face, his ex-wife's face, her lover's face, his former boss's face, his representative of Parliament's face, the pig's face on the gate, all leering at him in unison like that goddamned *Smile, Singapore* poster. He had to get rid of all those faces.

He put the gun to his own temple, smiled at a terrified neighbor, and calmly pulled the trigger. There was a click. And then he understood what it wanted him to do. Everything was clear now. He lowered the gun again, put the little red dot on the collector's face, and squeezed the trigger three more times.

# PART II

LOVE (OR SOMETHING LIKE IT)

# REEL

BY CHERYL LU-LIEN TAN

*Changi*

---

Ah Meng knew how it would end even before they appeared.

The *nibong* poles would have long been in place, a wooden labyrinth designed to attract and confuse. He imagined their hearts racing, surges of blood pumping through, adrenaline pulling them further into the buttery blackness, panic steering them along the rows of columns. They would sense then that it was too late. Even so, there was nothing left to do but swim, just keep swimming. It carried reassurance, even if false. By the time the nets closed in, snuggling them together in a tight slippery ball, there was no more point in trying.

This was stupid daydreaming, Ah Meng's mum would say. Fish so stupid—where got brains to think? The woman had a point. And the truth of that was what kept the family in business. Not good business, mind you—fish farming was becoming far more practical and lucrative than *kelong* fishing these days. But to start a new fish farm—expensive, *lah*. Maybe when Ah Long came back from Queensland with his *atas* business degree then they could discuss. For now, with the *kelong* that Kong Kong set up years ago, the family managed to catch enough each month to pass the time. Not good, not bad. Just can, *lah*.

Just can. That was what Ah Meng's days were, one flowing into the next. His only relief came one Sunday. Ah Meng was squatting on the jetty after a late breakfast smoking a cigarette, trying to see how long he could pull on it, how long he could get the ash to last before it fell off in one long tube. He was getting better at it—almost reaching one and a half centimeters now!—which made him feel a bit proud, *lah*, even if no one noticed or cared. Life on the *kelong* is just like that, he had learned in a year. If you don't notice the small things, there's nothing to notice at all.

Monsoon season had just started, which was both okay and not so okay for fishing. Sometimes the stormy waters pushed flotillas of tiger groupers and cobia into the *kelong* traps. But some days all he and Siva hauled in were nets of shrimp and tiny crabs. No matter how many of those you caught—no point, *lah*. The Chinese restaurants only paid big bucks for large fish—nice nice one they can display in fish tanks.

Ma had just scolded him for squatting and smoking like a *samseng* the week before, when she suddenly showed up again in her new secondhand Corolla to spy on him. It was true that Ah Meng never used to do it until he started copying his army mates. But once she scolded him, *aiyoh*, he found himself doing it all the time. He couldn't understand his mother sometimes—she always said she came by without calling first because she happened to be in the neighborhood. But hello, Ah Meng was her son—wouldn't he know that she lived in Faber Crescent, all the way on the other side of the island? Sometimes Ah Meng couldn't believe how *toot* she thought he was. He wasn't smart like Ah Long, *lah*—can go university in Australia all. But she should at least know that he wasn't stupid. After last week, Ah Meng started really enjoying squatting on the jetty smoking. He liked imagining the look on his mum's face if she pulled up in her Corolla at that exact moment. The thought of that made each puff all the more *shiok*.

Spotting the girls made him get up though. There were

two—one big, one smaller. Skinny beanpoles with long pale legs. The big one had a long tidy ponytail; the little one, one of those Japanese doll haircuts. Even before they got close, Ah Meng could see how pretty they were. He could tell they were sisters—same button nose, same slightly crooked smile, same cheeks the color of young dragonfruit. They even walked the same, each turning out her feet just slightly. Watching them stroll down the pier toward the jetty, slender legs purposely pushing out from their matching black Adidas shorts, Ah Meng imagined them as birds. Were birds as stupid as fish?

They must have come from the village hawker center— each clutched a clear plastic bag of sugarcane juice jabbed with a neon pink straw. From their slippers, Ah Meng guessed that they lived close enough to walk. He tried to recall if he'd seen them before—he didn't think so. Girls weren't that common on this jetty so he was sure he would have noticed. A little farther away, yes, near the government holiday chalets on Strawberry Hill or closer to the canoeing and windsurfing joints in Changi Village. Sometimes at night, you might see the Malay ladyboys pop up and loiter a little, some of them looking for a break from walking, some just looking for a good spot for their clients, *lah*. But mostly all you saw on this jetty were the morning fishermen and the few *kelong* oldies left. And Ah Meng.

If he wanted to see any *chio* girls he usually had to take the bus to the Bedok town center. If he felt in the mood for *atas* girls then go Clarke Quay where the high-class clubs were, *lah*. But the girls there were a bit scary for him. None of them usually wanted to talk to him. Actually, the ones in Bedok also usually ignored him. They could probably tell immediately that he didn't have anything. No car, no Tag Heuer, not even a credit card. He hadn't had a girlfriend since before the army days. Once he got posted to Pulau Tekong for three months of artillery training, his girlfriend dumped him for a neighbor who'd already finished his army duty—he would actually be around to bring her out and didn't have a *toot*-looking shaved head anymore. It had been so long since Ah Meng had seen one pretty girl, much less two. He sucked hard on his cigarette.

How to play this?

He flicked his cigarette out into the water and lit another, steadying himself against the railing as he leaned back on one foot, hoping he looked a little like Tony Leung in one of those moody Shanghai movies. He got no hat or gangster suit, *lah*, but can still act a bit. When the girls got close enough, he turned his face away, narrowing his eyes as he peered out at the water. It hadn't rained yet so it was still that time of day when the air in the village tasted like moist salt. The girls' footsteps were so light, the way they walked so high class that he heard no sounds of slippers flapping against their heels. He could feel his heart walloping his chest. He blinked and looked farther out, focusing on his *kelong* in the distance. The small platformed house in the slender strait that sliced a passage between Malaysia and Singapore was barely visible, encircled with an uneven skyline of tall *nibong* stilts. All was quiet—good. Siva and his two boys were off on Sundays, so if anyone was actually puttering around on his *kelong*, that means sure got trouble.

"Is that your boat?"

Slowly he turned around. It was the smaller one.

"Yah," he said as casually as he could. The small one was smiling slightly; the big one stared at him blankly. He wasn't sure what to do.

"Is it expensive?" The small one again.

A very Singaporean question, he thought, noting that she must not be very smart to imagine that his beat-up wooden boat might be expensive. It was fairly large, yes—big enough to transport nets and basins of fish—with a small sheltered section lined with painted benches. Ma had come up with the brilliant idea of *kelong* tourism a few months back, until she discovered how much cash she'd have to sink into fixing up the place before people would actually pay to come for a chance to check out "one of Singapore's last real-life working *kelongs*!" Not to mention the boat they had was so old and *lau pok* that Ah Meng couldn't see anyone wanting to risk even minutes on it.

"Er, no. This one very old one," he replied, desperately trying to think of something better to say. He took another long drag.

"Do you give people rides?" The bigger girl this time, smiling at him along with the little one.

Ah Meng wasn't supposed to—lawsuits, Ma had explained. Better don't risk anything funny. So even when his army *kaki gajiau-*ed him for evening joyrides, promising to bring a nice bottle of Black Label if he agreed, he always said no.

"Sometimes," he said, quickly adding, "but only if the weather's nice."

"It's nice today," the big one said.

That was true. Though the rains hadn't come yet it was bluish out. Even the sun was up in full force. There was nothing left to say, so Ah Meng tossed his cigarette into the still water and gestured for them to follow, leading the girls down the neat walkway to the boat.

Since it had been their idea, he thought they would be more excited about seeing the boat up close. From the looks of it, though, the excitement was all his. He hoped they couldn't tell. The small one peeked closely at the vessel before letting him take her hand to help her onto the boat. But the older girl simply stepped on, settling in next to her sister on one of the two slender benches. Ah Meng was thankful that he had spent the morning hosing down the boat and Cloroxing everything so the deck smelled more like the sashimi section at Cold Storage than the aunties' fish stalls at the wet market.

"Why doesn't it have a name?" the small one asked as he leaned over to cast off. "Usually boats got name—right? Always painted on the side?"

Ah Meng had never considered this and had no answer. "I can maybe name it after you," he said. "What's your name?"

The small one looked at the big girl, who shrugged.

"Yan—Xiao Yan," the little one said, smiling. "And she's Ling Ling. You can combine them and call it *Yan Ling*?"

She sounded so earnest Ah Meng suddenly realized how young she probably was. And her sister probably not much older. He felt a twinge. But it had been so long. And it's not like he really had anything so bad in mind. He just wanted to be friends. And it occurred to him that since he was only twenty-two, the age difference wasn't terrible. Hell, girls his age were meeting and fucking guys twice their age! In just a few years these two girls would probably be doing exactly the same. Those guys they would be fucking were much older than Ah Meng was now!

Ah Meng was sick of it. If a guy is just trying to make do, who can blame him? Isn't that what the government wants? His mum wants? For him to show some initiative? Fuck care, *lah*.

"Tell you what—if I can find some paint on the *kelong* I'll even let you paint it on the side," he said.

Both girls got excited. "*Kelong*?" Ling said. "We've never been on a *kelong*!"

This was easier than he'd thought.

"Okay, *lah*, since you two so nice, maybe I can take you there," he tossed out, ducking into the cabin to start up the boat.

The girls got up and followed him, watching and saying nothing as he put the throttle in idle, jiggered the gearshift into neutral, then turned the starter switch, cranking the engine for a few seconds before feeling it catch, throwing the floor beneath them into a thick trundle. Yan stumbled backward but Ling reached out so quickly to grab her that Ah Meng had no time to react.

As they left the jetty, Ah Meng wondered how he might impress them. Using one hand to steer—a move he was now glad he had practiced every day—he guided the chugging vessel toward the *kelong*. The ride wouldn't take long, five minutes at the most. The shortness of it stressed him out. Ah Meng felt as if this was his moment to make an impression. He wasn't sure what they had in mind but it probably wasn't a rickety platformed house surrounded by smelly nets of fish.

"You see that island over there?" he said, pointing toward the larger of the two that he glimpsed through the door of his dank room every day. The girls nodded. "That's Pulau Ubin."

The girls remained silent. Ah Meng tried to remember anything he might know about Ubin.

"It's haunted," he said. Yan and Ling looked bored.

Ah Meng decided to circle the *kelong* to buy a little time. He tried to remember an old story he'd heard from some of the fishing uncles in Changi the one time they invited him to join them for beers at the hawker center.

"I know it looks like nothing but trees and jungle, *lah*," he said. "But Ubin actually quite interesting one. Years and years ago there was nothing there. But then three animals from Singapore—a frog, a pig, and an elephant—decided to challenge each other to see who could swim across and reach Malaysia first. Whoever didn't make it would turn into stone. In the end they all also cannot make it, *lah*—the elephant and the pig turned into stone in the same spot, becoming Pulau Ubin. The frog was a little bit further from them and became Pulau Sekudu—Frog Island. You see that small one over there? The big rock in the middle looks like a frog, right?"

Ah Meng exhaled as softly as he could. He felt his heart chugging harder than the boat. This was the most he'd said to any girl he didn't know in a long time.

Something must have worked though—the girls went to the window and stared out. Ling was pointing, whispering and nudging Yan to look at Sekudu. The little girl said, "Wah!" and giggled softly. Ah Meng felt a burst of pride. He'd made her laugh!

The boat passed the nearest *kelong* to Ah Meng's, giving him a new thought. What if the boys over there were out and about? If they saw the girls on his boat, *susah lah*. People around here were damn fucking gossipy. With nothing happening every day, any small new thing—*wah*, people talked and talked about it for weeks.

He sped up as he passed. Let them think he was rude for not waving today.

The girls had returned to his side and were watching him steer. In silence, he circled his *kelong* and pulled to a stop at the landing. He gestured to them to stay in the cabin while he tied the boat to the *kelong* dock, jumped off, and tightened the connection, then waved to them to come out. Ling helped Yan off the boat before getting off herself.

Ah Meng looked around, squinting hard to gauge how clearly he could see into old Tan's *kelong* across the way. All seemed quiet over there—the boys must be on the mainland. Oh yah—day off.

Feeling much better, he led the way, wending down the slatted path that zigzagged around the series of sunken pools outlined with tall poles. A breeze was coming through now. He peered behind him; the girls were walking hand in hand, carefully treading in his footsteps. Yan seemed a little scared and was moving slower than Ling.

"Don't worry," he said, stopping and turning to face them. "People never fall in one."

"But if fall in, then how?" Yan asked.

"Not good, *lah*," he said, squatting down by one of the pools. He felt around for something to show them what he meant, patting his pockets and pulling out his pack of Salems. Ah Meng held a cigarette up for the girls to see.

"Inside here, ah," he said, pointing to a square of water, "got many many fish. Especially today—we holiday today, *mah*, so don't bring them to town until tomorrow. These fish, ah, anything also eat one. Small fish, each other, anything you throw in also they take."

Ah Meng threw his cigarette into the water and a violent vortex bubbled up. He imagined the swirl of fish below shoving and nipping at each other, trying to reach for what might be new food. The girls were giggling now.

"Do it again!" Ling said.

And so he did. Even if ciggies had become fucking expensive, he was sure this would be worth it. He flung the second one a little farther out. Even he was laughing along with the girls now.

Ah Meng glanced over at them—Yan didn't look scared anymore. He realized this was the happiest he'd felt in a very long time. He had been thinking recently about how ironic it was that the infamous Changi prison, where British prisoners of war were kept during the Japanese Occupation and now home to dangerous criminals, was so close to his *kelong*. Yah, sure— those guys in there now were prisoners. But hallo, so was Ah

Meng! What kind of life was this at the *kelong*? He was supposed to do it just for two years, until Ah Long came back from
uni. But from the way Ma had been talking, it seemed as if she
was happy to have him take care of business on the *kelong* for
good. Save money what—no need to hire a new *kelong* manager
all. *Kani nah.* Just thinking about Ah Long coming back and
getting to sit in some air-con office, planning the family business's future while Ah Meng sweated his balls off at the *kelong*,
made him want to vomit blood.

Ah Long had recently sent Ma some picture of a girlfriend—some small-small, cute-cute Singaporean girl who was
studying business in Queensland also. Ma was so excited, asked
Ah Long to make sure to bring her home for Chinese New Year.
Of course Ah Long could meet girls like that, *lah*—Ma send
him away to study all. But Ah Meng? Put him on the *kelong*,
how to meet girls? All the action he got most nights was
hearing Siva in the room next door whacking off. When Ah
Meng first started on the *kelong* Siva at least tried to be a bit
quiet about it. But now, after a year, the guy damn not shy one.
Ah Meng heard each long grunt through the thin wall between
them.

Now, though—who was the winner? Ah Meng looked over
at Yan and Ling, both of their faces bright, upturned, almost
glinting in the sun. He shook his head and smiled at his fortune. Just wait till Ma saw these two. When they were a little
older, perhaps.

"Come," he said, getting up and starting back toward the
house. "You girls hungry?"

Choosing not to show them his bedroom just yet, Ah Meng
led them to the small kitchen where he, Siva, and the boys
cooked instant noodles most days. Once a week they split a

fish—nothing special, just the first thing they netted that was large enough for the four of them. Ah Meng had caught one just that morning, thinking that he might have it all to himself tonight as a treat. He took it out of the fridge and showed it to the girls.

"You cook?" he asked.

Ling nodded. "Just helping Mum in the kitchen some-times," she said, opening drawers to search for a knife. She had never gutted a fish, so Ah Meng showed her how. Once that was done, he handed her the knife and let her chop up the rest. He didn't know how to cook so he usually just fried up pieces of fish with some green onions and soy sauce. When he explained this to Ling, she took over.

Ah Meng went to the fridge and grabbed two cold Anchor beers. He offered one to Ling but she shook her head. "Uncle—I'm only fifteen, *lah*," she said, laughing.

Fifteen. Ah Meng felt the twinge again. He'd come this far. See how, *lor*. If got chance then got chance. No chance then no chance. The gods would decide.

He lightly pinched Ling's cheek, a move that made her smile a little wider, surprising him. He felt himself start to blush and turned away. Opening a can of Anchor, Ah Meng sat down by the chipped square table outside the kitchen where he, Siva, and the boys had their meals. This day was turning out not bad, *lah*. But what next? He wasn't sure. When Ah Meng first saw the girls, he had thought he might say hello and maybe offer them a ride on his boat in the near future. Now that they were on the *kelong*, he had no idea what to do.

*Chuan dao qiao tou zhi ran zhi*—Ah Meng hadn't paid much attention to Chinese classes in secondary school but this old saying popped into his head. *When the boat reaches the head of the bridge, it will naturally straighten itself out.* He leaned back against the rusted metal folding chair and stretched his legs, getting settled before lighting up a Salem.

As his cigarette disappeared, he noticed the smell of fish frying in onions. Good girl, he thought. In minutes, Ling and Yan appeared bearing a plate of fish and three sets of chopsticks. Ling had tucked another can of Anchor under her arm, setting it down shyly in front of him. Ah Meng looked at the girl, blushing again.

They ate in silence. Feeling like he needed to thank Ling, Ah Meng said, "*Wah*, your cooking very good!" Ling just smiled and continued digging out plump little pieces of fish, using her fingers to remove hairlike bones, before offering them to Yan. This pleased Ah Meng. *She'll make a very good mother*, he thought, wondering how their first kiss might be, how her lips would feel on his, on his neck, more. He didn't feel guilty.

"You live here alone?" Ling suddenly asked, heading into the kitchen to get more beer when she noticed Ah Meng crumpling up his second can.

"I wish!" he said, laughing. "But no, *lah*. My workers here also. But today off day."

Ling, back with two cans, opened one for Ah Meng. "Isn't it lonely?" she asked. "Don't you have a girlfriend?"

Ah Meng wasn't sure what to say. Explain too much and she would think he was a loser. Tell her too little and she might think he wasn't interested in girls.

"Last time," he said, wiping his mouth with his palm and lighting another cigarette. "Now no more. No time, *lah*! Why? Want to be my girlfriend, is it?"

Ling said nothing but Ah Meng could see her smiling. Yan was absently picking at fish remnants, putting nothing more in her mouth. His mind was feeling a bit like cotton balls. He normally didn't drink this much so early—and usually not when it was so hot. Beer is nice in the afternoon, *lah*, but maybe when you're sitting in a shady hawker center or in your friend's air-con house. Out on the *kelong*, drinking in the afternoon sure got headache one. And he could feel one happening right now. Die, *lah*—like that how to perform? Ah Meng quickly finished the last swigs of his Anchor, crumpling the can. Too late, he heard Ling opening the other can on the table, pushing it toward him. He wanted to say no but she looked so deferential, her sweet face so much wanting to please, that he just nodded toward her, took the fresh beer with both hands, and had a few long sips.

Yan, bored, got up and wandered toward the slatted footpath near the fish.

"*Oi!* Be careful!" Ling shouted, jumping up and hurrying after her. Ah Meng did the same, falling in step with the girls after Ling had caught up to Yan, taking her hand, firmly guiding her to walk only in the very middle of the footpath, so narrow in parts it was almost like a gangplank.

When the path took them to the heart of the wooden maze, Ling and Yan picked a darker spot and sat down, cross-legged, staring out at the cloudy green water so calm that Ah Meng wondered if the fish were sleeping. He sat down next to Ling, getting as close as he could.

He felt the girl place her head on his shoulder. His heart started going like a motor. He knew there was no way she couldn't feel that and the thought made him blush again. He draped his right hand around her shoulder, pulling her closer, shutting his eyes to photograph the feeling.

A minute passed. Ah Meng was counting the time with his heartbeats. One one thousand, two one thousand, three . . . When he opened his eyes, Ling was peering up at him, her large brown eyes open and sweet and cool. He felt his left hand reach over to brush a long piece of hair away from her forehead so he could look closer.

Ling didn't move. The gods had spoken. So Ah Meng got even closer. He felt so full his chest hurt. He pinched his eyes shut, leaning toward her, lips extended.

He didn't realize his lips had never made contact until he opened his eyes, finding that he was falling over backward. The pain in his chest was still there—so was Siva's favorite fish knife. Ling was squatting by him now, casually watching him grope at the knife. He could see Yan standing behind her, covering her face with her little hands.

His T-shirt was so wet, his hands were so red. When Ling reached over and pulled out the knife, Ah Meng feeling each of the eight inches as it slid out, his first thought was to thank her for helping him. But too quickly, she plunged it back in, hitting a higher spot this time. Ah Meng gasped, feeling a tinny wetness coming up from his throat.

"Hurry up," he heard her say. "Help!"

His mind was a swirl of cotton. Dimly, he felt Ling pull out the knife and toss it into the water. Then the feeling of four hands pushing, rolling him. Once, twice.

Yan was crying, but very softly. Ling couldn't hear her over the boat's engine but sensed it anyway. Holding onto the steering wheel with her right hand and steadying it the way she remembered seeing the guy do it, she reached her left out toward Yan, gesturing for her to take it. The rains still hadn't come; the ride had been smooth. They would be back at the jetty in a few minutes.

Feeling Yan take her hand, Ling squeezed it. Glancing over, she saw that her little sister had stopped sobbing.

"Don't worry," Ling said. "Next time will be easier."

# MOTHER

BY MONICA BHIDE

*Kallang*

The Merdeka Bridge became Edward's home after the killing. He spent hours on it watching people go by. Nothing in this lonely city was his anymore; even the sky was different. But the water flowing gently under the bridge provided solace. The sound of the small waves, heard only when traffic disappeared, the gentleness of the ripples, those were the only things that reminded him of home. The home he left after the killing—or suicide, as some called it.

He knew better, the kill was neither a simple murder nor a suicide. But no one would understand that; they couldn't. They did not love her like he did; you had to love someone to the degree he did to understand why it had happened.

At the moment, though, he felt bad at having said something to the young woman—Ms. Ana, as he liked to call her—who had been running by him on the bridge. He saw her almost every night. She ran around the same time. Normally, she would stop and speak to him but today she seemed distracted; she even tripped and fell. He could see she was bleeding. He offered her a hand and was hurt when she recoiled. He was tall for his fifteen years, really tall for a Chinese kid. His time on the streets showed in the dirt caked in his ears. He had pulled several tufts of hair out of his head after finding lice crawling down his forehead and into the small, festering sores on the sides of his cheeks.

He knew what she was thinking; his friends told him: *Homeless man wants my money.*

He did not want her money; he liked her.

"Ms. Ana, it's me, Eddie," he offered, "Don't you remember? You gave me ten dollars last week."

"Yes, of course I do. How are you? Did you eat something?" Ms. Ana asked, wiping her chin with the edge of her T-shirt.

He smiled. "Yah, three times! Thank you."

"How do you feel today?"

"My friends, Ms. Ana, they are back. They went away and now they are back. I don't know why. I say to them to go away. Tell them to leave me alone, Ms. Ana, tell them to go away," he said, beginning to weep.

Gently, she sat down next to him and gave him a hug and then reached into her sock and pulled out a twenty.

"Keep this, Eddie, eat something." He smiled at her.

"The jacket you gave me keeps me so warm, Ms. Ana. It is so cold out here at night sometimes. The jacket is so warm."

"Come tomorrow, I will bring you some more clothes, but now I have to go."

Eddie tried showing Ms. Ana his friends. No one could see them. It made him so mad. They constantly talked to him. Never let him sleep. His brain tried to stop them from talking. But no, they knew better. They knew how to sneak up on him when no one was looking. Yah, they were sneaky, those friends.

He held onto Ms. Ana's hand as she stood up. She was so kind and warm. "Can you stay with me for a few more minutes?"

"I have to go, Eddie, I have to go," she said, tugging at her hand.

*Let her go, Eddie, she won't stay. Your hands are ugly, filthy. You smell. Let her go. She belongs in a different world.*

Truth was, he was hungry; he could not stand too well, his

head was spinning. He let her hand go and she turned to run and then stopped and came back to him.

He looked up at her surprised that she had returned so quickly. She bent down and gave him a gentle hug, then quickly turned around and ran off.

Most of the people he met could not get away from him fast enough and she had given him a hug.

*Be careful, Eddie, she may want something. You should watch her.*

Eddie pulled some more hair out; his friends were definitely back. The mean one had not started speaking yet. It was just a matter of time.

*Look around you, Eddie, you don't belong here. These people have perfect lives, big houses, shiny cars, lots of money. And they have good families. Not like yours. Their families care. They don't run around and let the kids fend for themselves.*

*Don't listen to him, Eddie. He is a* goondu! *She was a good woman, your ma. No, you tell him to stop, now. You wouldn't be in this shit if you listened to me and not him.*

Two older aunties were walking by now—Eddie watched as they moved carefully to avoid him. He felt lousy. He hated being on the streets. It was pathetic. He was homeless even though he had a home. He did not want to go home—the warmth of it reminded him of his mother. He did not want to be reminded of her. He missed her. No, he was better off outside.

*You know it is easier to be outside, Eddie. The house will be full of her things and there, they . . . they will be looking for you . . . they know what you did, they will try to get you. You need to stay out of the house.*

Eddie got up from the bridge and began to walk toward the lights of Kallang, away from the river, peering at the reflection of the setting sun as it glinted on the water.

A light breeze was rolling in. Luckily, Ms. Ana had given

him the jacket a week earlier. It was gray and blue with the word *Singapore* on the back.

*You know, Eddie, Ma would have loved your jacket.*

*No way, Eddie, she would be ashamed, you were her dream and now here you are wearing people's garbage.*

Eddie paused when he got to the bus stop. His hunger pangs had become an accurate indicator of time and they told him that Uncle Teo would be driving up soon in bus number 26 and Eddie would spend the next hour in its comfortable air-con before returning to the streets for the rest of the night. He thought for a minute about going home. But the house stifled him. Each time the phone rang, his heart jumped—maybe it was the police looking for him, or perhaps, just perhaps there was a miracle and his mother had come back. Neither ever happened.

The streets were better. No one knew him.

Uncle Teo opened the bus door and pretended not to notice that Eddie offered no fare—again. This was an older bus, one that wended a well-traveled route, and Eddie could always detect the familiar smell of dirt, sweat, and sometimes vomit lingering just beneath the scent of chemical sprays.

*This is what being unwanted smells like, Eddie, get used to it. This is the rest of your life.*

"Go to the last seat," Uncle Teo casually said, "someone left a McDonald's bag. Maybe inside got some *makan*."

It was the same routine each night.

*Maybe he poisoned the burger, Eddie. Who would want to feed you? You are such a waste of flesh.*

*No, no, Eddie. He loves you. You can repay him someday. Don't listen to that man. You are a good boy, Edward. Eat the Big Mac.*

Eddie clutched at his head. It was pounding, and the voices were getting stronger and louder.

He found the bag on a crackled cushion in the back of the

bus and inhaled the two burgers; his first and last meal of the day.

If only Ma had told him the truth.

He stared out the window at the spectacle of purpose on the street. People were busy, had places to go, things to do, goals to accomplish. He'd had it all too until Ma's rape. The rape changed everything. The voices, his friends, had shown up that day.

The day that changed everything was an ordinary day, a sunny one. After school, he had headed to the East Coast lagoon as usual, spending the afternoon helping tourists and schoolkids carry kayaks and canoes in and out of the water. The tips were good.

Eddie headed home only after the last of the canoes was put away.

"Ma! Ma! I home already," he'd called, as he entered their tiny ground-floor flat that sparkled on the outside thanks to his mother's hot-pink bougainvilleas. Inside it was cool. His mother had found a discarded air conditioner at the school where she worked and spent a lot of money getting it repaired. Then she'd had it installed in Eddie's room.

"Ma," he called again, but there was no response. On the dining table was a sardine sandwich with onions, his favorite. He hated eating alone but the swim had tired him out. Once the sandwich disappeared, he waited at the door for her to come home. Generally she arrived by nine. But that day she was late, very late.

He had fallen asleep near the door when he heard it open hours later. Then he saw her, in the stark fluorescent light from the deck outside—she walked through the front door covered in dirt. Her white blouse was ripped and she was clutching at it in the middle, desperately trying to keep it closed. She seemed oblivious to him as she entered. He averted his eyes so she would not feel the shame of having her son look at her in this state of undress. His mind was racing. He quickly glanced over to see if she was bleeding; he could see no red.

He followed her to her room. "What happened to you?"

"Nothing, *lah* . . . nothing. Go to bed, Eddie," she said very softly, "I'm okay."

He wanted to protest. But he just stood there, unsure of what to do. She sat on the edge of the bed, the white sheets now stained with dirt from her blue cotton skirt and open blouse. She covered her face with her hands and he noticed her nails were chipped.

"Go to bed, Edward. I am fine. I mean it, go to bed. I am fine." Then she stood up and ran into the shower. He understood. She was trying to wash away the sins of another.

Eddie went to the refrigerator. It was a wonder the twenty-five-year-old contraption still worked. Grabbing a packet of soursop juice, he sat down at their rickety dining table.

Had she been assaulted? Raped? What if it were rape? How would they ever get over it? This was not happening; it was like a scene from a bad movie.

He felt his hands crush the packet as anger flowed into his arms. He wanted to kill the bastard who'd hurt his mother. After all, he was the man of the house. He never knew his father, except through the pictures his mother kept around the house. He loved the one where his father beamed, holding his newborn boy. It was taken at the house when Eddie was just two days old. That was the last time his father held him.

His father's death was a testament to the times they lived in, his mother often said. He worked as a bank teller— a disgruntled employee and a knife told the rest of the story. Just like that, for no reason at all, his twenty-five-year-old father had been stabbed. Their only solace was he died almost instantly.

After his father's death, Ma seemed to forget everything except how to make sure that she and Eddie had enough to eat. She had no friends, preferring to spend all her free time with him. He was grateful that she was not interested in dating men. Unlike other kids in his school whose divorced parents were seeing other people, Ma seemed happy to be alone. She never seemed to need anyone besides Eddie.

Yes, he was thankful.

"You are like my tail, Eddie, always behind me," she would joke.

He rarely left her side, even when other kids and even some adults made fun of him. "Let her go, Eddie, she has to work. You can't be her shadow your whole life, you know—you have to be your own man," they would say.

Ma worked shifts at the primary school nearby, doing anything and everything disgusting—the clean-up lady no one noticed. She cleaned the toilets, collected rubbish, and even mopped vomit, feces, and urine off the bathroom floors. He felt sorry for her when he watched her cry herself to sleep each night. Someday, he hoped, he could give her peace.

Even so, everything was perfect when it was just the two of them, Ma and Eddie. Until that day when Ma came home with ripped clothes.

Eddie could still hear her in the shower as he left the dining table and walked into her room. She had such simple tastes, a tiny bed with a tattered mosquito net draped over it, a small side table where she always set down the romance novel she was reading, her prayer books neatly stacked on a narrow book-shelf on the other side of the room. He wandered over and ran his hand across the prayer books. His poor God-fearing mother.

What would this rape do to her? Would she be able to handle life now that she had been desecrated?

He saw the bathroom door open and fled. He did not want her to see his tears. He could not help but cry. After all, what could he do to help her?

His head began to pound. Voices that he had ignored for so long began to get louder, stronger; first begging and then demanding that he listen to them. They owned him and he could no longer ignore them.

*You are the man of the house, Eddie. You have to help her. Find out what happened.*

*How can you leave her in there alone?*

*You are a coward, you cannot do anything. You should have died in the womb.*

*Yes, Eddie you are a loser.*

He left the house and ran across two wide streets, down the passage beneath the highway, and emerged on the beach clutching at his head and screaming, "Stop it, stop it, go away, go away, I don't hear you, go away, go away!"

As he sat on the dark beach throwing rocks into the water, gentle cold waves washed his feet, calming him down. The emptiness of the beach reminded him of his mother's life. She had nothing except him and her honor. Tonight she had lost the more important of the two. He could never restore that.

As the sun came up, he decided to go home. Ma was sound asleep.

*Sleeping?! How can your ma sleep, Eddie? Has she no shame? She should be praying to God and asking for help. She should be cleaning herself. How can she sleep at a time like this?*

*What woman sleeps after being raped? Why hasn't she called the cops?*

*Maybe she liked it, eh, Eddie? Maybe your ma misses having a man around.*

"No, no, no!" He covered his mouth and then his ears as the voices began to take over.

The next morning, he tried to talk to her: "Who was he? What happened? Were you attacked? Is it someone we know?"

She would not answer.

Her purity had been lost and she seemed not to care.

*She has become a slut. She liked it with the strange man. Or men. Why else won't she tell you what happened? You don't know her anymore, Eddie. She was with a man—a man, Eddie, who was not your father. She was with a stranger.*

*No, no, Eddie, she was possibly raped. You need to take care of her.*

*Yes, Eddie, you need to take care of her. She needs to be cleansed of all the filth, the sins.*

He had too much on his mind to go to his ridiculous special school so he wandered off to the arcade in Parkway Parade. He needed to think and school was not the place to be. Fortunately, the voices left him alone at the arcade.

Around noon, he decided to head home. His mother was usually at work at this time, but this day was different, he knew she would be home.

He saw her back first; she appeared to be on the phone. She turned toward the door, but did not seem to notice him. She was staring at the ceiling and talking very quickly.

"I can't believe this happened . . ." she was saying.

He stopped. Perhaps now he would hear what had occurred. She would reveal the name of the bastard to her friend, he thought. This would be good, he needed to know and he would find out right now. She began to cry and her words got muffled. He could barely make out what she was saying, and he stared hard at her lips.

"We were walking through the park . . ." She was clearly getting more and more agitated. "It was so quiet and no one was around. He turned and kissed me and then . . . and then he pulled at my blouse . . . in the dirt right here in the park. I can't believe it happened. I think I'm—" She stopped mid-sentence when she saw him and quickly hung up the phone. "Would you like something to eat?"

He said no. Her question surprised him; usually it would have been a torrent of, *Why are you not in school? Where have you been?* Today she seemed uninterested.

*Told you, man. Told you, she is hiding something.*

*She is seeing a man.*

*Eddie, don't listen to him. You don't know what she said. You did not read her lips all the way through. You don't know the whole story.*

*There he goes, Eddie, calling you stupid because you can't hear properly. Yes, he is calling you stupid—are you going to let him do that?*

*No, I am not stupid.*

*I never said you were.*

Thoughts clawed at his brain like tiny crabs taking over the shoreline.

He remembered that day even more clearly than the day of the rape. Because after that phone call, her behavior began to really change.

Ma began to stay out later after work each day. When he asked why, she made excuses that made no sense. She seemed constantly lost in thought, and he hated the fact that she ignored his questions. She began to scout local resale stores for silk blouses and bright skirts. She even started wearing makeup. Perhaps, he thought, she feels like she has been prostituted so she needs to dress and behave like one. He wondered how he could help her. He asked her constantly about that day; she never responded.

Although she did still go to the Holy Family Church, he noticed that she had stopped praying in the mornings. She was more concerned with the way her hair looked than with reading the Bible.

*I told you, she is turning into a prostitute.*

*No, she isn't. She is a kind, gentle woman, don't forget that, Eddie.*

*She is a prostitute, Eddie. Ever wonder where she goes out at night? Why is she so late? Who is she with? Why won't she tell you?*

The final straw was when she began to have people over several times a month. Men and women came to his house for what she called a reading club, to discuss some book. He hated them on sight, and hated the fake attention they showered on him. She thrived on it. A cleaning lady in a book club—it was a joke. The people came and talked to her, they ate and drank together and laughed. They were stealing his mother from him, and she was letting it happen.

"Why are you trying to be so *atas?*" he asked one day, and she slapped him. It was the first time.

*She doesn't need you anymore, Eddie. She has them.*

*A cleaning woman—what does she need to read for, Eddie?*

*She is becoming atas, Eddie. Soon she will think you aren't good enough for her.*

He began to withdraw.

He knew it was all because of the rape. It had changed her; she was no longer the beautiful, pious woman he had loved. She was now a cheap slut, flaunting herself in front of these people in her new clothes and makeup, laughing out loud, pretending to be someone she was not. He was sure she was in a lot of pain.

*You are right, Eddie, she needs help.*

*Her soul has been desecrated, you need to cleanse her. She is in pain. Evil is making her hide the pain. You need to help her, Eddie, she is your ma. She would do the same for you.*

*Help her, man, help her.*

The decision was made. The voices were unanimous. He decided he would help her. He would put her out of her pain.

He picked a day about two weeks later, telling her he had saved enough to treat his mother to a nice meal.

Then he began to plan, meticulously writing down each step.

When the day finally arrived, his mind was calm. He was prepared.

Even though God had not given him the best ears or brain, he had given him several advisors who dwelled in his head.

His mother dressed down for the dinner, which pleased him.

At five p.m., he told her he was ready to go.

Together they walked to a little beachside restaurant nearby, one he knew she liked. Because it was right by the water, you could feel the sand under your feet at the table. Ma loved it, and he wanted her to enjoy this evening.

She ordered her favorite, fermented shrimp-coated fried chicken wings, for the two of them, the extra large basket that they had shared many times before.

As they ate, he began to tell her about the new place he had discovered—it would be his present for her birthday.

"It's beautiful, Ma! You have to see it, will you come with me?"

She smiled at him. "Yes, of course."

She reached into her purse to pay. He protested. It was his treat, he said. After he paid, he took her hand and started walking.

They had been strolling along the water for about fifteen minutes when Ma started worrying. "Where is it, Eddie? I'm getting tired and it's getting dark."

"Just a bit longer, Ma," he said.

They reached a tiny jetty, a long slender walkway that cut a swath far out into the blue.

Eddie squeezed his mother's hand, gently tugging her along as he stepped onto the jetty and headed toward the edge. "Happy Birthday, Ma!" He beamed as he pointed toward the panorama at the end of the pier.

She had lived on Singapore's East Coast all her life, but even in the dimming light of the evening, she was stunned by the view. He had managed to find a view of the sea that she had never seen before. Shades of blue looked like flowing silk, the shadowy tankers twinkled in the distance. All the colors and sights melded together to form a perfect seascape.

She stepped further toward the edge to take in the beauty. She never saw the push coming.

*This is for you, Ma, this will save your soul.*

*Yes, Eddie, you did it, you have cleansed her of her sins. Now she will be with Him, she is safe.*

When she screamed, he began shouting along too: "Ma. I love you! I'm coming, Ma! I love you!" In a new pure world, they would be together. No unhappiness.

He closed his eyes and took a step forward. But then a bony hand grabbed him and pulled him back.

"Ah, boy!" he heard a stranger shout. "What happened? Did your mother fall in?"

Eddie began to cry.

Her funeral was held a few days later. It was a quiet ceremony. There was no body; it was never found.

When her new friends, the ones he hated, showed up, he sidled up next to them to hear what they were saying.

"Pity," said one.

"Yes," agreed another, "she was so in love and ready for her new life. What a waste."

Love? In love? What were they saying? His mother in love?

"Yes," whispered the first. "She told me about him a few months ago. Their first encounter made me blush! They made love in Fort Canning Park! She said she was a mess when she got home."

The jolt of the bus stopping brought him back to the present. "Time to get off, Eddie," Uncle Teo said. "I'm sorry."

Eddie thanked him and walked out into the night breeze. The bus had dropped him off where he had started, by the Merdeka Bridge.

He pulled the thin jacket closer to his body, heading to his usual spot in a corner. When he closed his eyes, he knew he would see his mother, the jetty, her back, his hands. Slowly but surely the dreams would come; dreams filled with snakes. Some nights they would slither up his legs first—on others, they would simply coil around his stomach. Just before the bites, he would wake up screaming.

# KENA SAI

BY S.J. ROZAN

*Bukit Timah*

O n Monday afternoon the old man with the *erhu* was
at the corner again.

In the soft shade of a *tembusu* he sat on a folding stool,
the ancient battered instrument held upright. The knobby fingers of his left hand slid along the strings while his right arm
worked the bow. A tight-stretched cobra skin fattened each
long slow note before releasing it into the air.

Watching through sinuous heat shimmering up from the
concrete, Ed was caught. Davey stopped also. He stared, let go
of Ed's hand, balanced for a moment on not-quite-steady tod-
dler legs, then plopped down on the grass of the verge, never
taking his eyes off the old man. Ed smiled and slid down against
a mahogany tree. It would make no difference when they arrived at Ellen's. They could stay here for now and drift on these
melodies, alien and alluring.

The old man's hands gained speed, racing, nimble as the
macaques in the park; then they slowed, slipped supple and
flowing, like the water in the Strait. The macaques had ruled the
island once, dancing through the trees, screaming by the water
holes. The Strait had washed the shores of island and mainland,
tying them together as it held them apart. Now the few macaques
left were confined to the reserve and the Strait was causewayed
and ferried, narrowed by landfill and curbed by barriers. But
the monkeys were still monkeys and the water was still water.

The music sounded sad to Ed. That was the minor scale, he knew. Probably these were not sad songs, just his Western ears that made them so. The old man did look sad, though. Because he was far from home? Or because he was old? Or because no one but Ed and Davey stopped to listen, and he knew Ed didn't understand?

No one in Singapore stopped to listen, or stopped for anything. No one played music on streetcorners, either, and on a less out-of-the-way sidewalk the old man would've been arrested for interfering with the public progress, for distracting citizens from their daily rounds, for being unnecessary. But on this hot afternoon in Bukit Timah, no one other than Ed and Davey were on the street to be distracted.

Ed wondered if the old man lived here, in this sweet, treed expat enclave where Westerners dwelled to be reminded of home. He doubted he did, thought it more likely he traveled to this corner by bus, to other corners of the island also, other quiet empty suburbs where he could sit and play his quavering melodies in the damp heat. Maybe he lived with his family; maybe his daughter was a banker, his son-in-law a doctor, his grandchildren energetic high-achievers who ran off in their school uniforms in the morning, none of them with time for the old man's music or his memories. Maybe, long ago, young and energetic himself, he'd come to Singapore from South China, from heat like this, and now he was old and an expat and he, too, wanted to be reminded of home.

Ed didn't. Home was worlds, years, lives away. He didn't miss it and he didn't want to go back there, back to New York, back to winter slush and politics he had to pay attention to and buses that didn't come. It was ten years since they'd left, since Ellen had called, so excited, the promotion had come through and they were headed to London. No more taxi drivers who didn't know the way, no more slithery roaches, pretentious hipsters, brown smothering clouds drifting over from New Jersey.

"I think they have roaches," Ed smiled, kissing her at the door that night. Her eyes had been glowing. "And I'm sure they have hipsters."

"My God, what smells so great in here?"

"Roast beef and Yorkshire pudding. I thought I should learn the exotic cuisine."

All through dinner she talked, making lists, assigning tasks. She would tackle this and Ed should follow through on that. He sipped his wine, enjoying her incandescence, her mad caroming. A month later they'd settled into a West London flat. "You've got to call it a *flat* now, darling," she told him as she breezed out the door her first day.

Ed's own clients were people he'd never met and they didn't care where he was as long as their websites got designed, updated, and populated, a word that delighted him: as though each page were a tiny village, *JoeJones.com, pop. 313*. He methodically took care of them and then took long midday walks, as he had in New York, as he always had.

In their new suburban London home Ed saw himself as one of the islands revealed when the tide of commuters swept out each morning. His walks took him to the greengrocer, the locksmith, the fishmonger, islands also, each one craggy or forbidding or gentle, each one worth exploring. The cars driving on the left-hand side of the road he found interesting to watch, like choreographed dancers in a number new to him. He wondered whether England had no tornados because her traffic went counter-clockwise. He learned to differentiate the subtle variations of fog and rain and he liked the clinks when he jingled the coins that made his pockets heavy.

Ellen didn't. The money exasperated her and she couldn't

get used to traffic coming from the wrong direction. The gray
weather was draining. The cabbies never got lost but there
weren't many places, she found, that she wanted to go.

"New York made such sense," she sighed over lamb chops
and green beans one night. The chops were particularly good;
Ed had made friends with the butcher, a fat man from Sussex.
*I've given ye the best ones, tender and tasty if ye cook 'em right.*

"London," Ellen went on, shaking her head. "It's so . . .
medieval." Her response was to buckle down and work harder.
Eighteen months later she called home one morning, an hour
after she got to work, thrilled once again: they were going to
Prague.

In Prague Ed liked the tensions between the past and the
present, the red roofs, the smell of yeast and cinnamon from the
bakery. He couldn't master Czech but the baker spoke English.
*From Madagascar, the vanilla, she's cost too much but nothing else
worth having.* Ed cooked chicken with onions and paprika. Ellen
railed against the narrow streets and the traffic. In London, she
said, it rained all the time but at least you could get around.

After Prague, Buenos Aires, where Ed paused in his walks
to sit in cafés on wide boulevards. *Try first without milk, señor, you
drink Argentine coffee now.* He grilled butter-tender steaks and
Ellen felt nostalgic for buttoned-up Prague where ragtop cars
didn't pound out music twenty-four hours a day. Then Nairobi,
to Ed a never-still metropolis of old jeeps, bright cloth, musical
speech (*Fresh pineapple! Come buy it! You can do much wid it!*),
and dark, glistening faces. He learned to make *ugali* from corn-
meal and served it with roast goat. To Ellen, Nairobi was dust
that made her cough, bottled water, failed Internet connections
(in Buenos Aires the technology worked), and armed guards.

In Nairobi, she got pregnant. It was time, she said; they
didn't want to wait until they were too old, until conceiving

was a chore and delivery a risk, did they? Ed thought perhaps she'd want to go home, at least to have the baby, but she was working on some major deals and so Davey was born in Aga Khan Hospital three months before they moved to Singapore.

Singapore astonished Ed.

Ellen's colleagues envied the assignment because, they said, Singapore was Asia Lite. Not like being sent to Shanghai or Tokyo, with their illegible street signs, illegible menus, illegible manners. Everything worked in Singapore. Crime barely existed, the water was safe. Everything worked, and worked in ways you understood. Not that life was perfect. The trees were groomed and the sidewalks practically polished, traffic flowed—but be careful, they were warned: Singapore, it's Disneyland with the death penalty. Jaywalking, gum-chewing, free-thinking: just watch yourselves.

Ellen didn't care about jaywalking, or free-thinking either. She was happy to be an expat among expats, to mix only with other Westerners, to live as though she weren't in Asia at all. The safe, clean, functioning Singapore was the one she came looking for, the one she found, the one that—for a time— pleased her.

Ed saw all that—how could you miss it?—but it wasn't his Singapore. More than anywhere they'd lived, more than where they'd come from, Singapore instantly felt like home.

He loved the damp heat, the daily rain, the bright and gray skies alternating, striping the day. The storms that blew through and scoured the air. The breathless young Singaporeans in the business of business; the expat community constantly churning, impermanent, strangers arriving and friends departing every day. Cultures mashing into one another in heady confusion: the swirling scents of curry, coconut milk, and coriander, the roast Cornish hen with fingerling potatoes in one café, the *nasi lemak* in the next, the chicken *tajine* a few doors down. Singapore had four official languages, but the one Ed loved was the unofficial one, the one everyone spoke: Singlish—in vocabulary, in grammar, and in syntax, a knotted combination of them all. In Singapore you could live your life in English, but Singlish was what the locals spoke, and the transplanted, the settled-in. Ed set out to learn it.

He also set out, as always, to learn the local cuisine. In Singapore that very idea was funny, because all recipes except the oldest Malay ones were immigrants and none were pure. He wrapped Davey in a quilted cotton infant sling and took him along to the markets, collecting the dozens of umber, ochre, black, and gold spices that went into curry, depending on whose curry you were cooking. He made pineapple tarts and oyster omelets, yellow egg noodles, coconut-stewed beef, and fish head curry.

Ellen started to drink.

"Singapore," she sighed as they sat over the remains of vegetable dumplings and pork rib soup. She poured herself more wine. "At least in Nairobi when it was this freakin' hot, it was dry."

"I took Davey to the reserve this morning. We spotted a baby macaque in a tree. I don't know which thought the other was funnier." He told her this because she never asked anymore. Somewhere between Buenos Aires and Nairobi she'd stopped wondering how Ed spent his days. In Singapore she'd briefly become curious again, because of Davey, but it turned out baby news bored her. She cooed over Davey in the morning, once Ed had him dressed and in his high chair. She sang to him at night if she was home before his bedtime, though those early evenings slowly grew rare. She read parenting books, but not, as Ed did, to learn what to do, how to be a new person with the new person that was Davey. Ellen read to find out what Davey should be doing, what his accomplishments ought to be in this month, and this and this. She compared Davey with the child in the books—an average child, and shouldn't Davey be more advanced than that?—and with the children she met, children of expats, of transplants, of locals. On weekends, before the midday heat chased her indoors, she'd walk with Ed and Davey in the Children's Garden or to a breakfast of noodles at a hawker center. Davey's chubby friendliness made the cooking aunties cluck and chuckle: what a *buaya* he was, a little flirt! Ellen basked in their adoration, but Ed understood: admiring Davey, they were admiring her. She was *kiasu,* Ed thought, cutthroat competitive, as she always had been. He used to admire her fire and drive, having little ambition of his own; but now that Davey had become her proxy, it began to trouble him. The aunties asked to hold Davey, which Ellen affected to think about and then graciously permitted—Ed always allowed it—and at first they tried to give him sweets but they soon learned that was only for weekdays, when Davey was alone with Ed.

Ed, enchanted with Davey's first smile, his first tooth and first word, suggested on his first birthday that they think about another child. Ellen barked, "Are you crazy?" and went off to bed alone. Ed took a folding chair out onto the walk in front of the ground-floor flat and sat in the evening breeze. Ellen kept the air-conditioning cranked up high; Ed didn't like it, living in a temperature Singapore never felt. *Crazy?* He considered. *Well, maybe.* Huat sio oreddy. *The man's mad.*

Across another year Ed took Davey to the garden and the reserve, to the market and to other kids' homes to crawl and then walk and then run around in a chattering tribe like monkeys. He cooked fried dough, sweet potato leaf stew, biryani, chili crab for holidays. He told Ellen about Davey's day while

Davey laughed and mashed his hands in his rice and Ellen nodded and floated farther away. At the end of the year she told him she'd found someone else and she'd like him to move out.

He wasn't surprised. Though he wasn't happy, he knew his unhappiness stemmed largely not from the loss of Ellen, long since lost, but from her insistence that they share custody of Davey.

"What mother would just totally give up her son?" she said, blinking.

*What mother doesn't know the names of his friends?* Ed thought, but he understood. Ellen resisted Asia in Singapore, as she had Africa in Nairobi and old Europe in Prague, but still, this was about that most Asian of notions: saving face. Not with the cooking aunties, who would have mattered to Ed but meant nothing to Ellen; but among her colleagues. This ornament, this piece in the game that Davey was to her, it would make her look bad, cold-hearted, to give him up.

Ed didn't protest, though, because he saw immediately how it would be and he was right. Ellen hired a nanny. A smiling Filipina named Maricor, who lived in the ground-floor flat three nights a week in the room that had been Ed's office. Ellen made no adjustment in her life for Davey, still left for work early in the morning when the light was clear, and Maricor didn't mind at all that Ed usually appeared an hour or so later, to go with them to the reserve, the garden, shopping at the market for spices and fruits. Ellen knew, and Ellen didn't care, as long as Ed waited until she was gone so she didn't have to see him, wasn't required to make small talk and act as though they were still connected. They were, of course, because of Davey, who would connect them forever. But Ellen, as always, was eager to leave one life behind and begin the next.

Twice, on weekend days—weekends were always Ed's, because, as Ellen explained, if she wasn't working through a weekend she needed *Me* time—Ed and Davey ran into Ellen and her someone else in the Smith Street wet market. The someone, a boisterous Russian with a big smile, was a client of Ellen's firm. He tickled Davey's chin and seemed happily baffled by the noise, the bright colors of signs and stalls, the profusion of spices and fruits he called "foreign" and "exotic." Ellen kissed Davey, smiled thinly, and steered her Russian away as soon as they'd exchanged enough substance-free sentences so that everyone could see she was perfectly comfortable in Ed's presence. Watching her examine fine powders, peeled bark, and round berries in spice stalls, seeing her make purchases he was sure she had no idea how to use, Ed wondered if she was hoping to learn to cook. Ellen, he thought, cooking: none of their friends back in New York—or anywhere else—would believe it. But Singapore did strange things to you.

Ed settled into the new arrangement and found it not uncomfortable. The nights Davey spent at Ellen's, Ed missed him, missed cooking his rice porridge in the morning and teaching him his new word of the day. Ed worked late into those nights, so his days were free for Davey and for Maricor, whose calm company he was coming to enjoy. Maricor had good English— one of Ellen's criteria for a nanny—but Ed also spoke with her in Singlish, Maricor laughing with delight when he surprised her with a new phrase. Ellen had rolled her eyes when he'd used Singlish words: "It's not a real language, you know."

Six seasonless months drifted by. Ed and Ellen were quietly divorced, Davey adjusted easily to his double life and started to speak in full sentences, both Singlish and English—with the occasional Spanish word thrown in, and sometimes Russian—and the languid heat of Singapore seeped deeper into Ed's pores, melted the suits out of his wardrobe and the hurry out of his steps. Expats and young people raced around him, career-building, but the old, true life of the island was indolent and slow and kind, and that was the life Ed lived until Ellen called one morning to say she'd been promoted again. She was going to Moscow.

Ed congratulated her: he knew she was happy. Moscow was the plum placement in Ellen's firm and she'd worked hard for it.

"Sergei says he can get you a work visa, no problem." Ed heard the pride in her voice about her well-connected Russian before he understood what she was really saying.

"I don't want to go to Moscow."

"We can't very well share custody long-distance. I know people do, but study after study shows that's not the best thing at all for the child."

*Study after study? Best thing for the child?* "You're taking Davey?"

"Of course. I'm his mother."

Phone to his ear, Ed stared dumbly out the window. He lived now in another ground-floor flat a few blocks from Ellen's, a place with a small patio where Davey and Maricor sat on the paving stones building a tower from wooden blocks. Davey wore khaki shorts ("Like Daddy's!" he'd shrieked with glee when they'd been presented to him) and Maricor's red sundress pooled around her knees. "Davey doesn't want to go to Moscow."

"What are you talking about? He's a child. He has no idea where he wants to go."

The patent error took Ed's breath away. He tried to picture Davey, who'd never worn a sweater, all bundled up in parka, scarf, and boots, with a no-nonsense Russian nanny pulling his mittens on. He wondered where a child would play if nine months of the year it was too cold to be outdoors. Like New

York, he realized, but worse, and what did New York parents do? Sent their kids to preschool boot camp so they'd be fast-tracked to MIT or Yale.

"There's an American School in Moscow," Ellen was saying, "and a couple of international schools as well that would be good for him. Sergei looked into it already. I start the fifteenth of next month—that's more than four weeks, that gives you plenty of time. You can stay in a hotel until you find an apartment. My firm might help."

Ed hung up thinking, *Kena sai, lah. Kena sai.* Hit by shit.

Early Sunday, when Maricor went to Mass at Good Shepherd Cathedral, Ed and Davey went to Malaysia. They made the trip every few months, always by ferry because they were in no hurry and Davey liked the boat ride. Sometimes they went right on through Johor Bahru all the way to Kuala Lumpur and spent the night. From time to time they went to the beach at Desaru. Almost always, whatever else they did, they shopped at the Larkin wet market for spices and vegetables. The market aunties in Singapore laughed at Ed about this, for they scorned Johor Bahru because of its dirt and crime and general not-Singapore-ness, and claimed everything found there was available in Singapore. Ed would shrug and smile and say, "Most can, some cannot, *lah*," and join them in laughing at his Singlish.

On this trip he bought some things he had seen previously but hadn't had a reason to pick up. He took Davey to the beach and they got home quite late, Davey sleeping in Ed's arms, the heft of him at once heavy—he was getting big—and weightless. Davey didn't wake up when Ed put him to bed and slept soundly while Ed organized his purchases.

The next afternoon, Monday, was the day of the week when Ed delivered Davey to Ellen. In practice it was almost always

Maricor who received him, Ellen staying late at the office. This night, while Maricor gave Davey his bath, Ed inspected Ellen's kitchen, noting the increased number of bottles and shakers and jars of spices and herbs, the powders and chunks and leaves and liquids Ellen had never paid attention to when he was cooking. He was careful how he handled them. If there was an organizing principle he couldn't see it, but Ellen had systems for everything and had never liked Ed to disturb her things. When Davey was all scrubbed and sleepy, Ed read him a bedtime book from the pile he'd brought over, Ellen having no idea what children, or her own child, liked to read. After Ed kissed him good night, Ed and Maricor sat down as usual for a cup of *kopi-gau*, Singapore's signature condensed-milk extra-strong coffee that had driven Ellen, from the day they arrived, to thank God that Singapore also had Starbucks.

"Has she been cooking?" Ed asked Maricor, waving his cup toward the shelves.

Maricor's smile was sweet, but also amused. "On Sunday, she tell me. *Ella necesita el fin de semana,* the whole weekend, to prepare. She mix curry spices herself, *lah.*"

"Is it good, the food she makes?"

"I come Monday. She and Señor Sergei, they eat it all up before I get here." She added, "He is very polite, Señor Sergei. He always eat what she make."

Ed smiled too, understanding: if the curries Ellen made were good, Sergei wouldn't need to be polite.

Not much changed over the next two weeks. Ellen's conversations with Ed, ever short and to the point, were about nothing now but the impending move. It was a good thing the furniture in the flat was all rented, and whatever wasn't (a few mirrors: Ellen had thought the flat needed more of those) the landlord could inherit. Ellen never brought anything from one life to the next. In his flat Ed had carved masks from Nairobi, *matryoshkas* from Prague. Ellen had her Russian work visa, her plane ticket; she was taking the last few days off work before she left, to accomplish her final errands, and she suggested Ed do the same.

Ed spent half a day getting Davey a passport and bought two tickets, for himself and Davey, for a few days after Ellen's. "I need time to get settled before you two come," she said. Ed's answers didn't matter so he hardly offered any. He met Maricor at Ellen's on midweek mornings, took Davey home with him Thurdays, brought him back Mondays. He shopped at the market and cooked beef *rendang* and jicama-filled *popiah*. They didn't go back to Malaysia; there was no need.

Now, on this Monday afternoon, the last before Ellen's moving date, Ed and Davey sat entranced before the old man with the *erhu*. Because of the impromptu concert, they'd get to Ellen's later than usual, but now that Ed thought about it, it was probably better this way. The old man would see how relaxed Ed was, how sweet he was with Davey; that would be useful if the police found him and asked. It would be hard on Maricor, the shock of finding the bodies when she arrived; Ed had been hoping to save her that but it occurred to him now that after she called the ambulance she'd probably ring Ed and tell him not to bring Davey into the flat. That would be easier on the boy. Ed would rush there in any case, and leave Davey outside with her, and go inside and try to take charge, though by then the police would be there and he'd be interfering. He'd be unnecessary, except to tell them, in low, shocked tones, that Ellen absolutely didn't know her way around the kitchen or the market; that he'd warned her once or twice that not everything sold in the wet markets was edible, and that some herbs were easily mistaken for others.

Later, once the poison was identified as *cerebera odollam*, suicide tree, he'd shake his head blankly and say no, he had no idea where she'd gotten it, nor any idea what she'd thought its use was, though when it was ground it probably looked like any number of the darker spices used in curries and maybe that was her mistake. He'd tell the police he'd heard suicide tree could be bought in Malaysia but he hadn't seen it here, which didn't mean it wasn't for sale, but that no, no, there was no possible way this was a suicide, double or otherwise, because Ellen had been promoted to Moscow and was very excited and planning to go.

Ed ruffled Davey's hair. Yes, things were *buay pai*. No, better than not bad—everything was *shiok, lah*. Great. He settled more comfortably against the mahogany tree, wiped sweat from his face in the hot, rich air, watched the old man's macaque hands, and waited for his phone to ring.

# TATTOO

BY LAWRENCE OSBORNE

*Geylang*

When he was hired by Hiroshi Systems, Ryu was offered a family apartment in Bayshore Park for himself, his wife, and his son. Relocated from Japan, they had little idea where they were, but the condo faced the sea over the East Coast and a cooler wind swept through the private roof garden where he and his son Tomiko grew pepper plants in pots and arranged a little Zen enclosure of white pebbles within a square of white tea shrubs.

At thirty-two, Ryu was viewed favorably by his cynical superiors, though he was never quite fully aware of the degree to which he was being groomed for more exalted responsibilities at the commading heights of Hiroshi Systems. He was given a company car and a Malay driver to take him every morning down to Orchard, where he stayed until late at night working at a seven-floor HQ decorated with silk scrolls and antique samurai swords.

More conscientious and puritanical than his peers, he rarely joined the raucous drinking parties that were held at Orihara Shoten or Kinki. He was never seen paralytic under a table chewing on a napkin or ramming yen notes into tassled hostess bras. He punctually called Natsuo an hour before he left the office to make sure that when he got home Tomiko was not yet in bed. He prized the hour that he could spend with his son, reading in bed or watering the shrubs on the roof, the seven-year-old following him around with a watering can. After he had put him to bed, he and Natsuo ate together in their ocean-view dining room and afterward, according to their mood, enjoyed an hour together in bed or watched old Zatoichi movies animated by the incomparable Shintaro Katsu. They were the same movies his mother used to watch.

Their life went on like this for six months. Natsuo's mother visited from Osaka, and Ryu's father visited from Hiroshima. They went to the movies in Orchard once a week while the Filipina nanny looked after Tomiko, and on Wednesday nights he took Natsuo to Gordon Grill for an English meal followed by a Baked Alaska, a dish so lavishly outmoded that it felt startling and arousing to them. Once a month they sat behind candles at Tong Le and peered out over the lights of a city they did not understand and never would. It seemed like a place they should be enjoying, but which they did not know how to enjoy. The most enjoyable, the most sensual thing about it for them, was the heat.

Natsuo worked part-time at a Japanese food consortium, and she had more hours to feel out her adopted city than her husband did. But that same enjoyable heat dogged her when she spent time in it and she too often felt her will sapped as soon as she hit the streets. During the rains, she went to the movies by herself and grew a little plumper on daily servings of *kaya* toast; she went to spas in five-star hotels and had her nails done after her massages and wondered if this was decadent or virtuous. There was no way of knowing. Whether or not she was a typical expat Japanese wife never occurred to her. It was the passing of time that was the great problem, the riddle with which she had to grapple. And then there was the buying of lavender-flavored Hokkaido milk and sake from Meidi-ya supermarket.

Ryu had little time to himself. One night, however, when he had finished work earlier than expected, he got into a cab on Grange Road and asked, as usual, to be taken home. While they headed eastward, the driver caught his eye in the rearview mirror and offered him a smile.

"Tired go home, *lor?*"

"Why—do I look tired?"

He touched his face and caught a glimpse of the wan specter in the same mirror. It was true, he looked appallingly sapped.

"No fun after work, bad time, *lah.*"

Fun after work? The concept, so ubiquitous around him, had never really occurred to him. Yet the driver's surprise made perfect sense. He was hurrying home to the same routine he enjoyed every day, but as it happened the word *enjoyed* was a slight exaggeration.

Feeling suddenly resentful, he fired back: "So, what do you suggest?"

"If you like it, I'll take you for some relax."

"I think I'd like that," Ryu blurted out, and before he could change his mind the driver had shifted lanes and then turned away from the usual road.

"Where, then?" Ryu asked, leaning forward weakly.

"Don't worry, san, a place where Japanese gentlemen like."

They drove west. It was a Thursday night in the rainy season, unremarkable in every way, the streets swept with wind and rain, and Ryu didn't ask again where the driver intended to take him. It seemed so innocuous and unexceptional that he felt embarrassed to ask something that would make him appear a rube. He sat back and enjoyed a ride into Geylang, and soon they were passing along streets of what looked like suburban villas and shop houses.

Some of these were clearly brothels, with dark red lights

and a couple of girls sitting outside on metal stools, watching the cars floating by. So that was what the driver had in mind. And yet he was neither surprised nor put off. His curiosity was lightly aroused. The area away from the white neon of the main streets seemed calm and matter-of-fact, and the red-light houses with their girls gave off no energy that could be interpreted as menacing. When they came to a quiet halt in front of one, halfway down a leafy street, he got out with a falsely cheery wave and wondered what commission the driver was given for bringing naïve expats there. The man, holding open the door for him, told him that he would wait for him and take him home afterward for a set price, to which Ryu agreed at once. There didn't seem any point complicating things unnecessarily.

He went up to an entrance where an older woman sat reading a paper by a garage light, and when he had gone through the bead curtain into the foyer there was a quiet commotion, a pleasurable rustle, and a mama-san appeared with a kettle in one hand and a pair of glasses wrapped around her neck with a glittering string. He had to use his awkward, slightly broken English to make it understood that he did not have much time. That it was his first time, however, was easy enough to disguise.

The room was half-dark, with a Guan Yin shrine in a corner and a walnut coffee table piled with travel magazines. He was served tea while five girls were brought out from the room beyond, all of them dressed in below-the-knee black silk skirts, and from these he had to choose his one-hour paramour. It would have been easier, he reflected, to do so with his eyes closed, not seeing the way they subjected him to their own smiling scrutiny. But as it was, he had to look each one in the eye and cast a quick glance over her shoulder, the obscured curve of the breast and stomach, the hips in their locked poise, the angle of the mouth. Though the air-conditioning had been turned up as soon as he entered, he began to perspire and mopped his forehead with one of the napkins which had come with the tea.

Then he turned his eye back to the girl at the dead center of the row, whose shoulders were bared by her strapless dress. She was the shortest of the line-up and her hair was dyed a curious dark blond at the tips. Her eyes looked green from a distance, as though she were wearing colored contact lenses. She did not smile, but in any case his eye had not returned to her face but to a small tattoo on her left shoulder.

It was a dark blue Chinese character which did not correspond to a *kanji* which he could decipher. Suddenly prompted by something in this spidery character, with its radiating lines and disciplined geometry, he nodded to her without a moment's further indecision and rose unsteadily, unsure as to whether his equipment would rise to the occasion of so pretty and relaxed a girl. Such an unflappable professional.

*And on top of that*, he thought, *you're a swine and a low-life, and now you have a secret, the first secret you have ever had from Natsuo—*

The world of secrets. As he followed the girl—he just about caught her name as Cheryl—he wondered if every man had this moment of grim initiation into the world that lay beyond and around marriage.

Certainly, nobody ever talked about it until they were older and it no longer mattered as much. But as soon as one had entered it, there was no going back. It was an irreversible decay, a one-way slide. Everything one had known up to that point as sexual happiness and wonder became instantly foreshortened and relativized. It was this that was arousing. One of his more lewd colleagues at work, now that he thought about it, had expressed it crudely when explaining why he had gotten divorced from his wife in Tokyo: "Like the wondrous and fastidious panda," he'd said, "I found it impossible to mate in captivity."

They went into a small back room garishly adorned with a small droplet chandelier and silver-framed mirrors.

"You like short time one hour?"

"I think so, yes."

"Take shower together."

He paid her, and they disrobed under the absurd chandelier.

Naked, she was far more beautiful. In the claustrophobic shower she soaped him from head to foot and nestled against him as she used the shower head to disperse the suds from his chest and back. As she did so, he looked down at the tattoo. It seemed to have been carved into her marvelous skin with a laser, the lines crisp and elegant. They washed each other's hair and began to laugh. She held his erection with one hand and caressed the back of his neck with the other soaped hand, running her nails into his hair.

He had the impression at once that this one would not keep a faithful eye on the clock by the bed. When they were half dry they rolled onto the bed in their white towels and his guilt subsided and he plunged his face into her hair, holding a shoulder in each hand, and kissed her throat.

During the hour his ear picked up what seemed like distant sounds. Cars passed in the rain, men walked along the street looking into the brothels while a soft thunder rolled across the city. His initial hysteria also calmed and he realized that to take this sort of pleasure one needed a measured coolness, a sense of righteousness. That was the trick. The jittery fear and guiltiness of the newbie were faintly ridiculous to these girls who saw so easily beneath the male surface and who, unlike other women, did not heap facile scorn upon it. But now he also realized that this diversion away from Natsuo was in fact a boomerang motion back toward her. It didn't matter at all, and nor did it matter that if she discovered his pecadillo she would not understand it in the least. It was one of those things that only explanations and expiation make sordid.

The people we think we know the most are always the people we know the least. They carry their secrets within them with a greater discipline, that is all, but those secrets can be larger than oceans, deeper and more critical by virtue of being skillfully kept out of view by a surgical paranoia.

Afterward, he lay on the bed exhausted while she brought him tea. The girls chattered in Mandarin in the next room.

"I was wondering," he said at last, while she carefully combed her hair in a dresser mirror, still naked but for a towel wrapped around her hips. "That tattoo on your shoulder. Is it a Chinese character?"

Without turning, she caught his eye in the mirror. "Of course it is. But it's an old character."

"I thought so. What does it mean? Do you mind me asking?"

"I don't mind you asking, but I won't tell you unless you come back to see me again."

They smiled.

"That seems fair," he laughed. "You'll tell me next time."

"Maybe, if you make me happy."

Ah, the tip. He would make it a handsome one.

"Maybe you'll tell me where you are from?"

"So curious, *lah*! I am from Penang."

He guessed it was not quite true. He had heard her speak a quick, native Mandarin to her sisters in the other room. *Whatever*, he thought in amusement. *She is allowed to lie, given what she has to do for a living. She can lie to me, or any man she likes. It's not the same as a real lie.*

He accepted it and admired instead the almost military tension of her spine, the vertebrae visible through that delicate skin. She had a smell like bergamot tea. When she half turned toward him, her eye moved like that of a gecko, ironic and quick.

On the way out, he kissed her more warmly than he should have and was sure that she responded in kind. It produced in him a grateful moment of crackpot pride. There was, then, the hitherto distant possibility that this hour in bed had not been merely a financial transaction, and even if this was an illusion, he clung to that moment of pride all the way back to Bayshore Park.

He ate dinner with Natsuo as usual, Tomiko quietly asleep.

"You were late," she observed as they were halfway through the curry their maid had prepared. "Are management leaning on you?"

"A bit."

"That means they want to promote you."

"Perhaps," he said absently.

He was still thinking about the shoulder scented like bergamot tea and its ancient tattooed character.

"It's just a thought," she said tactfully. "It would be wonderful if they promoted you. We could get a jeep."

"What would we do with a jeep?"

"I don't know," she shrugged. "Couldn't we drive to a jungle somewhere and swim in a waterfall?"

*What a foolish idea,* he thought. *Why would anyone want to buy a Jeep and swim in a waterfall?*

"Whether they promote me or not," he said instead, "I am quite content. The salary is more than enough but I might have to work a little later on some nights. It's normal, I guess."

"Then I'll contact Koyabashi and ask her if she'd like to

play cards at the Raffles. They have a group that plays there every week. Just the girls."

It was a ridiculous idea but maybe it could have its uses. He kept his mouth shut. Then looked into her cool, restrained eyes and wondered if she had instinctively understood the manner in which his mind and heart had wandered off for a while, without saying a word. It would be a small miracle if she had not, but he let her talk on about her atrocious cards party until she ran out of steam, and her eyes rose suddenly, enormous with a distant grief.

They lay mutually antagonized and distant in the bedroom that night. Storm clouds amassed on the horizon, momentarily visible when lightning flickered below them. When she had fallen asleep, Ryu continued to think about his unexpected evening and the mystifying antiquity and elegance of the tattoo. He wondered about the other girls in the establishment, the leafy streets of Geylang and the calm that seemed to possess them at a certain hour. The calm, perhaps, of a thousand individual lusts rushing toward their premeditated satiations. The city had suddenly acquired a new dimension for him, and he had time to enter it again and again.

The following day, he worked alone in his seventh-floor office. He was filled with a hurried concentration. Come noon he took a punctual bento lunch with his immediate superior at a small Japanese place on the street and talked about the accounting software they had just installed at a well-known supermarket chain.

"Everything all right at home?" Mr. Inoue asked halfway through the dreary meal. "How is Natsuo adapting to her new city?"

Ryu shrugged. "She seems fine. The heat bothers her a little."

"The heat, eh? Well, the heat bothers everyone."

This wasn't exactly helpful, and Inoue pressed on with a few more questions. Did the alienness of the new culture oppress them?

"Oppress?" Ryu shot back irritably. "It's as good a place as we've ever lived. We even have lavender milk from Hokkaido."

Ryu's days began feeling longer. Between bouts of intense work he gazed through double-glazed windows at the sadly luminous monsoon skies alternately drenched with sunlight and flurries of rain. Out of their depths, huge atomic clouds materialized in slow motion, filled with a supernatural light.

Four days later he went back to the same house in Geylang; he had taken their business card on the previous visit. *Golden Lotus Happy Massage.* Now it was late afternoon and he had taken off an hour early so as not to arrive home late. The street sank into a watery dusk as he walked up to the outer door and rang the musical bell.

The same mama-san opened. Cheryl, however, was not there. He decided to wait with his tea and read the magazines on the tables. No other customers came or went. The mama-san explained that it was the unstable weather. His time was slipping away but after a half hour Cheryl appeared, dropped off by the parlor delivery car. She was dressed like a secretary, buttoned up and crisply prim, in a tartan skirt and glossy heels, a strawberry umbrella folding itself as she burst through the colored beads and showering the linoleum floor with water. She saw him at once; he rose and, with absurdly correct Japanese etiquette, bowed at the waist.

"I didn't think I see you again, *lor*," she said as they undressed with the windows open onto a small lawn. "Shall I close them?"

"No, leave them. I don't mind the heat tonight."

A quiet purr of cicadas came from the trees, the wet shrubs.

They felt more familiar to each other, the humor came more spontaneously. This time he forgot the hour and relaxed into their play, and when it was done he saw that three hours had passed. She said it didn't matter, it was not a busy day of the week, and they showered together at the end with a slow-tempoed affection and deliberation. He asked her again about the tattoo.

"What if I said I didn't know?" she said, smiling. "I just saw it in a tattoo shop in town."

"What a strange thing to do."

"Tattoos are always a whim. Maybe I was drunk. At least it's only on my shoulder."

"Your beautiful shoulder. It looks very at home there."

"It's a spell, you know—I know that it's a spell. The man who did it said it was."

"Why would you want a spell?"

They walked out lazily into the reception area, where the mama-san was asleep in a corner.

"It's protection," she said with a mischievous smile. "One never knows who one needs protection from, *lor*."

"Not from me, anyway."

He kissed her cheek and promised he would come back at the same time the following week. His courtly manner seemed to charm her. At least he told himself that it charmed her, that between them there was a quick, subtle bond which had matured with a beautiful suddenness. This unpredictable swiftness had created its own delicacy.

It was remarkable, he thought as he drove back to his office in a taxi, how the bonds leap from one skin to another without any prompting. Like the tropism of plants. He went up to the empty office and called his driver, pretending that he had worked late. He must always arrive in Bayshore in the company car.

Tomiko was still up when he stumbled into the apartment, oddly disheveled and incoherent, complaining as he now always did of the overwork. Natsuo was in an evening dress, pointless in the circumstances (had she gone out by herself?), and slightly tipsy from gin-and-tonics which she had been making for herself. The boy ran up to him and asked him at once to go up to the garden and water the bonsais.

"All right," Ryu said, quite relieved. "Let's go make our garden grow. If Mummy will let us."

He went over to kiss his wife on her cheek. "Did you go out?"

"The card game at the Raffles, remember?"

"Ah, yes. Did the Japanese girls have a good gossip?"

"We played bridge and missed autumn in Kyoto."

"You know," he added softly, "you shouldn't drink when you're alone with Tomiko. It isn't necessary. He can sense everything—"

"There wasn't anything else to do," she retorted, flaring up. "You were two hours late. Are they really working you that hard?"

"We'll talk about it later."

"Or not at all—I don't want to talk about it."

He went up to the roof with Tomiko. The act of watering outdoor plants during the rainy season was purely symbolic, but for that very reason the boy loved to do it. He was prospering at the American School and his English was now almost fluent. Into his flowing Japanese he would drop entire English sentences as if they were universally understood. They puttered around the bonsais they had set up and then stood on the parapet and watched the jittery lightning ever present on the horizon. He was a neat and punctual boy, somewhat like his father in that respect, and there was something neat and punctual about the way he approached the small events of his life. He took his father's hand now and asked him why Mummy was drinking so many sodas by herself—could Ryu not come back a little earlier from work?

"Maybe you're right," Ryu admitted. "I've been held up at the office rather late, I couldn't help it. I'm sure you and Mummy can understand that."

"But why is she drinking so many sodas?"

"I don't know. Maybe I'll ask her."

He took Tomiko in his arms playfully and kissed his overgrown mop of hair. He told him not to worry about Mummy and her sodas, or about his coming home late. Daddy always came home as soon as he could.

Week after week, the routine repeated itself. He saw Cheryl every Wednesday night now, assuming that this regularity would conceal his movements more effectively, and on the weekends he took Tomiko to the resorts on Sentosa and to Luna Park. It was, on balance, more or less the life he had always expected to have, if one excepted the gradual falling in love with a massage parlor girl. He had even foreseen moving to a foreign tropical city as a rising young executive living in a luxurious highrise by the sea.

What he had not expected was the gradually encroaching sense of dissatisfaction that now began to gnaw at him at the very moment when he should have been happiest.

Or at least most content. But something in his meetings with Cheryl had accelerated a crisis more typical of middle age. Now he saw how grimly predictable it was. The gaudy, fantasizing romance which had sprung up, but which existed only in his own head, the little lies and evasions with which he made his marriage continue to tick.

It was a machinery which he himself had assembled unconsciously but which had now begun to work as he'd intended. The machine lurched forward—the lies were its gears. Increasingly, he could not stand having sex with Natsuo, for all the increased desire which his initial adventure had inspired. He would think, *I can't imagine her permitting herself to be tattooed. She would never do that. It would go against all her rigid principles of cleanliness and self-regard. That tattoo is everything that she is not. It would fill her with contempt and horror, just as the idea of a massage parlor whore would.*

He began to show up later for dinner and when he played with Tomiko he was slightly brusque and more impatient. He yearned for his Wednesday evenings when he was alone with Cheryl on the far side of the city, with the smell of the mango tree coming through the open window. His work, too, began to slip. Mr. Inoue sometimes called him in to see if an explanation was forthcoming. But Ryu dismissed his superior's concerns; he said the wet season did not agree with him and that he had trouble getting to sleep at night.

"Take some Ambien," Mr. Inoue replied tersely. "Your figures are dropping a little. Are you worried about financial matters?"

"Not at all, sir."

"Then see if you can't get yourself back on track, Ryu. We all know relocation can be a tough time."

In reality, Ryu had never felt more alive. He bought extravagant presents for Cheryl, watching her face carefully as she opened them. He masturbated himself to sleep thinking about her while Natsuo snored next to him. The lovemaking on the side street of Geylang had become more fluid and indifferent to time, more childishly wild. He had fallen in love.

Sometimes, because he was stubbornly awake, he heard Tomiko stirring in the room at the end of the long corridor, crying out in his sleep, and he would creep into the corridor for a moment and listen before returning nonplussed to his bed. It all seemed increasingly unreal. When his insomnia grew more severe, he sat in the front room looking down at the operatic tropic sea and the empty beach wondering what his mother would think of him now. The dutiful good son had turned on an enigmatic axis; the city had played a delicious trick on him and his jolly old character had begun to erode.

Natsuo was now aware that something had changed. His behavior was becoming erratic and he no longer spent as much time with Tomiko. Ryu smelled strange as well. It was as if his aftershave had suddenly turned sour. One night, during a storm, it was she who woke up and heard the boy slamming his door, and she went quietly down the corridor to see what was wrong. Tomiko was wide awake but lying in his bed. He had been drawing in the dark, and the sheets of paper lay all over the floor. She went in and calmed him down and asked him why he was awake.

"Bad dream," he said.

"What kind of bad dream?"

He turned on his side to look into her face, and his lips were pressed in a half-smile, his eyes suddenly malicious.

"Can't remember, Mummy. Something nasty."

"All right, but now you can go back to sleep and not worry about it. It won't come back."

"How do you know it won't come back?"

"Because I know. Do you want your rabbit?"

Slowly, he shook his head. "You don't know," he said.

She scooped up one of the sheets and took it with her into

the corridor, then closed the door behind her. To her surprise, her hands were shaking. It was impossible to imagine from where the merry malice in his eyes had come. Glancing down at the sheet, meanwhile, she saw that it was covered with scribbled *kanji*, but the more she looked at them the less she could read them. They were Chinese, and not familiar at all. As she returned to her bedroom she felt a subtle unease. It was not a variety of different characters but the same one repeated over and over. She folded the sheet of paper and put it away in a drawer in her closet. If it happened again, she would have to see if a therapist might have an answer.

But as it happened, Tomiko's performance at school was exemplary. When he was at home he sat quietly in his room learning English words on a laptop. His behavior was so unremarkable that before long she forgot about the sheet of paper folded inside her closet. She became more and more immersed in her weekly bridge games at the Raffles—where the ladies played in a parlor as white as an iceberg—and she even began to think a little less about her husband. How boring his stress and their now nonexistent sexual intimacy were. The other Japanese wives assured her that this lugubrious situation was normal. Their men were overworked by their companies and it was the wives who paid the price. Such was life.

"Yes," Natsuo burst out one night, on the brink of tears, "but is that what I was born to put up with? Is that all there is?"

Reassured in the end, however, she busied herself as these other women did, with part-time work, shopping, and Bridge, with daydreaming and fantasies and books of Buddhist aphorisms. This self-distraction would not last forever, she calculated, but for the time being it was a kind of pain reliever. She organized their household as briskly as she could. When Tomiko started waking up again in the middle of the night, she made sure she had enough chocolate milk in the fridge to calm him down and told him he would stop dreaming of the Chinese character soon. Ryu, she thought, hardly noticed anyway. More than ever he was "detained" at the office, and she knew he was lying.

To compensate for this dreary absence of her husband, she decided one night to take him out to one of the city's better restaurants and pay the nanny extra to babysit. She insisted that he come home early from work (it was a Wednesday and he had to cancel his tryst at the Golden Happy Massage) and made him cocktails as they dressed for their now unusual night out.

Ryu was in an irritable mood because of the cancellation. But he had enough sense to realize that if his wife was putting on a show it was important for her, and, indeed, for them. Miserable and hokey as it was, he had to go along with it.

They got tipsy from the first drink—a particularly strong version of a Mai Tai which she mixed poorly—and got dressed in the vast master bedroom in a state of antagonistic confusion. She lay down for a while and asked him to go into her closet and pick out a pair of stockings for her, ones that would match her red Pucci dress.

"And don't fuck it up and bring back something green."

He went to the walk-in closet and fumbled around with the drawers in a slightly drunken annoyance. Why could she not organize her drawers at least? He had to open several of them, and as he did so he came across the folded sheet of paper which she had placed there weeks before and which she had since forgotten about. He opened it and saw the character, which he recognized at once. And yet, it seemed impossible.

A cold panic swept through him as he stood staring down at the crudely drawn characters, which looked as if they had been made by a child. Immediately he understood that Natsuo must have had him followed and the massage girls investigated. So she had been lying and fooling him all along. She was not as oblivious or rigidly naïve as he had believed. After his momentary astonishment, he felt a new and quite fierce respect for her. *Admirably done*, he thought grimly, and peered back into the room to make sure she was still lying on the bed. She was probably only pretending to be drunk, watching and observing him when he was off his guard.

*That clever bitch*, he thought, smiling in spite of himself and refolding the paper and putting it back exactly where he had found it. *She's been one step ahead of me the whole time!*

He came back into the room with the wrong stockings; she smiled indulgently and he stroked her face.

"I'm glad we're going to dinner," he said. "It's been awhile— what an inspiration on your part to book us at Tong Le. I've missed the old place."

They went to Tong Le and drank a bottle of Argentinian wine. Natsuo had revived, and he found that she looked savagely appealing in her mismatched stockings and heirloom earrings that had once belonged to her grandmother, a glamorous consul's wife in Pusan. It was something unheralded. He reached over and took her hand, which was now soft, sly, cunning, sexualized once again. He was secretly bemused and amused. His wife had never scared him before, but now that she had done so, he was intrigued. He wondered how she had done it.

She must have "read" his body language, with a feral intuition, and it seemed not unlikely that she had prepared a vengeance that would be equally surprising.

On the spur of the moment, then, he made a resolution to call off his secret rendezvous in Geylang. He would tell Cheryl by means of a written message that he would send by courier

and he would say it in a gentlemanly way. She would understand without hesitation, as such girls were bound to do, since
it was, presumably, a cruel aspect of their metier.

He wondered whether Natsuo knew he had seen the sheet of
paper. If she did, it was a marvelously elegant and disciplined way
of restoring her marriage and chastizing her ridiculous husband.

*Yes*, he thought, *a man in captivity is always a fool ten times
over. He doesn't see anything.*

Across the bay, dark with clouds and rain, they saw the
flickers of lightning faintly green against the horizon. They divided a salted century egg and laughed about their parents. In
his mind, he formulated the letter he would write to Cheryl,
and as he did so he became forlorn. This was alleviated only
by the thought of the sex he would enjoy with his wife later
that night, and for the first time in four months. He thought
about the tattoo itself, and the meaning which had never been
divulged to him. It must indeed have been a spell, he reflected,
and this explained the girl's reluctance to tell him what it was.
Inoue was right after all—it was a culture he didn't understand,
and which he secretly despised.

He saw the ghostly reflection of his own face in the wet
glass, and sensed the restaurant rotating slowly, one complete
revolution every two hours, as they advertised. They drank
quite heavily and a violet violence slowly came into her eyes;
his hand began to shake and he felt himself beginning to suffo-
cate behind his collar and tie. *So it is*, he thought, *secrets always
lead to other secrets.*

Far away in Geylang, the girl was leading another man into the
back room, opening the window so that the scent of rain and
grass could enter the boudoir and give it some natural life and
charm.

Like Ryu, he would notice the tattoo and wonder what it was. Afterward, he would ask her what it meant, and she would shake her head. She would smile in genuine denial and then tell him that she didn't know, only that it was a spell of some kind, a spell which someone had given her long ago and which she had accepted as some kind of supernatural truth but which ever since had served her well.

# PART III

GODS & DEMONS

# MEI KWEI, I LOVE YOU

BY SUCHEN CHRISTINE LIM

*Potong Pasir*

## 1

Two hours past midnight, Cha-li was sitting inside her gray Toyota, watching the corner house in Sennett Estate. There were nights when she wanted to call it quits, but she didn't because she'd given her word. Keeping her word was essential in her business. It was what drew women to her. The scarred, the abused, the cheated, the exploited, the rejects, and the victims. Single or married, they came to her at the temple. They knew by word of mouth that her specialty was adultery and infidelity. Not for her—the commercial investigations or surveillance of employees or insurance fraud or missing persons. A specialist in unfaithfulness, that's what you are, a client had told her. Cha-li liked the phrase. It made her feel she was more than a private eye. She was the PI who peered into hearts seething with dark secrets and contradictions. But she was cautious about making any claims. A private investigator deals with hard facts—the what, the when, and the where—not the speculative whys and wherefores. That was what she told Robina Lee, who'd come to see her two weeks ago.

Where is Charlie Wong? Robina had asked in a peremptory voice.

I am Cha-li Wong, she answered as confusion clouded the young woman's eyes. Cha-li was used to such reactions. Before meeting her in person, many people thought her Mandarin name, Cha-li (Beautiful Guard), was Charlie, because they'd expected the investigator to be a guy. Just like they'd expected a guy to take over as the medium of Lord Sun Wukong's temple. Ah well, such things no longer bothered her.

Robina Lee, the woman introduced herself. Not my married name, she added, and sat down across from Cha-li, who reckoned her age to be thirty or so. Robina was tanned, slim, and looked tense. Her lips were rouged a deep pink, and her eyes had dark rings around them. Cha-li noted the smart black stilettos and expensive black leather handbag, and wondered if Robina was one of those high-flying execs from the towering offices in Shenton Way. The look that Robina gave her seemed haughty at first. Seated with legs crossed and hands clenched tightly around the arms of the chair, she said in pitch-perfect Mandarin, My husband is seeing another woman. I would like to engage your services to find out who the woman is. What hold she has on him. What black magic, and here Robina switched to the Hokkien dialect and said emphatically, what *kong tau* the vixen used to ensnare him. I need a private investigator and a medium. I'm told you're both. I will pay you well above market rates if you agree to handle the case.

Taken aback, Cha-li muttered that she'd stopped conducting séances. She was more of a caretaker than a medium of the temple these days. No matter, Robina Lee said, and would not take no for an answer. She desperately needed a private investigator with knowledge of the black arts and *kong tau*. But what proof did she have that her husband had eaten *kong tau*? Cha-li asked. Robina stared at her hands, still clenched. Her husband was always distracted at home after dinner each night. At times he was glassy-eyed, distant, and vague. He shot out of the house the moment his mobile rang. The family's business and reputation were suffering. But that did not necessarily prove he was bewitched, Cha-li pointed out. Robina's voice rose. Proof? You want proof? Then you tell me. Why else would a young man desert his young wife for a woman old enough to be his mother? Look at me. I am not yet thirty!

Cha-li calmed her down, agreed that it was an uncommon case. Far more common for a man to leave his old wife for a young mistress. But as a private investigator, she had to suspend judgement. Observe, listen, gather and assemble the facts, objects, people, and events without adding or subtracting, explaining or interpreting. That should be the PI's objective, she explained to Robina. The temple medium, on the other hand, could go beyond the realm of fact and information to things hovering in the shadows, at the corner of one's eye.

Look, I don't care what you do. Just be discreet. I will pay you well. Those were Robina Lee's parting words.

A black cat jumped onto the bonnet of Robert Lee's white Mercedes and disappeared down the other side. Cha-li glanced at her watch. 2:38 a.m. Was he spending the night in the corner house? Could he be so bold as to leave his car parked in front of the house till morning? Cha-li rolled down her window and settled in to wait the whole night.

Butterfly Avenue was hushed, and the air was cool under the thick canopy of trees and bush. All the houses down the road had switched off their lights except the corner house at the end of the row of two-story terraces, each with a fenced-in garden, driveway, and a car under the porch, the symbols that spelled *middle class* and *private property ownership*. Cha-li doubted she'd ever be able to own one of these prim-looking terraces. She was familiar with this private housing estate known as Sennett Estate in Potong Pasir, which had made history when it voted in Singapore's sole opposition MP in 1984. A teenager then, she saw how Prime Minister Lee Kuan Yew tore into and shredded the academic record of the opposition candidate, Chiam See Tong, and that had so roused the residents of Potong Pasir that they voted for the underdog. That year her heart had swelled with pride as she watched Kai-yeh, her adoptive father and medium of the Lord Sun Wukong's temple, rally the villagers to vote for Mr. Chiam. 1984 was also the year she crossed Upper Serangoon, the busy main road that separated her village from wealthy Sennett Estate, to attend Cedar Girls' School, not far from Butterfly Avenue.

Cha-li reached for the night-vision binoculars in her glove box and trained them on the house at the corner. The front door had opened and two figures had emerged. Robert Lee was with a woman silhouetted against the light from the living room. The woman was laughing and pushing him toward the gate. Cha-li's heart stopped. She couldn't breathe. Is that Rose? But Rose was dead. Died in Macau. That was what her sources had told her years ago. Were they wrong? Cha-li watched the woman in the red housecoat open the gate, push Mr. Lee out, and shut it. Her eyes following the woman's retreating figure, she failed to catch the sound of a car engine starting. She didn't even see the white Mercedes drive away. Something was unraveling inside her head.

*Mei kwei, Mei kwei, wo ai ni.*
Rose, Rose, I love you.
A song she hadn't heard for years.

They had grown up together, she and Rose, in Lord Sun Wukong's temple in Potong Pasir village. She was the medium's adopted daughter while Rose was the unwanted mewling waif fished out of the temple's bucket latrine. Throughout their childhood, Rose was caned often, while she, Cha-li, was spoiled rotten by Kai-ma, her adoptive mother, and Kai-yeh, her adoptive father who channeled the spirit of Lord Sun Wukong, the Monkey King.

In those days, Potong Pasir was a stinking labyrinth of filthy lanes, muddy ponds, duck and vegetable farms, *attap* huts, and outhouses with bucket latrines. The latrine is in your flesh! Kai-ma railed at Rose. Go and bathe, you filthy rag! But no matter how often Rose took a bath, she could never shake off the stench that seemed to seep into her clothes, her hair, and under her skin. Rose cursed the mother who gave birth to her and dumped her in the temple's outhouse. The children teased her. *Sai! Sai!* they yelled in Hokkien. Even the adults called her *Ah Sai*—lump of shit. The village boys would kick open the door of the outhouse whenever Rose was crouched inside. One day, Cha-li heard a loud quacking and flapping of wings. The bullies had jumped into the duck pond splashing and yelling as they frantically washed themselves—evidently, Rose had suddenly opened the outhouse door and hurled several brown lumps at them. You are the *sai*! Not me! I am Rose the beautiful! she screeched. Cha-li laughed.

Rose ran away from the temple several times, away from the stink and choke of joss and other incense. Away from Kai-ma's caning and the boys' taunting. But the trail of rot pursued her wherever she went. The faster she ran, darting this way and that among the huts, the more lost she felt. Sometimes Cha-li found her crying in Yee Soh's outhouse with the mangy bitch snarling outside. Sometimes Rose hid under the bushes after Kai-ma had caned her. Once Cha-li found her on Upper Serangoon Road, a wiry urchin gulping exhaust fumes from the city's buses as though they were fresh air. The fumes overwhelmed the stench in her flesh, Rose said, her eyes bright as stars. The world outside Potong Pasir was a heady mix of new smells, speed, and ceaseless motion to her. She gripped Cha-li's arm. Run! she yelled, and pulled Cha-li along. Cars honked as they dashed across the busy road, dodging bicycles, motorcycles, hawkers' carts, and trishaws ferrying women and children.

Once across, Rose demanded: How much you have in your pocket? Show me. Come on, you monkey. She twisted Cha-li's arm. I know you've got money in your pocket. Her nails dug into Cha-li's flesh until she cried out. Then all of a sudden she felt Rose's hand stroking her face. Don't cry, little monkey, please don't cry. A thrill shot through Cha-li's heart. It was pounding so hard against her rib cage she had to shut her eyes to stop the dizziness coursing through her, the better to savor the sensuous feel of Rose's hand on her cheek. She took out all the coins in her pocket and dropped them into Rose's hand.

I knew it! You little monkey! Forty cents! Let's go and buy *tau huey*!

Sweet bean curd was Rose's favorite dessert. She ate tubs of it in those half-forgotten days, which was why her skin was so smooth and fair, and smelled so sweet that Cha-li almost swooned when Rose held her in the kitchen the night they both turned fifteen. Prostitute! Kai-ma's broom hit them on their heads. Rose sprinted out of the kitchen, and didn't return for three days and three nights.

Cha-li sighed, and returned the binoculars to her glove box feeling as if she had crawled out of a black hole where time had warped like a rattan mat left in the sun too long. How long had she been sitting in the car lost in her own thoughts? She was ashamed. This was uncharacteristic. And worse, she'd lost her quarry. Robert Lee's white Mercedes was gone. The gate of the corner house was shut, and the woman who looked like Rose had disappeared back inside. The house stood in darkness. But-terfly Avenue was wrapped in silence at three a.m. The night air was soft and sweet, as though this avenue was not part of such a densely populated city, as though it belonged to a time when there were few cars and migrant workers from China, India, or Bangladesh hadn't yet squeezed Singaporeans out of the crowded buses and trains.

Cha-li took out her black notebook, wrote down the time, date, and her observations, and then shut it. It pained her to think of what she'd tell Robina Lee the next day. The woman had phoned earlier to say that she was coming to the temple tomorrow. Cha-li had no wish to see her yet, but an operative must maintain close contact with her client just as a medium must maintain close psychic contact with the spirit she is channeling.

She got out of the car. She had to clear her head. She walked past the corner house and followed the road beyond the silent gated bungalows, their orange roofs gleaming in the ghostly night sky. There was no moon. Just banks of ominous gray clouds. Her mind returned to the woman who looked like Rose. If it was Rose, what was she doing back here? Had she moved up in the world through Robert Lee, son of a hotel chain tycoon? Was he her young lover? Was he bankrolling her?

Information was scarce at this point. Robina Lee was re-luctant to tell her more. You are the investigator. You find out, she'd said at their last meeting. And let me remind you of your high fee plus expenses. In return, I expect the strictest confidence.

Cha-li grimaced at the memory of that voice. No, she didn't want to see Robina Lee tomorrow, and looked up, surprised that her feet had led her to the gate of Cedar Girls' School. She must have turned onto Cedar Avenue without thinking. This was their secondary school before Rose was expelled for what the school called "unhealthy relationships."

Monkey! Rose had yelled on the first day. Did you see the school toilet? No shit! No flies! No smell! So clean! You just pull the metal chain. And whooooosh! The water flushes away everything! Rose's face was glowing. The toilets aren't like those in Potong Pasir village. When I grow up I want to live in a beautiful house with a clean toilet just like this. And me? What about me? Cha-li asked. Oh, you? You will live in the temple, *lor*! You will be Lord Sun Wukong's medium. No, Cha-li protested. But it was not a very strong protest.

She turned away from the school and returned to Butterfly Avenue. A dog barked at her, strident and querulous. Cha-li crossed over to the other side of the road just so the stupid Alsatian wouldn't wake up the neighborhood. The avenue was U-shaped, and where it curved, there was a small playground with a slide and a swing under the trees. Their shadows fell across the park where a girl's soft giggles broke the night's calm. She saw a young Rose and herself on the swing. Rose was pushing her higher and higher, and she was laughing and screaming, Stop! Stop!

What must you say? What must you say?
*Mei kwei, Mei kwei, wo ai ni.*
Rose, Rose, I love you.

The Alsatian's barking grew louder, joined now by the yelpings of other dogs. She quickened her pace. Just as she was about to reach her gray Toyota, a glimpse of black hair caught her attention. Near the red car. No, the black one. No. It's a mirage. An optical illusion. She must be hallucinating. Go home, Cha-li. Get some sleep!

She parked her Toyota in the wasteland next to the canal, formerly known as the Kallang River, that meandered through

Potong Pasir village. Wild grass, bush, and creepers grew around the old temple. The wasteland became a fairground every August during the feast of the Monkey King when an open-air stage was erected and a street opera was performed for the gods and devotees. When Kai-yeh was the medium, the entire village of Potong Pasir would gather at the temple to pray, eat, and watch street opera for three days and three nights. These days, however, like the slow-flowing Kallang River that had given way to the rapid Kallang Canal, the street operas had given way to *getai* in which scantily clad women sang and danced, not for the gods but for the younger devotees who loved MTV. The wasteland had also shrunk, and the concrete blocks of housing board apartments had moved closer to the temple each year.

Cha-li unlocked the side gate, collected the mail from the red letterbox, and opened the door to her private quarters. Exhausted but hungry, she cooked a bowl of instant noodles and ate it while sorting through her mail.

What's this? She tore open the letter from the National Development Board. Her application to renew the temple's lease had been rejected. *We regret to inform you that the temple's site has been rezoned for public housing . . .* Cha-li swore under her breath. Lord Sun Wukong's Temple had been here forever. This was her home. She must see Kai-yeh and let him know the bad news at once.

## 2

Outside the ward in the Goddess of Mercy Home for the Aged Sick, Mr. Singh, the night watchman, looked flummoxed. The gate, which he had padlocked the night before, was unlocked again this morning.

"The third time this week, Mr. Singh," the staff nurse said.

"But Miss Tan, I lock the gate last night!"

"No, you didn't. The gate was open when I arrived. And you weren't at the gate."

"I had to go to the loo."

"We have residents here suffering from severe dementia. The gate must be locked at all times. I have to report this to the matron."

"If you report, then I *susah-lah!*"

"If I don't report, and something happens, then how? I'm not going to be responsible, you know!"

Sitting on a chair next to the bed, arms resting on her lap, Cha-li stared out the window and pretended not to look at Kai-yeh's wizened face. Curled like a shriveled fetus on his side, Kai-yeh was following the altercation outside his ward with avid interest. Neither of them spoke until the nurse and watchman walked away.

"Troublemaker," Cha-li hissed. "You did it, didn't you?"

Kai-yeh's eyes lit up. For a second, Cha-li saw the simian features pass through his wrinkled face like a wind moving across water. Then his lungs seized up. His chest heaved with the effort to draw in air. Fourth stage, the doctor had told her. The cancer had spread to his lungs. When his coughing worsened, Cha-li summoned the nurse. An oxygen mask was placed over his nostrils. Aahh . . . ah, Kai-yeh dragged in each breath of air. Cha-li placed a hand on his chest. Gradually his breathing quieted. He waved off her hand, and pointed to the mask clamped over his face. Cha-li took it off.

"I . . . I . . . Rose. Bring . . . her . . . back here."

"What? Kai-yeh. Did Rose visit you?"

He coughed again and again, and could not stop. Each explosion was worse than the one before. The young Malay nurse strode into the room and clamped the oxygen mask back on. "You should go. The patient has to rest."

Cha-li bent down and whispered in the old man's ear, "Kai-yeh, you hang in there. I'll find Rose."

His eyes remained closed; he gave no sign that he'd heard. Cha-li knew he wouldn't last long. She had to find Rose before Kai-yeh entered the eternal Peach Garden.

She drove back to Potong Pasir via Aljunied Road, past Mount Vernon where the crematorium used to be, where the Christian cemetery and its dead slept in peace, where love had made the evening air fragrant when Rose held her hand as they walked among the tombstones and kissed in front of the dead.

She slowed as she turned onto Serangoon Road, and let the trucks and buses roar past her. New condominiums and shopping malls had replaced the black-and-white colonial bungalows. No remnants of the dairies, duck farms, vegetable gardens, and *attap* houses remained. Rural disarray and abundant greenery had given way to concrete flyovers, congested roads, and blocks of flats built by the Housing and Development Board. The only real village left in Potong Pasir was St. Andrew's Village, a school complex with a chapel and an artificial rugby pitch. Butterfly Avenue and Sennett Estate, on the other side of Upper Serangoon Road, were part of the Potong Pasir constituency now, although this could change in the next general election when boundaries would be redrawn, and the authorities would once again deny that such redrawing of electoral boundaries was gerrymandering.

Cha-li thought of going to see the opposition MP, but changed her mind. She doubted that the old man, Chiam, could save the temple sitting on land slated for development. The temple was famous for its support of the opposition. Since the early 1980s, Kai-yeh had invoked the spirit of Lord Sun Wukong to help Chiam See Tong win in every general election, and Chiam's success was credited to Lord Sun Wukong's benevolence to the people of Potong Pasir. Cha-li smiled. So many stories had circulated to explain how Chiam, a humble lawyer with less-than-stellar school results, had held his own against the might of the PAP in general election after general election. No, the temple was doomed. The authorities would sooner bulldoze it to the ground than preserve it.

Cha-li parked her car and went into the temple, surprised to find Robina Lee among the women praying at the altar of the Monkey King.

"Good morning, Wong Sifu," the women greeted her.

In their eyes, she would always be Sifu or Master Wong, who channeled the spirit of the Monkey King. That she was also a private investigator was irrelevant to them; it was just a job to fill her rice bowl. Periodically, Cha-li suffered pangs of unease. She was a fraud burdened by a sacred duty that had been imposed on her as a child. As the chosen one, selected by Kai-yeh, who had consulted the Monkey King's spirit before anointing her as his successor, she had to serve in his absence. Years of performing the rituals, the chanting, and the comforting had won her scores of grateful devotees, women who respected and adored her. Some had even been her lovers when she was young, handsome, lonely, and pining for Rose.

"Good morning, Sifu!" the women called out to her again.

"Good morning, good morning!" she said, laughing as she opened the door to her office. Robina followed her inside and closed the door. She was wearing a dark pantsuit and sunglasses. When she took off her glasses, Cha-li saw the wretched look in her eyes. Her face was puffy, and there was a dark bruise on her right temple.

"Did your husband do this?"

Robina shook her head, and Cha-li didn't press her.

"He slept in the baby's room last night. He didn't want me

near him." Robina's voice was flat. "You must give me a ritual cleansing. Please."

Shocked by the request, Cha-li tried to focus her attention on the case instead.

"I have checked out your husband's new office in Shenton Way. His clients are all Indians. Rich fat cats who are buying up our luxury condos."

"Robert is repulsed by the sight of me."

"He's running some kind of consultancy that includes real estate."

"Help me, Wong Sifu," Robina pleaded, kneeling suddenly.

"No, no, please. Please stand up."

"Our little boy is only six months old. Robert owes people a lot of money. My father-in-law does not know it yet. I fear . . . I . . ."

"Wait, Robina. I know. I ran a check—"

"He's bewitched. It's that vixen. Please, Wong Sifu, help me. The family . . . the . . . the scandal will ruin his father. Please, Sifu!"

Cha-li sighed. She was hoping it wouldn't lead to this. "Go into the prayer hall, Robina. I have to change."

She did not move until the woman had left the room. Then she locked the door.

The anointed are never free. They must respond to the cries of the broken and lost—Kai-yeh had drilled this into her from a young age. They sought her, these broken hearts. She had tried to tell them that Lord Sun Wukong, the Monkey King, was a figment of an author's imagination, but all to no avail. Besides, there were the women's testimonies. *Lord Sun Wukong answered my prayers*, some claimed. *He granted me a son*, declared another. *He made my husband stop seeing that woman and come back to me.*

She sighed. The women's beliefs had tinted their percep-
tions and shaped their universe; Lord Sun Wukong was the
godly spirit who came to their aid. If she was tempted at times
to tell them to pray to a rock, which would work just as well,
she restrained herself. If praying had helped these women to
sit still long enough for their problems to work themselves out,
what right had she to destroy their faith in something higher
than themselves? No bloody right at all! She yanked off her
blue jeans and pulled on a pair of gold-colored silk pants. Then
she took off her red checked blouse and slipped on a white silk
shirt and the Monkey King's bronze headband. She gazed at the
woman in the mirror, dressed in silk pajamas.

Would her features turn simian when she was as old as
Kai-yeh?

She was six when Lord Sun Wukong, through the intercession
of Kai-yeh, chose her to be his young messenger. Thrilled and
scared that she, and not Rose, was the Chosen One, she had
knelt before his altar and drunk a cup of tea mixed with holy joss
ash. Lord Sun Wukong was a wise, courageous, shape-changing
god in the Taoist pantheon of deities, Kai-yeh told her. Capa-
ble of forty-nine changes; he could change himself into a fly, a
beautiful woman, a monster, or a rock at the blink of an eye.
That's what I want to do, she declared. Kai-yeh laughed: That
you will, my child. That you will.

Later, in school, she discovered that the English storybooks
referred to the deity as the Monkey King. In the temple, however, he was respectfully addressed as Lord Sun Wukong. His
altar was covered with a red velvet ceremonial tablecloth embroidered with the Eight Immortals. The cloth reached down
to the floor, hiding anyone under the altar from view. This was
where she and Rose had slept as teenagers, hugging each other

close each night, especially after Kai-ma's death when Rose refused to sleep in the kitchen alone. Kai-yeh sleepwalks and touches me, she complained.

The temple's drum boomed. Her assistant called out in a loud voice: "Make way for His Excellency, Lord Sun Wukong!"

Cha-li took her rod and glided into the prayer hall.

### 3

The following week, on Monday evening, Cha-li waited in the parking lot of Tower Block One, Shenton Way. Outside, a thunderstorm was pelting the city hard. After two weeks of blistering sunshine and high humidity that caused her shirts to cling to her back, the weather had finally turned. The storm raged as she sat in her car, watching Lift Lobby Two and the white Mercedes parked near it. Robert Lee should appear at any moment. By seven, the storm petered out. Several men and women walked out of the lift, got into their cars, and drove off, leaving large gaps between the remaining cars. Bored, Cha-li continued to keep an eye on movements in the lift lobby as a light drizzle started to fall on the city's gray towers now gleaming wet in the lamplight. Another hour passed, and still no sign of Robert Lee. Lift Lobby Two was brightly lit and empty, most of the executives having left the building by now. For the past two weeks, Robert had left his office between six and seven. Tonight he was late, but he could dash out of the lift any minute. Two evenings ago, she'd had to duck her head and pretend she was reaching for something in the backseat when he'd come out of the lift suddenly with an Indian client in tow. Tonight she was better prepared. She had donned a wig and changed her glasses.

At 8:46 p.m. Robert Lee came out of the lift, alone. He drove out of the parking lot with Cha-li tailing him through heavy traffic to Orchard Road and the Hilton. She did not follow him into the hotel this time. Instead, she drove home to collect Saddam Hussein. Tonight she would try a new strategy.

At ten p.m. she parked her gray Toyota near the playground on Butterfly Avenue and got out. "Come on, Saddam boy. Okay, okay! Let's go!" Her fox terrier jumped out of the car, pulling at its leash. Laughing, Cha-li jogged after Saddam Hussein—taking the dog out at night was good camouflage. Running down the lanes gave her a chance to observe the corner house on Butterfly Avenue from different vantage points. She could see a pattern beginning to emerge.

As she came around the corner, Robert Lee's white Mercedes stopped in front of the corner house. His passenger, a well-groomed Indian male in a long-sleeved blue shirt and dark trousers, stepped out and pressed the buzzer on the gate. When it opened, Robert Lee drove off.

Back inside her gray Toyota with Saddam Hussein panting in the backseat, Cha-li checked her notes again. For the past several nights, Robert Lee had brought a different Indian male to the house. Sometimes, Robert went in with his guest. But last Tuesday night, he had dropped his Indian guy off and driven away, and Cha-li had tailed him back to his home. Last Monday, Wednesday, and Friday nights, Robert had parked his car and followed his Indian guest into the house. About two hours later, the two men had returned to the car and driven back to the Indian's hotel. Just this week alone, she had followed Robert to several high-end hotels. On Monday night, it was the Fullerton. On Wednesday night, it was Marina Bay Sands. On Friday night, the Ritz-Carlton. On Saturday night, the Shangri-La. But all these details hardly spelled adultery. Robert Lee was simply the chauffeur for his rich Indians. She'd not seen any women coming out of the corner house yet except the one in red who looked like Rose.

She flipped over several more pages in her notebook. Nothing important in there. Her surveillance of Robert's office had yielded little except a list of his dinner appointments with Indian clients, who inevitably ended up going to the corner house for dessert. Which was interesting. Is the house a brothel? Unlikely. Butterfly Avenue was not Geylang Road. Sennett Estate was in one of the city's respectable middle-class areas. It's true that some wealthy Chinese had bought houses here for their mistresses, but this had not dented the estate's respectability. Besides, Cha-li had not seen any young women emerging from the corner house. Was the woman in red the sole magnet that attracted the Indians? But if the woman was Rose, she'd be fifty-five and considered over the hill, no? Unless . . . unless she was offering something kinky.

**4**

On Sunday the matron phoned. Kai-yeh had taken a turn for the worse. When Cha-li arrived at the home, Kai-yeh was hooked up to a ventilator and drip.

"Is he in pain?"

What she really wanted to know was: *Is he going to die?* He was all the family she had.

"He's stable for now. The doctor has given him an injection."

Cha-li slumped into the chair next to the bed. She stroked the old man's hand. His eyes opened. He raised his forefinger with some effort, and tried to speak. But all he managed to croak was "Rose." After that, he had to breathe hard to make up for that expense of energy.

"Kai-yeh, I'll find her."

Cha-li parked the rental van outside the corner house. Pulling a cap on her head, she got out, pressed the buzzer on the gate, and shouted into the intercom, "*Karang guni!* Collect old newspapers!"

The gate opened, and she walked up the driveway. The front door was ajar.

"Come in!" a woman shouted from the kitchen.

Cha-li stepped inside the spacious living room. Its walls were apple white, and the floor was made of white marble. A large white sofa and two armchairs upholstered in white leather sat on a thick beige and gray carpet. The woman who came out of the kitchen didn't seem surprised to see her.

"I knew you'd find me sooner or later."

"Rose." That was all Cha-li could manage. Her throat was dry.

Rose, meanwhile, said nothing. She had not moved from her spot near the kitchen. Cha-li peered at her. Wearing a pink housecoat, she looked like the aunties who came to the temple to pray. At fifty-five, Rose was no longer the young dark beauty queen who had held men spellbound as she gyrated onstage with a python in the Great World Cabaret and broke Cha-li's heart. A hard glint appeared in Rose's eyes as she looked at Cha-li, who searched for something to say now that she was face to face with the girl—no, the woman—she had once loved.

Scenes from their past came and went in her head. She saw their two naked bodies, tinted red by sunlight shining through the red tablecloth covering Lord Sun Wukong's altar, as Rose's fingers reached into the deep moist recesses between her thighs, stirring feelings of love, guilt, and shame. Ashamed of what she felt, and conscious that she was Kai-yeh's chosen successor, while Rose was just the temple's waif, she fought hard to suppress her feelings. Until one day, Rose was gone. Gone without a word. Frantic with worry, and sobbing her heart out,

Cha-li went to the police. A missing person's report was filed but nothing came of it. She wept long and hard every night. For months she haunted the places they used to visit. Kai-yeh was philosophical. Rose is a temple stray. Strays come and go. It's their nature, he said, and encouraged her to study hard.

Five years later, Cha-li became a private investigator. She was on duty in the Malaysian town of Ipoh when she chanced upon a large black-and-white photo of Rose in the Great World Cabaret. It showed a scantily clad sultry beauty with long, dark tresses, and a large python curled around her. Shocked, Cha-li sat through Rose's show before charging into her dressing room backstage. Fuck off, Cha-li! I don't owe you an explanation! The cabaret! Now, that's *my* temple! It's where I dance like a woman. Sexy and beautiful. You! You prance around that temple like a dressed-up monkey! Stung, Cha-li left the cabaret, and hadn't seen Rose again.

"You might as well take off the cap."

Cha-li pulled off her hat and stuffed it into the pocket of her jeans.

"Why have you come?" Rose asked in a hard voice.

"Kai-yeh is dying."

"Good! May he rot in hell!"

"He gave you a roof over your head, Rose."

"Keep your pious shit, Cha-li. You're blind, and a fool. He gave me more than that. Come."

Cha-li followed her into the kitchen. Rose threw open a door, and Cha-li walked into the kitchen of the house next door. She followed Rose into the dining room where an old woman was trying unsuccessfully to feed a young man strapped to his chair. The young man's large shaved head was lolling on the back of the chair as though his neck was too soft to support it. Spit was dribbling from the corner of his mouth, which was making guttural sounds. The old woman wiped off the spit with a washcloth, and shoved another spoonful of rice into the gaping hole as though to stop the ugly sounds coming from it.

"Ugh! Ugh! Ugh!"

"What your Kai-yeh gave me."

Cha-li stared at the head and vacant eyes. "Did he . . . ? Did he . . . ?" Helpless, she turned to Rose.

"He raped me. Then I tried to abort him."

Rose patted the lolling head, which said, "Ugh! Ugh!" and more spit dribbled.

"Good morning, Madame Mei Kwei! Good morning, Ugh-Ugh!" two girls called out in Mandarin as they came down the stairs, their nipples showing under their skimpy nightdresses. Cha-li remembered seeing them when she was walking Saddam Hussein. One of the girls approached them and planted a kiss on the lolling head. "Ugh! Ugh!" The distended mouth dribbled more spit, and the wrists strained at the belt that strapped them to the armrests.

Rose turned away. "Let's go back. They're getting ready to eat."

Cha-li followed her back to the first house. The sun had come into the living room, and the light that bounced off the white marble floor hurt Cha-li's eyes. Her head was swimming.

"Is Robert the mastermind?"

"No. Robert has to settle his gambling debts. I . . . ah! I need the money and so do these China girls. They have something to sell that the Indians want to buy. Robert brings the Indians. I bring the girls. Everyone is happy. It's not a crime."

"I don't know about that."

Rose drew the curtains. "Report it to the police if you want. I don't care what you do."

"Why? Why didn't you tell me what he did?"

"Tell you?" Rose's laughter bordered on the hysterical, a wild gleam in her eyes. "Tell *you*? The bastard's monkey girl? The Great Lord's Chosen One with a paper gold band on your head? And a fake gold chain around your neck? The bastard was holding the bloody chain while you pranced before the devotees, drunk in their adoration. Strike me dead, Cha-li! I couldn't tear open my heart to a prancing monkey in silk robes!"

She wanted to slap Rose, but walked to the front door instead and stopped at the doorway, surprised at the sudden weight in her limbs. Her shoulders sagged. The memory of the gilt headband that she'd worn in those days made her cringe. It was made of cardboard and cheap plastic, painted gold. Later, she had bought the bronze headband to replace it.

The sunlight outside hurt her eyes, which were beginning to tear, the same eyes that had remained shut when footsteps were shuffling in the middle of the night into the kitchen where Rose slept. Rose's mouth was moving, saying something to her, but she couldn't catch the words. She kept thinking of the lolling head and dribbling mouth next door.

"The . . . the temple will be demolished. Very soon," she said without turning around. She couldn't face Rose. She wanted to shut her eyes, shut out the noonday glare, but she forced herself to keep them open, fixed on the green lawn outside sizzling in the midday heat. "I . . . I can get a flat big enough for the three . . . three of us . . . er . . . you and him . . ." Her voice trailed off.

# SPELLS

BY OVIDIA YU

*Tiong Bahru*

W e were minding our own business! Never causing no trouble! And then, for no reason, you came and cursed us! You are wicked—evil!"

The accusation bursts out of the figure lurking by the vase of welcoming lilies on our rooftop terrace as we come out of the lift.

"Please—not another suicidal teen!" says Renee, my flat-mate, only partly in jest.

Living in a modern condo in a heritage conservation district where walkups are the norm means an unexpected visitor to our private penthouse lobby is a potential mugger.

The woman turns on Renee: "You busybody slut, this is all your fault. You made this one curse me! Now my husband is gone and my boy has diabetes and the doctor says he has some lump growing inside so he has to go and operate!"

Renee retreats before the barrage of Singlish and spittle.

The woman has the fierce, focused intensity sometimes seen on people verging on insanity. Her hair looks dirty and she smells . . . a stale, sour odor of unhealthy, unwashed flesh and fabric envelops and moves with her.

If I were meeting her for the first time, I would classify her as crazy.

"Should we call the police?" Renee asks quietly from behind me.

"Call Gary," I say. I stay between Renee and our visitor. Gary, chairman of our management committee, lives in the other penthouse in the Banyan Tower and is a reliable witness.

"It's all your fault! You destroyed my family! And now you are making my son get sick and—and—"

Tears and memories overcome her words. She cannot make herself say the word *die*. But I know it is not only her son that these harsh raw sobs are for as she twists herself in agony against our front door.

"And that stupid maid. Can you believe the girl had the cheek to offer me money for my boy's treatment? Whoever heard of such a thing? I told her, if you so *laowah* and got so much money to throw at people, why are you here washing toilets? I told the police, I told the maid agency, if the girl got so much money she must have stolen it from me! Those useless people come and tell me I'm the one that owes her back pay!"

Renee, ever softhearted, moves over to comfort the intruder. Instinctively, I reach out an arm to block, to protect. The blue ceramic vase shatters on the wall rack beside her head and—

"Did you see that?" The madness in the woman's voice rises and she shrieks again. "Did you see what she did? I didn't break that—but I know you are going to blame me!"

"No one is blaming you . . ." Renee says, but she retreats to safety behind me. She obviously doesn't recognize the woman.

It is not surprising that I remember her. After all, I remember everything about Tiong Bahru since the 1930s and it was only a year ago that I first encountered our not-yet-mad visitor at the newly reopened market. The old stigma of subsidized government housing is forgotten in our district's graceful curved balconies and pastel wooden shutters, and the vegetable patches between rows of terraced walk-ups are tended by a mix of original inhabitants and recent arrivals. In the prewar days the buildings were called *mei ren wu* or *houses of beauty* because mistresses of wealthy businessmen lived here. Now that coffee bars, modern bistros, and retro bookshops have moved in, property prices have gone up, attracting real estate agents like this woman.

The first time I saw her was at the market when she cut in front of me at the *chwee kueh* stall. *Chwee kueh* is rice flour and water steamed into delicate discs and topped with fried pickled vegetables and sesame seeds. It is still one of Renee's favorite treats.

The woman had her husband, maid, and two children in tow and was talking loudly about the profits she intended to make. "I don't see why this place is supposed to be such a big deal. People buying to rent to homos and foreigners—that's why the prices are so high!"

She complained about the quality of the *chwee kueh*. She complained about the seating and the birds and she scolded her daughter for not eating, her husband for not listening, and her maid for not stopping her son from throwing his fork and plate and water bottle at the birds.

Then she slapped her maid for trying to collect their unfinished food in a plastic bag. "So dirty! People will think we don't feed you!"

The maid had not been given anything to eat or drink. But the maid was not as thin as the daughter, who had transferred the food from inside her bowl to under her plate, bypassing her mouth. I noticed, even if her mother did not. She might have been a pretty girl, I thought, if not dwarfed by her mother's size and manner.

That would have been the end of it had the woman not appeared in front of the Seng Poh Road ground-floor flat I was living in then.

I recognized the smug, strident voice mocking our simple wooden doors and painted window grills even as she stuffed *Best Price Offered for Your Property* flyers through them.

"I tell you, these days all the rich homos and poor *ang mohs* want to live here. These stupid old people don't know what they are sitting on—eh-eh-eh, boy-boy, don't throw!" A crash followed.

I opened the door to find her pale pudgy son had smashed the *arowana* tank on the five-foot way with a cup cactus. Water and broken glass were mixed with porcelain fragments and the pink-tipped petals of the crushed *Sedum rubrotinctum* were being smeared on the cement walkway by my two desperately flailing fish. The boy had already picked up another pot off the wall rack, a three-inch Tiger's Jaw in a clay pot, and was looking around for his next target. When he saw me his eyes gleamed; he raised his arm in my direction but squeaked and dropped the plant as its needles twisted around and jabbed him. The husband and maid were nowhere to be seen, no doubt distributing flyers elsewhere, but the anorexic daughter was standing there looking both sullen and alarmed.

The woman smacked the girl on the back of her head, making the chubby boy forget his pinpricks to crow in glee. "Why didn't you watch your brother? This is all your fault!"

Now the lift doors open again. Handsome, efficient Gary appears with his two Filipina maids and chauffeur, assorted neighbors, and an apologetic security guard. They are armed with kitchen knives, Gary's golf clubs, and a Koran.

"Police are on their way," Gary says. "Renee just said you had a psycho up here—I didn't know if she meant psycho as in suicide, murderer, or opposition party member."

"She's the wicked one! She took my husband away! She's killing my son!" the woman shouts at them.

Here, at last, we have arrived at the heart of the woman's bitterness. Not surprisingly, Renee still doesn't recognize her. Instead, stress and incredulity burst out of her in a sudden spurt of laughter.

"Her? She's not into men and she won't even eat meat because she won't kill animals!"

Now the woman stops, her attention caught, and really looks at Renee for the first time. "And she took you too. I never knew you were so serious about singing. I thought you were just playing the fool. For once in your life, listen to me. Tell her to stop killing your brother!"

Renee looks confused. Fortunately, Gary steps in and directs his chauffeur and our security guard to take the woman downstairs. She is still struggling with them when the police arrive.

The policemen take the woman away, of course. One of them shyly tells Renee he has all her CDs and always watches *President's Star Charity* when she sings on the show. She gives him a can of chrysanthemum tea and an autographed photo and he goes off happy, promising he will make sure she is never bothered again by this "whacko nutcase."

The woman is still shouting. We can hear her at street level, the desperation in her voice growing with the distance.

"She cursed me! She cursed my whole family! She stole my daughter!"

I had not cursed the woman or her damned family. As her daughter had helped transfer my poor suffocating fish into a tub, I had spoken quietly to the woman, outlining the future coming to her. There is no need for harsh tones when your words hold power. Even her daughter, measuring capfuls of water conditioner into the tub as she held the plastic hose steady, had not heard a thing.

Besides, it was already clear to me then that her husband had left her bed for another months before and was well on his way out of her life. Likewise, her son's cancer had already been hovering, a dark miasma of stickiness in the air around his soft, sickly body. All I had done was name it and bring it to the surface. I know the smell of sickness very well. I was only twenty-seven years old when I died of diphtheria during the Occupation.

Some things hang in the balance and a word spoken is all it takes to tip it . . .

"Will she be all right?" Renee says. She looks beautiful and concerned. "She's crazy, isn't she?"

No, the woman is not crazy yet, but she will be soon. And she is likely to find herself labeled crazy long before that happens. Perhaps after she tells her story to her boss—her shift supervisor at McDonald's who, though sorry for her, will be forced to fire her because of parents' complaints that she frightens their children. And of course the police and the court-appointed psychiatrist will label her delusional and psychotic.

I decide it is safe to forget her.

But Renee still looks shaken. "What she said just now—for a moment I almost seem to remember—" It is as though some bitter echo remains in her. "I don't want to end up like her," she says a second time.

When my Renee first said that a year ago she was referring to our uninvited visitor's hard, calculating eyes and the harsh lines etched around a discontented mouth stained with cheap lipstick. That was when I decided to save her from her life. I called her "Renee," meaning "reborn." Because I rescued her, I will protect her.

"I love you," I remind my Renee. "Nothing else matters. I will always keep you safe."

My words protect and bind her securely to me again. Renee's lovely face clears and she smiles and turns and goes into our home. I will follow.

But first I heal the shattered vase and its contents. I bless the shimmering koi in their new unbreakable tank. I adjust the sand, the salt, and the watching seeds that shield our entrance. The smooth, hard, shiny golden-brown shells of flax seeds in their box with two whole dried chilies will protect us from forces stronger than a desperate human, but I know better than to take them for granted. As I stir my energy into the seeds, I feel subtle barriers of protection rise and hear Renee laugh. These items are more for show than anything else, of course.

The most powerful magic still lies in words—
Not in words spoken but in directions heard.

# SAIFUL AND THE PINK EDWARD VII

By Damon Chua

*Woodlands*

It is past two a.m. and Saiful stands outside the Church of St. Anthony on Woodlands Avenue 1, smoking one *kretek* after another as he nervously tugs on his long, greasy hair. He has been waiting for the better part of an hour and is ready to bolt. But he can't. It is ridiculous to think that all this trouble has been the result of a stupid postage stamp. But the stamp—a rare Straits Settlement misprint from 1902 featuring a pink-colored King Edward VII—is all that Saiful has. On her death-bed, Saiful's mom, dying prematurely of liver disease, told him to hang onto the family heirloom at any cost. *At any cost*— that was what she had said, and he had promised her that he would. Now, he is beginning to understand the gravity of his commitment.

Saiful was once considered a *mat rocker*, a somewhat derog-atory term referring to a young Malay who is into heavy metal. With his tight leather jacket, gold-rimmed Ray-Bans, and long sun-bleached hair, he used to be a fixture at Studebaker's disco in Pacific Plaza. But now that he is reaching the ripe old age of thirty-five, other priorities have surfaced. For one, he has begun to think seriously about getting married and starting a family. After all, his childhood friends Ismail and Khamsani are both hitched and have seven children between them. Plus, the government is extending all sorts of monetary incentives to increase the fertility rate of Singaporeans; though, of course, the unspoken truth is that the bureaucrats are hoping to have more Chinese babies, not Malay ones.

Still, the thought of getting married gives him a headache. He knows only too well that the lovely Aishah, his longtime girlfriend, is averse to the idea. It is not about money—Aishah has said as much; but Saiful feels ashamed that he is unable to afford a condo, car, or country club membership. Sure, it is always possible to sell the stamp and potentially net a six-figure sum, but that would expressly go against his mother's dying wish. *At any cost*—the words continue to ring in Saiful's mind. The truth is, Aishah has other priorities. As much as she appears to love him, her career as a stewardess with Singapore Airlines currently takes center stage.

Saiful takes another drag of the *kretek* and glances at his watch. At that moment, a creaky, badly scratched Mitsubishi Lancer appears around the bend. The car stops, the door opens and dislodges a petite Indian woman wearing a sari and sporting a pair of sparkly gypsy-style earrings.

Before Saiful can say anything, Leela, for that is the woman's name, comes right up to him and jabs her index finger at his nonexistent pecs.

"First of all, shut the fuck up. If you want your fucking stamp back, do as I say. And no fucking comments on my brother's pimp mobile."

Saiful takes a closer look at the Lancer and decides to keep his opinion to himself. He sees that the driver is Indian too, and correctly assumes that this must be the brother, whom Leela refers to as Babu. Saiful and Leela hop into the vehicle and it trundles off.

Almost immediately, Saiful senses there is something wrong with the baby-faced Babu, but cannot put a finger on it.

When he sees the siblings communicating animatedly in sign language, his discomfort builds.

"Doesn't he speak?"

"What do you think?" Leela retorts.

Then it occurs to Saiful—Babu is a deaf-mute. He isn't allowed to drive, of course; but Saiful can see that Babu is the perfect chauffeur and getaway driver—his heightened visual sense makes navigating the confusing Woodlands thoroughfares a cakewalk.

"Should he be driving?" Saiful tries again.

"Just keep your fucking mouth shut till we get to the temple."

As the Lancer chugs along, Saiful peers out onto the empty streets. All he is concerned with right now is getting his stamp back. And whatever he needs to do to make Mr. Rao happy. He has no choice.

Illuminated by the mercury flare of the endless rows of streetlamps, Woodlands looks nondescript and anonymous. Yet this is where Saiful feels most at home. Cars and trucks zoom past this forsaken bit of Singapore toward the checkpoint and onward to Malaysia via the causeway. No one stops here, not unless they have to fill up their gas tanks. And those that do make sure they don't stay too long.

Saiful knows Woodlands well, having grown up in nearby Mandai village. He knows, for example, that it has a higher proportion of unsolved murders than anywhere else in Singapore. A few years ago, a schoolgirl from Si Ling Primary School was found near the train tracks, raped and strangled. The perpetrator was never caught. Several months later, the body of an Indonesian maid was discovered decomposing in a water tank atop one of the HDB apartment blocks along Woodlands Street 73. Even though a Bangladeshi worker was quickly arrested, Saiful heard rumors that the murderer was in fact some rich

Singaporean who paid the worker off to take the rap. And what about the famous case of the *char kway teow* hawker who was found dead in a pool of blood at Old Woodlands Town Centre?

In all fairness, it isn't surprising that there is a preponderance of unsavory activities here. After all, this is as far away from downtown Singapore as one can get, and here at the fringe, marginal characters find a home. A quick escape to Malaysia is always an option. And if you cannot take the causeway for whatever reason, a brisk swim across the Johor Strait is not impossible.

Saiful's troubles started when he accepted an offer to work for Madame Zhang, who runs a small fruit stall midway between Marsiling and Kranji. Madame Zhang likes to hire Malays, for she knows they hardly ever complain, work hard, and pretty much keep to themselves. And even though she can only muster a few words of *bahasa* (her English is equally deficient), she quickly developed a liking for the quiet and dependable Saiful, and groomed him to be one of her top runners.

Apart from selling pineapples and papayas, Madame Zhang makes much of her income peddling forged passports and visas. And with Saiful's help, she has been making a killing distributing traditional medicines to her wide network of mostly mainland Chinese customers. Be they tiger penises from Burma or human placentas from Vietnam, she has a steady stream of cash buyers for her smuggled goods. Her specialty is rhino horn from South Africa, which, because it is banned, can often fetch up to two thousand dollars per ounce. As the horn is widely considered an aphrodisiac, it is not unheard of for a syndicate of buyers to make an order in the tens of thousands of dollars. Once bought, the prized item is shaved into delicate ribbons of cartilage, boiled in water, and presto, the result is liquid Viagra.

But Saiful is far from thinking about aphrodisiacs. Babu

has stopped his car in front of an ugly 1970s-style warehouse somewhere in the concrete maze of Woodlands Industrial Park. Leela signals Saiful to get out and leads him over to a bolted steel door. Babu waits in the Lancer, playing to the hilt the role he knows like the back of his hand.

In the dim moonlight, Saiful can just make out the words: *Sri Vinayagar Temple.* It certainly doesn't look like a temple to him, but what does he know?

"First, you have to agree to everything Mr. Rao says," Leela pipes up. "That being understood, you have to kiss his elephant."

"Elephant?"

"Just fucking do it, all right?" Without waiting for an answer, Leela rings the doorbell. After several seconds, the door cranks open and a temple guard who is no more than four feet tall shows them in. The midget bows and quickly disappears.

The interior of the warehouse is unexpectedly opulent. Saiful feels like he has stepped into a mini–Taj Mahal, with incense and patchouli candles burning at various corners. Rich silken fabric adorns all four walls, and the dropped ceiling is covered with hammered gold leaves. Everything is cast in a soft, deceptively reassuring glow.

Then Saiful notices the elephant. Almost as big as a real specimen, this is the Hindu god Ganesh, carved out of a single block of blue-green granite and inlaid with bands of moonstone and red garnet. It stands toward the rear of the room, glittering surreptitiously. The animal's scowl tells all worshippers it is something not to be trifled with.

"Kiss it," a high-pitched male voice rings out, and from the shadows Mr. Rao appears, looking like a cross between Fat Albert and Salman Rushdie. Mr. Rao is a fleshy, effeminate man. Once he sees Saiful, he begins to examine the thin ex-rocker with undisguised sexual interest.

Mr. Rao appears to be carrying a white mink stole in his left arm, until it opens its eyes and purrs.

"Fernando, say hello to our guests," Mr. Rao prompts his snowy Persian cat. The animal stares around the room lethargically with its blue crystalline eyes. All at once Saiful feels much more at ease, for cats are by far his favorite animal. As a child, he collected feral tomcats and mated them with the village tabbies in Mandai, and then sold the kittens as purebreds to rich townsfolk. To him, the cat is the ultimate symbol of resourcefulness.

"You may be wondering why you're here, and who I am," chirps Mr. Rao, "but none of that is important right now. What is important is that we do what we must do. But first, the elephant."

Saiful, who has been staring at Fernando to calm his nerves, almost opens his mouth to ask where he should kiss the beast. But he seems to have lost his voice. Moving close to the bejeweled mammoth, he gently places a little peck on the trunk. Saiful feels like he is performing a perverse sexual act.

Leela, who has not said another word, suddenly snaps to. Her face contorted in fury, she approaches Saiful and slaps him across the face.

"When you kiss Ganesh, you kiss his feet, asshole."

Somehow, this amuses Mr. Rao greatly and he is sent into a paroxysm of giggles. Even Fernando the cat seems to find levity in the situation, and relaxes his formidably impassive face for a moment.

Saiful does what he is told, his nose registering the fact that the elephant feet are scented with sandalwood oil. Then, as he looks to Mr. Rao, the wide smile on the Indian's face vanishes. With a theatrical flourish worthy of Houdini, Mr. Rao whips out a leather-bound stamp album. Fernando hisses at the abrupt movement and jumps out of its master's arm.

"You want this, don't you?" Mr. Rao opens the album and shows Saiful the pink-colored stamp. "Such a beautiful thing. Do you know that Edward the Seventh was a notorious womanizer and loved visiting high-end brothels whenever he was in Paris? His dick was quite famous."

Saiful stares at the album and can only dumbly nod his head. He has no idea where any of this is going.

"This is what we must do." Mr. Rao begins to describe a complicated scheme involving the removal of Madame Zhang and his takeover of her smuggling racket, including the inception of a new side business dealing with the importation of *yaba*, among other things. Mixed in with that, there is also what Mr. Rao refers to as "the pleasure industry." He speaks continuously for more than ten minutes, but Saiful quickly loses the thread of the narrative and his mind starts to wander.

"So, how would *you* get rid of Madame Zhang?"

Saiful snaps out of his stupor. "What?" he says, his eyes beginning to tear from the thickening incense vapors.

"The ball is in your court, as the saying goes. Do it . . . if you want your stamp back." Mr. Rao shuts the stamp album, nods almost militaristically, and sashays off into the gloomy recesses of the temple.

"I hope you value your life," Leela whispers ominously into Saiful's ears. With that, she too disappears. He is left alone in the candlelit temple. He looks again at the elephant, and wonders how and when he fell down this rabbit hole.

That night when he gets home—after walking for almost an hour—Saiful has a dream. In it, he is with the lovely Aishah, who is all dressed up in a form-fitting sarong *kebaya* that shows off her ample curves. One minute they are frolicking on a white sand beach, the next they are kissing passionately in the shower.

He wakes up in the middle of the night with a raging hard-on, and proceeds to touch himself. But it is just not the same without his girl, who is on a plane to Frankfurt.

Saiful begins to reconstruct the events that led to his meeting with Mr. Rao. The problem is, he has no idea how he could have lost the stamp. He had always kept it in a safe in his HDB apartment, under lock and key; no one had access to it—at least, no one other than he and Aishah.

Is it possible that Aishah . . .

No, he tells himself. There is no reason she would do a thing like this. After all, hasn't Aishah always insisted that she has no desire for money, and in any case, didn't she just sell her one-bedroom walk-up in Kolam Ayer? The woman should be flush with cash.

But wait, why *did* she sell her apartment? It had surprised Saiful then but he didn't think it proper to pry. With his heart thumping, he suddenly realizes there are too many unanswered questions. He has to get ahold of Aishah immediately.

When he finally reaches her, the entire airline crew has just checked into an airport hotel in Frankfurt. Saiful never calls when she is traveling, not because he doesn't want to, but because of the expensive phone charges. But this time when Aishah picks up the call, it is clear she isn't surprised to hear from him.

"What happened?" she asks quietly.

For a few long seconds, Saiful cannot get the words out.

"I had no choice," she starts again.

An ache spreads from his chest and envelops his body. He doesn't need to hear any more; her explanations are like distant thunder in a tropical downpour. The thing is, Saiful has always been mistrustful of people, and Aishah is one of the very few who penetrated his shell.

For a long time after, Saiful sits on his bed trying to calm himself. The stamp has been passed down through four generations and he is determined to keep it. It doesn't matter if no one else cares; it is about legacy and family history. Saiful looks out the window and sees that the sun is rising. A new day, and hopefully a better one. He changes into a fresh set of clothes and sets out to find Mr. Rao.

The temple looks very different in daylight, and except for a few colorfully dressed Indian devotees deep in prayer, it is bereft of activity.

"Mr. Rao!" Saiful shouts at no one in particular. The words bounce around the room and merely attract stares from the devotees. There is no sign of the man. Saiful shouts again and this time the midget appears.

"Leave now or else I call the police," says the man in a surprisingly deep voice.

Saiful cannot help but laugh at the comical sight. But then the midget pulls out an impressive-looking machete. One of the devotees starts to scream and in the blink of an eye all of them have vanished. The midget stands in front of Ganesh with his weapon, looking like a figure from a Disney cartoon.

"As I said, leave now or else I call the police."

Saiful assesses the situation calmly and decides to retreat. He will come back later that night and take Mr. Rao by surprise. He will have the last laugh.

On his way to the nearest bus stop, he walks past a long row of parked cars. In the middle is a beat-up Mitsubishi Lancer. Saiful does a double take—the color, the condition, and especially the deep scratches are all unmistakable—this is Babu's car. Saiful does a quick 360-degree scan and immediately spots Babu sitting at a nearby *sarabat* stall, drinking tea. This is his chance.

Approaching from behind, he swiftly puts the unsuspecting boy in a headlock. Babu starts to struggle; but the more he does, the harder Saiful applies the pressure. After a while, when it is clear that resistance is not getting him anywhere, Babu simmers down.

"I can break your neck, but I'm not going to do so. When I release you, you're going to cooperate and write down Mr. Rao's home address for me. Is that understood?"

When there is no response, Saiful realizes that Babu has not heard a word. He has to spell it out. Motioning to the *sarabat* stall owner, who is cowering behind the service counter, Saiful gets ahold of a piece of paper and a pen. As he releases Babu to start writing down the instructions, the boy picks up his cup of tea and flings the remaining hot liquid into Saiful's face.

Saiful grabs his head and screams in pain. By the time he recovers, Babu is gone. Left on the table is a written note.

*Fucking loser,* it says. Saiful grabs the paper and crumples it. He can only curse at his bad luck, yet again.

Later that evening, recharged and with a renewed sense of purpose, Saiful makes his way back to the temple. The moonless sky is full of stars, so quiet that they seem to be part of a larger conspiracy. He tries the door up front, but finds it locked. After a quick search, he locates a side entrance with a wooden door. That door is also locked, and as he tries to figure out what to do next, a shadow appears behind him. Saiful quickly turns around, and finds himself face to face with Madame Zhang.

Standing almost five feet nine and with a sharp angular face, Madame Zhang is an unmistakable presence. Saiful sees that she is carrying her fake good-luck Gucci handbag.

"You're still alive," Madame Zhang proclaims in broken Malay, revealing her two gold front teeth.

"Why wouldn't I be?" Suddenly a thought occurs to him. "Mr. Rao wants to take over your business, but I can protect you if you help me get my stamp back."

"Stamp? What stamp?"

"It's mine, but he took it."

"Mr. Rao is a religious man," Madame Zhang says, apropos of nothing.

Several things then happen in quick succession. Madame Zhang lets out a whistle, and four Chinese men appear, wielding machetes. They proceed to knock down the side door, and in no time everyone is in the temple.

As the men fan out in all directions, Madame Zhang takes a compact from her handbag and starts to powder her nose and forehead. One of the men comes right back with the midget, a machete placed against his tiny neck. Soon, two others are escorting Mr. Rao out from the depths of the temple. Fernando the cat is nowhere to be seen.

The negotiations begin. Though Madame Zhang has the upper hand, she remains a shrewd businesswoman. She quickly outlines how her black market operations can be expanded, especially given the Indian community's predilection for ayurvedic preparations, many of which are banned. Madame Zhang has no doubt that a mutually beneficial agreement can be reached. Of course, she wants an above-market commission; and, in fact, she already knows of at least one supplier in Kenya who can ship the illicit merchandise.

A deal is hammered out in no time. As the Chinese men relax into their sullen selves and the midget again assumes his cartoon pose, a look of unvarnished admiration begins to wash over Mr. Rao's face.

"I like how you do business, Madame Zhang. Quick and to the point."

Madame Zhang smiles for the first time that night, her gold teeth gleaming. Later, when all the handshaking is done, Mr. Rao lets Madame Zhang and her posse out the front door. It is done with such ceremony that it makes Saiful uncomfortable; still, it would appear to anyone looking on that the unlikely duo have become the best of friends.

"What about my stamp?" Saiful shouts after Madame Zhang, who doesn't even turn around.

"I'm going to keep it," replies Mr. Rao instead. "It will be my insurance that you keep your mouth shut."

"I will keep my mouth shut anyway."

"Just want to make 100 percent sure. Unless, of course, you have something valuable to trade."

"Like what?"

With a wave of his hand, Mr. Rao dismisses the midget. It doesn't take more than a split second for the Indian's eyes to shine with carnal anticipation, as he sidles up to Saiful and places his moist, fleshy hand on his crotch. Saiful flinches in disgust.

"Quite tragic, isn't it, to have a girlfriend who betrays you?" Mr. Rao intones. "I can't blame her really. She owes me quite a bundle, and she truly loves the roulette table at Sentosa."

Saiful wants to spit in the man's face. He wants to get as far away from this den of depravity as possible. But he is frozen to the spot, overwhelmed by a deep sense of shame and revulsion. And there is another feeling, one that Saiful is trying hard to decipher. He starts to think about his stamp, and he recalls his mother's dying words. *At any cost.* The phrase echoes like a phantasm in his conflicted mind.

From nowhere Fernando appears, jumping onto the elephant's head and purring as if it has something to say. Fernando looks at Saiful, who looks right back.

Then Saiful stares straight into Mr. Rao's eyes, and shapes his lips into a half-smile, half-sneer. The first jab lands squarely in the Indian's solar plexus, and the next catches him in the rib cage. But before he can make good on his third punch, Mr. Rao pulls out a revolver and points it straight at Saiful. Simultaneously the midget appears, wielding his trusty machete.

"You think it's going to be so easy?" Mr. Rao's voice is thick with unctuous venom. A rivulet of blood makes its way down his chin.

With an earsplitting cry, Saiful lunges at Mr. Rao, and in the ensuing melee, four shots ring out. The first two miss completely. The third goes right through the midget's heart, killing him at once. The fourth and last clips Fernando's tail, scattering a puff of white fur.

What happens next seems to Saiful like a scene from a Hollywood action flick. He clamps his hands down on Mr. Rao's neck, squeezing with all his might. As his opponent thrashes about like a maniac, desperate for a gulp of air, a feeling of euphoria sweeps over Saiful. It is in this heightened state that he sees Mr. Rao's body erupt into spasms and then go limp.

By the time the police arrive, Saiful is already halfway across the causeway, the pink Edward VII carefully tucked away in his back pocket. *Welcome to Malaysia*, a sign says. He sees the city lights of Johor Bahru ahead, beckoning to him like a virgin. Calmly, he takes out a fake Malaysian passport and approaches the immigration kiosk. From now on his name will be Eddy bin Abdul Halim. Saiful quite likes the sound of it.

# PART IV

THE HAVES & THE HAVE-NOTS

# CURRENT ESCAPE

BY JOHANN S. LEE

*Sentosa Cove*

The first strike is a slap across her left cheek, but Merla barely flinches. She has learned to anticipate.

His glare still fixed upon her, he steps backward slowly, assessing the situation for a way to force a reaction. There is the faint sound of water lapping against the private berth outside the house while he stands by the designer lamp that has been switched on for the night. Then a flare of inspiration. He turns his eyes to the gaudy Swarovski collection arranged on the console table. A calculated pause, to grant her time to read his next move. His hand hovers over his first choice. She stiffens.

The heavy ornament hits her hard just above the right eye, triggering a mad scrambling of her arms. Even as it lands in her hands, the next projectile is already hurtling toward her, aimed to make her sink to her knees to catch it. The two objects collide in her small palms with a mercifully soft clink, so soft it infuriates him. He grabs another and takes an exaggerated swing, flinging it high up at the wall behind her. As Merla's chin drops, she feels falling fragments bounce off her back. He strides toward her, seizes her by the hair, and clubs her over the head with his clenched fist. The blow instantly hurling her onto the marble floor, she rolls into a fetal position, disoriented, both ornaments clutched to her chest. Though her eyes are shut, she can feel his obese form looming over her, more so than the pain, which she recognizes as not being the kind that means blood.

She does not know what set off this latest attack, but she knows he does not need a reason. She knows to keep still.

You do not walk away. You wait for Sir to go.

Later, when she thinks—prays—that she has seen the last of him for the night, Merla sweeps up. Then she goes to the garage where the Saab and Ferrari are parked, picks up leftover grayish-blue paint and a damp brush from the corner cupboard, and returns to the lounge to cover up the mark on the wall where the crystal smashed into pieces. The paint blends easily. In this opulent house, flanked on either side by similar ones which are still unsold, everything is still new. She has had plenty of practice covering up wall stains, mainly left by him and his guests in the den, for which the paint color is Dulux Black. She tries not to think about that room; these days she tries not to think at all.

Meticulously, she rearranges the Swarovski collection, predominantly birds. Most of them are seagulls, birds that she has never seen in her two years in this country, even though the waterfront villas are nestled amidst lush tropical foliage, on an isle within a cove of an island off the Singapore shore. Perhaps there are no birds because the vegetation is landscaped, the isle built from Cambodian sand and the cove artificially carved. Or maybe because there are never any crumbs to be found.

She picks up a small crystal seagull and looks at it more closely under the lamp. It has tiny red gemstones for eyes—rubies? How much is it worth? she wonders, as she has in the past. Enough, surely, to pay for half a year of round-the-clock care when her mother's Alzheimer's takes full grip. Enough to buy time for her younger brother to complete secondary school.

Look after Nanay. Study hard. I'll send everything I get.

A sound from the floor above startles her. He is clearing his throat, his usual noise like a skanky alley cat coughing up fur and filth. His noxious spit will follow. She turns off the lamp and briskly heads back to the servants' quarters. She does not run anymore.

Merla locks herself in her tiny room, behind the utility area where the washing machine and dryer are kept. She has a single bed with a thin mattress, a low chest of drawers, an unreachable window near the ceiling facing the side wall of the compound. The cicadas are quiet tonight. In the adjoining bathroom, she removes her blouse and winces as she lifts her bra away from her scalded breasts. The skin is still raw. She showers quickly, with cold water. She knows she should have seen him coming the other night, when he appeared in the kitchen doorway just as the kettle started to boil.

As she towels herself off, she stops to touch her back, where the deep burn from a few months ago has dried and hardened into a large triangular scab. Not the way to do collar! he had yelled. He yanked the cord, grabbed the iron away from her, and rammed her face against the wall. Hot metal. Fabric stuck to melted skin. As she writhed on the floor, trying to muffle her own cries, he ransacked her room, leaving with her battered old Nokia, her address book, and her passport.

At least that time there was a reason. The luxury of a reason. But sometimes there is no reason, or logic, or fairness. Only faith. She kneels and surrenders her eyes—one swollen, both weary—to the framed picture of Mother Mary on the bedside unit. Five hours to go before she is expected to toil again, but she knows that as always there will be little sleep. Still in need of solace, she recalls her long-dead father. The year His Holiness visited the Philippines, her father emptied his savings account to travel from their remote village by bus to Manila, bringing his teenage daughter with him. His wife and newborn son stayed at home. Young Merla watched as he wept in Luneta Park during closing Mass. She felt forever changed. From a roadside stall, he bought her first rosary beads, made of wood. Now the beads remind her not just of home, but of the time they were shoved into her mouth and forced down her clenched throat. The time she was left gagging, her shaking hand pushing through her open jaws to get a grip of the chain, her esophagus cut as she pulled out the metal crucifix.

The rosary beads are where she always keeps them—coiled around a corner of a small mirror, next to the picture of the Virgin Mary.

Gray meets gray where the mackerel sky merges with the South China Sea on a blurry horizon. A light breeze blows across the upstairs balcony of the vast master bedroom. She prefers it like this. When the sun blazes, the light catches the thousands of specks that fly and float with every desperate stroke of her feather duster, making her work seem an impossible struggle; she is certain she has lost battles of several lifetimes. As she is alone in the house, she allows herself a minute. He left hours ago—she saw his red Ferrari speed down the driveway and swing right at the gates with a haughty *vroom*. His wealth, so incomprehensible to her, so inescapable, seems to be the only topic he deigns to speak of when he has no intention of abusing her. More than once he has described with glee, in his broken English, the expression on the real estate agent's face when he turned up with a suitcase stuffed full of cash from Chengdu, and every retelling concludes with a rant about how the conveyance should have been completed then and there. FAH-king bu-raw-CRASSY!

Just as Merla is about to shut the sliding door, she is jolted by the sound of a splash from the pool below. By the time she takes tentative steps toward the balcony railing and peers down, all she can see is a trail of wet footprints on the path leading into the house. The fact that he never uses the pool heightens her alertness. As she tiptoes along the landing and down the glass stairs, the stereo comes on at full blast. This is no burglar. Then the stranger moves into view.

For a second, the unexpected sight of near nakedness and bright yellow swim trunks makes her avert her eyes and retreat behind a wall. But when she peeks again, she sees that he is more boy than man, though blessed with the promise of every physical glory of male adulthood. His wide-eyed good looks and not-too-tanned complexion remind her of the Pinoy pinups that adorn the celebrity rags she has seen in Manila. Not yet eighteen, she reckons, or else he would already be conscripted for national service. There is only one connection she can draw between the boy and the house. The den. She never lingers in that room long enough, never raises her eyes from the tray long enough, to see or remember faces. She cannot be sure. She has seen many young men in that room, and witnessed things that remind her that there is at least one kind of wickedness that will not befall her in this prison. For that, she thanks the Lord.

The boy notices her and calls out, affably. My name is Zhi-wei, he yells through the loud music with a grin, but everyone calls me Zach. Sensing her discomfort, he covers himself with a white bathrobe from the pool hut. He turns down the volume and talks as he runs his fingers through his shortish hair. About him being a lifeguard at the beach on the far side of the island, near the Cafe del Mar where he got to know the owner of this house. About how *amazing* this place is, how you can definitely fit the *entire* flat where he lives with his grandmother into just half of the lounge from *there* to *there* . . .

She feels she should hurry away but his voice, with its rise and fall, so strange in a house of oppressive silence, takes an easy hold of her; so she stays, busying herself with her duster and cloth. He crisscrosses the room aimlessly, glancing at the paintings, now and then touching the sculptures. He speaks in the local English slang, his jumbled syntax interspersed with the occasional big, misused word. He tells her he is from one of the oldest housing estates, went to the neighborhood school—*What's the point?*—from which he got expelled—*What to do?*—and that he has big plans for the future. There are other ways to make it in life, Zach says, as he slips his hands into the robe pockets; just look at the guy who owns this villa, he comes from some province in China and can't be *that* well-educated. The boy emphasizes this with a shrug.

Interrupted by the ringing of his mobile, Zach leaps onto the nearest oversized sofa to take the call, burrowing into the plush cushions. From what Merla can make of it, it is the man on the line. They converse in Mandarin for a minute or two before hanging up, after which Zach passes on the message that the man will not be coming home tonight, and that she is to serve the boy dinner. Their eyes meet for the first time, for just an instant.

You don't talk much, says the boy.

When evening comes, Merla prepares the kind of meal she normally does—three dishes and rice. Zach hangs around in the kitchen, mostly perched on a stool by the breakfast bar, swiveling from side to side as he chatters away while she stir-fries. Eventually growing tired of talking to himself, the boy reaches into his worn-out rucksack and removes a large black folder and a copy of the day's tabloid. She stops and stares. It was months ago when she last laid eyes on a newspaper, in the study, transfixed by an article on the front page of the *Straits Times: Maid Tries to Flee, Jumps from Fourth-Story Condo*. Merla did not hear the footsteps coming until it was too late. The man grabbed her wrist in a vicelike grip. I kill you, he said.

Do you want this? Zach asks. She turns away. Feigning nonchalance, he moistens his fingertip and flicks through the tabloid, in truth trying to find something that he thinks might start a conversation, eventually settling on the single finance page. Look, he says, holding up the paper. *Philippines to Become Sixteenth Largest Economy by 2050.* No response.

Merla sets a place in the middle of the long dining table, positioning the cutlery with painstaking precision. As she serves the food, he asks casually, And you? As he has not seen her put any aside, the response Zach anticipates is that she will eat what he leaves behind. She is visibly thrown by the question, her glance at the food too furtive. At last he sees her bony frame, dry complexion, sunken eyes. She shrinks further under his plain gaze. Zach weighs his options. He moves everything from the dining table to the utility room where he finds, tucked away at the back, a set of folding chairs and a plastic table. Merla watches in astonishment. He sets down the dinnerware and saunters back to the kitchen, rummaging around for a second bowl and an extra pair of chopsticks while she trails along like a lost creature. Finally, his eyes light up as he finds what he is looking for. The boy returns to where the food is, sits down, and peers at her expectantly.

Over a fortnight passes without them seeing so much as the man's shadow—one of his occasional spells of unexplained absence to which Merla has become accustomed, and for which she prays. Zach comes and goes as he pleases, suns himself by the pool and in the manicured garden, where this boy who grew up in a shabby high-rise is enjoying the novelty of figuring out how to use a lawnmower. He has been sleeping over some nights, in the master bedroom, whether or not with the man's consent Merla cannot tell. It is not for her to ask. But she changes the bed linen and plumps up the pillows after each time, leaving the sliding doors wide open to clear the room of the tang of male adolescence. It is the same smell that pervades the upstairs gym which he has taken to using, just next to the room with the closed door.

Can I have a look inside? he asks, not really for permission—since he wanders freely—but because it is the only door in the house that is locked. Merla shakes her head and hurries away.

When they eat, it is in the utility area, him engaged in one-sided chitchat, her with eyes cast down at her lap. He always helps with the washing up, though only after he has placed the man's iPad in a stand and set it on the kitchen counter, with the screen facing the sink, playing an episode of *America's Next Top Model*. He pretends not to see that she pretends not to watch. Tonight, however, he surprises her. No iPad. Instead, he sets his black folder on the counter. It is a portfolio, the kind every model, or aspiring model, possesses; this one filled with photos of Zach, the most striking among them amateurish at best. What do you think? he asks, slapping his palms together childishly. Merla returns her gaze to the soap suds. She shrugs.

He knows people, Zach says after a while.

Later, while Merla is ironing, Zach engages in a series of phone calls. With his mates, he sounds jovial and frivolous. To his presumably deaf grandmother, he shouts in deliberate, slow, monosyllabic dialect, though Merla can tell the exchange is tender. Then comes a theatrical coyness in his demeanor which immediately fills her with dread. He is talking to the man, in increasingly excited tones. Zach mouths to Merla: He's coming back tomorrow! The conversation is in Mandarin mingled here and there with a word or two of English. One particular word is all it takes to propel her into a further state of panic.

Party.

Fumbling around her apron and withdrawing from one of the pockets a single key, Merla walks away with uncharacteristic speed, carrying with her his puzzled stare. It is not long before she finds Zach standing beside her in the den, slack-jawed. To her, this room, with its black walls, black rubber flooring, and blackout curtains permanently drawn, is as unholy now with all the lights on as it is when lit with only garish candlesticks and lava lamps. She looks down, focusing on twisting the key around in her fingers while he takes it all in. Everything has been contrived with care, from the racks of chains, handcuffs, whips, to more bizarre equipment and instruments of bondage and torture that neither of them can name. Here was the scene of her first beating, within minutes of her becoming acquainted with the house, sparked off by the involuntary, almost imperceptible shaking of her head when she was told she was to clean everything in the room, every day.

Oh my god, says Zach, barely audible. His line of vision is directed toward the ceiling, where large mirrored panels cover every inch, magnifying the depth of the chamber. In spite of herself, Merla glances up, instantly flinching at the sight of their reflection. In her earliest encounter with this room in its intended use, when strangled cries and hoarse growls and cigarette smoke and chemical fumes invaded her senses, she lifted her head so her eyes could dodge the bare bodies, only to be shaken by what she saw in the mirrors as a bloodcurdling negative of the frescoes of the Sistine Chapel.

You must go, she says to Zach. She is taken aback by the sound of her own voice. He has already left the room.

The following day, there is no sign of Zach. She does not dare to call out for him, for anything, so she searches around the house, floor by floor, room by room, every hour. Nothing. Just after nightfall, the Ferrari appears, at the front of a small convoy of trophy cars carrying about a dozen people, all male. The man leads his guests through the doors. Only three of them are young. Raucous laughter reverberates through the house, cigar and cigarette smoke spreading, thickening. A glint from a Rolex watch. A flicker off a heavy gold chain. Overpowering eau de cologne. Behind the kitchen door, Merla goes about filling the large tray. A bucket of ice, cognac, and bottles of mineral water. Two vials of Viagra, four bottles of GHB, a large bag of pure cocaine. She prays that tonight she will only need to do this once. Bent low and with eyes down, she carries the tray past the lounge where the men are gathered and makes her way up the stairs toward the den, slowing down a fraction when the doorbell suddenly chimes. Seconds later, she judders to a halt from the sound of Zach's voice. An Evian bottle tumbles off the tray, hits the glass stairs, and rolls noisily down . . . one . . . step . . . at . . . a . . . time . . . She freezes. The laughter dies.

Leave it! she hears the man shout.

Her heart at once pounding and heavy with dismay, Merla finishes the task at hand as swiftly as she can, and withdraws to her room, latching the door behind her. She wraps her rosary beads around her wrists and clasps her hands tightly around the crucifix. A feeling threatens to engulf her, the sense that she is fouled, like a beached seagull overwhelmed by slick. But even the black swell of a spill cannot sully the red of a seagull's flesh and blood.

*Holy Mary, Mother of God, pray for us sinners . . .*

She waits for the minutes and hours to go by, stares through the small window at the moon behind a shifting veil of clouds. Between here and the soundproof room, there is a wall of impenetrable silence. She pads into the kitchen and from a tin can picks out the one tea bag she is allowed for the month. More time passes. At long last, she hears men's voices and the sound of heavy car doors, engines revving, tires on concrete, gradually fading to nothing. Zach appears before her, disheveled and pale, his pupils dilated. His robe, wrapped tightly around him, is stained. Blood trickles from his nose. Merla sets down her mug of cold tea and reaches into the cupboard for the medicine kit.

I'm okay, he mutters. I had too much . . . stuff . . .

More familiar with what the box offers than she wishes she were, Merla sets to work. Within minutes, she has done all she can.

Go, she says quietly. Don't come back.

He takes the soiled cotton wool from her hand and rolls it between his fingertips into a tight ball.

He knows people, says Zach.

The twelve-meter yacht at the front of the villa used to have a different name. The day it was delivered, not long after the house was bought, the man stood impatiently on the berth, using his hand to shield his beady eyes from the sun. When the boat cruised into view from around the sharp curve of the isle, he did a little jump. From behind the curtains in the lounge, Merla watched, agape. She had never been anywhere near a yacht. When the awe receded, she wondered what this luminous white vessel would mean for her existence. How was she to clean it? With a sponge and bucket? Would the hose from the tap by the pool stretch far enough? As it drew nearer, she witnessed an abrupt change in the man's body language. He waved his arms about wildly as if to say, NO! TURN. BACK. The Malay guy piloting the boat looked confused; he tugged at the peak of his baseball cap and approached closer still, until the man began to stamp his foot irately, point at the lettering inscribed in gold, and holler—something about the FAH-king dealer forgetting that he had changed his mind about some word. When the message ultimately got through, the Malay guy nodded apologetically, offered an awkward sort of salute, turned the vessel around, and sped off. Merla kept watching until the yacht and its trail of foam disappeared from view. That was the last she saw of any boat by the name of *Current Escape*.

Now, on the murky waters of the cove, the *Current Asset* gently bobs, moored alongside the berth. A light wind blows and on the sea far beyond, the crest of a wave is spotlit by a few rays breaking through the clouds. On an unstoppable advance, the northeast monsoon.

Merla traverses the full length of the berth a third time, the mop in her hands just damp enough to capture what little dust there is on the varnished brown of the wooden boards. Having had his offer of help silently declined, Zach is on the deck of the yacht, sprawled out on the chaise lounge, deeply engrossed in a magazine—an untouched copy of *Singapore Tatler* which he stumbled upon in the cabin below has been keeping him occupied longer than he expected. Not being a magazine he's heard of, it was at first eschewed in favor of *Vogue Hommes* and *Jaguar World*, later picked up and marked for study only when he grasped that it is about rich people. He leafs through the glossy spreads and, at times, when laboring through some of the wordier columns, wishes he made more of an effort in school. If only, he thinks, there was someone to push him. All of a sudden, his eyes widen. He slides his shades up over his head. In front of him, on a back-page story about some charity gala event, is a photo of the man, fitted in a tuxedo, posing with a bevy of extravagantly gowned socialites. I knew it! thinks Zach, feeling utterly vindicated. Magazine in hand, he bounds off the chaise lounge and leans over the side of the yacht, waving to catch Merla's attention.

Someday I'm going to be *super* loaded! exclaims Zach, his tone playful, arms stretched out wide. I'm going to be a *megastar* actor. I'm going to travel the *world*! First, I have to make it as a model!

Merla is no longer ill at ease at the sight of him with his shirt off; she has seen it enough times. As she glances up at his perfect yet still developing form and his beaming face, she suddenly feels—dare she say it—grateful for the respite of not having seen the man for weeks since the party, for Zach's unfettered optimism, and for the relief he unknowingly provides for her pain of not seeing her own brother grow from boy to man.

Where would you go? Zach asks. If you could go anywhere in the world?

Not pausing for her to respond, because she never does, he rattles off a long list of faraway cities and exotic resorts, his flights of fantasy becoming ever more unrestrained. As for Merla, her imagination, so rarely fed and now drawing off vague memories of photographs she may have glimpsed ages ago, lifts and carries her thousands of miles to Vatican City. She forms a hazy picture of the dome of the great basilica, the glorious symmetry of the colonnade spreading out around the towering obelisk. What she would give to see His Holiness at the library window and be blessed . . .

. . . and Rome! she hears Zach call out. For the hot guys and fashion!

Merla has not completely slipped out of her reverie. Show me, she says.

Zach leans back a bit, completely taken by surprise. What do you mean? he asks.

Putting aside the mop and pail, Merla sits on the wooden

boards, her legs hanging over the edge of the berth. You, she says indistinctly. Modeling.

Zach is hesitant at first. The images from the *Vogue Hommes* are still fresh in his mind, so he proceeds to pump up his chest and give his best version of brooding sexiness. Standing, arms folded, gazing into the far distance. Lying down on the chaise lounge, propped up on one elbow, knee artfully bent. Dashing aft to do an exuberant star jump on the diving platform. When, from the corner of his eye he clocks that Merla is looking more amused than impressed, he decides he may as well segue into outright comedy, so he begins to mime—a guest at a cocktail party, air-kissing, snootily turning away a waiter carrying champagne. Merla's features begin to betray the faintest of smiles, which she tries to hide with her hand; then a mere whisper of a giggle escapes from her lips, and taking the cue, Zach bursts into laughter.

In a flash, Zach's countenance morphs into impassivity. Merla turns and immediately notices the man on the upstairs balcony. She rushes to get onto her feet, loses her balance, and stumbles into the water with a yelp. Zach springs to the edge of the boat but Merla is already clambering back onto the berth. She stands there, shoulders hunched, arms straight down by her sides, not knowing what to do next, shaking her head at Zach's offer of his robe.

At the balcony, a poker face. The man prolongs the silence. All Merla can think of is how shameful it is that her undergarments are visible and how disgraceful it must be that they are gray and threadbare. The man looks at Zach and, as a lewd signal, grabs his crotch, tilting his head in the direction of the bedroom. Zach silently obeys. Merla is just about to scamper into the house behind him when the man shouts for her to stop. He asks, You finish? So she continues to mop—mopping up the water dripping off her, with her head down, until the sun begins to set.

When she returns to her quarters, she recoils at a smell coming from her room. She traces the stench to the toilet, where she finds, awaiting her, human waste and, half-buried within, her rosary.

---

The air is thick and heavy. It is that strange, deceptive kind of electrical storm where the lashing winds by turn wheeze and howl but no rain ever comes. The yacht rocks upon the dark currents, the corner of its stern thumping heavily against the side of the berth. Jagged edges of water lurk on the surface of the pool. Upstairs, the candles are lit, the lava lamps switched on, and the contents of the tray have been laid out. With another rumble of thunder echoing in her chest, Merla shuts the last of the sliding doors, the thick glass vibrating in its frame. No better time to use her one tea bag.

She stands in the dining room with her hands around her mug. Partly concealed by blinds, she watches as the Ferrari screeches to a halt. Out comes the man in wobbly steps, while Zach emerges from the other door, straining against the strong gusts of wind. Seconds later, only one other car passes through the gates and pulls up close behind. Merla has not seen it before. The driver is tall and lean, with a narrow face. The three of them make their way toward the house, the stranger looking sober by comparison to his host. Zach catches Merla's gaze, and turns almost instantly. She frowns, unable to read the expression she just saw. Suddenly she is aware that the man is pointing her out to the stranger, who nods in response and stares directly at her. Merla backs away to the kitchen and stays there, not moving, her ears pricked. She hears the front doors open and shut, voices mumbling, footsteps heading toward the stairs.

The long period of quiet which follows is not what it seems. Out of thin air, the stranger appears in the kitchen before her, holding the mug she left on the dining room table. He asks for more ice, a request which she tends to immediately. Then he tells her she must have forgotten her tea, and places it on the counter within the outline of his shadow. She hesitates. The weight of his stare shifts from her to the mug. He picks it up and moves a step closer toward her. Merla takes her tea and darts off, ignorant of the fact that he lies in wait, not knowing that his eyes never leave her, and too quickly disregarding an obscure instinct that this man is unlike the others.

Darkness which hurts. Light-headedness. An escalating awareness of being roughly shaken. Through hooded eyes, Merla sees the stranger thrashing against her body, feels the searing pain below. Terror pierces right through her. She cannot breathe. She tries to scream but her mouth is gagged. She struggles but her body is weak. He pounds the side of her head with his bare knuckles, flips her over, and pushes her legs apart. Another jab of agonizing pain. Tears start to stream down her face. She passes out.

Nausea surging over her, she rolls and tumbles onto the floor of the cabin. Vomit spews from her dry mouth. The stranger is nowhere about. Hands trembling, she pulls up her underwear; she cannot see her skirt. On her hands and knees, she moves slowly toward the way out, feeling the yacht sway beneath her. She crawls halfway along the berth before finding her feet, the heavy wind swirling around her. In the lounge, she collapses onto a sofa on which she has never sat. Blood seeps into the fabric. She does not know when the spasms cease, is oblivious to the passing of time. She feels nothing. She rises unsteadily to her feet and staggers past the console table, her flailing arms sending the Swarovski crystal crashing onto the floor. In the dark of the kitchen, she picks up a knife. Then she heads up the stairs.

On the landing, she sees that the door to the den is ajar and hears a strangled cry. She approaches, her mind and body disconnected. Through the gap, a partial sight. A grotesque heap of obese nakedness on the floor, slurring and slobbering. She pushes the door open. Zach is strapped to the wall with his hands pulled high. His bare frame is limp and his cries have turned into feeble sobs. Merla's vision adjusts to the dim light. Covering Zach's torso and limbs is a gruesome mass of lashes and deep cigarette burns. Merla starts to convulse with anguish. Finally unleashed, she lurches into the room, knife raised high, and plunges the metal deep into the man's shoulder blade. He yelps and reels away on the rubber floor in shock, staring up at Merla, at the knife in her hand. Uncharted waters. Shaking violently and barely breathing, she drops the knife and unstraps the boy, never taking her eyes off the man. Zach collapses onto his knees. In a split second, a tidal wave of rage thrusts him back onto his feet. With a primal scream, he lunges. Grunting through clenched teeth, he punches and kicks with all his might at the man's face and crotch.

Merla crumples into a corner, slamming her palms over her ears. She can still hear the tumult of blows. Blow after ruthless blow. With each one, she is hit again by the force of every strike she has ever suffered, every injustice. In her defiled body, her spirit burns. She shuts her eyes tight. Now she wants to scream. The cry is there, the beginnings of it, still caged in her chest, straining toward her vocal cords to smash through her muteness. In her head, a chasm of whirling darkness. Beyond the den, in the black skies over the cove, a vortex rages. A slash of lightning. She opens her eyes to see that Zach has suddenly stopped. Spit trickling down his chin. Horrified disbelief etched into his features. On the floor, a few feet away from Merla, the man's blood-smeared lips are distorted, twisted into something obscene. A smile. From his mouth, a hideous sound—an animal growl, erupting into profane laughter. Zach, his brutalized, bleeding chest still heaving and eyes ablaze, turns to Merla. She sees him glance at the thing in her hand. She feels her grip tighten. She is adrift, in turmoil. Did she not let go of the knife?

Outside, a lone boat battles through the turbulence from the treacherous open sea into the cove, crashing through the waves, passing the house at desperate speed. An eleventh-hour mooring. Man's creation against God's wrath. Its headlights sweep and penetrate the black curtains through a thin crack. A shaft of unearthly light stabs the floor. Merla's wild eyes are dragged along as the light beckons and taunts, as it slides over the wall, the straps, and the chains, moving relentlessly toward the ceiling mirrors, going up and up.

# BEDOK RESERVOIR

BY DAVE CHUA

*Bedok*

I t was around four a.m. and the cupboard-sized room was, as always, unbearably warm. Natalia could feel herself choking on her own breath. She climbed down from the bunk bed and glided to the door on cotton slippers, past her belongings and the photographs of her family in Java. Her employers were still asleep.

The security guard did not notice her leaving the compound. Her only witnesses were the pair of green stone fish that spouted water even in the middle of the night. She walked along the gravel jogging path toward the reservoir, a street away, intending to make herself tired enough to sleep.

A Bangladeshi worker was wedged on a bench, asleep, his light blue phone still pressed between his shoulder and ear. There were pink plastic bags and condom wrappers on the grass, and lamps blazed around the perimeter of the water. Too much light would draw complaints from the condo dwellers, so there were unlit patches, and Natalia liked to disappear into them.

Soon enough she found a spot that would do, settling down on the grass a foot away from the water, staring into the blackness of the reservoir. This gleaming scentless lagoon with its circle of manicured greenery, hive-like concrete dwellings, and evenly spaced trees could not have been more different from the lake of her village. Yet it made her think of home, of her mother, her aunties, her friends, scrubbing their blouses in the water, swimming. Any moment out of her bosses' apartment gave her joy, but it was these quiet ones stolen in the early hours of the day that she relished. There was hardly any breeze. She wanted to hear waves but the waters remained silent.

Natalia felt herself falling asleep when she spotted a man in a cap about twenty feet away, approaching the water. Trees obscured him, but from the way he was hunched, he seemed to be carrying something. A fisherman trying to catch something early in the morning? She had seen those once or twice this early in the day, but it was rare. Then there was a splash, and for a moment she saw the surface of the water rippling in response.

From the corner of her eye, she saw the man walking away. He was almost at his car, parked in a bus lane, when he abruptly turned and appeared to be looking at her. She ducked, hoping the foliage would hide her.

The man was now walking toward her; she stood up. Surely she had done nothing wrong. The city's many laws confused her. Perhaps she should not be so close to the water's edge? But she was just taking a breather. She walked up the slope and onto the gravel path. Her movements woke the Bangladeshi worker; he sat up and scratched himself, his phone still stuck to his shoulder. He looked dazed and mumbled a few confused words. It sounded like he was calling for his parents.

When Natalia glanced back at the man, he had turned around and was now jogging back to his car. He drove off without turning on his headlights. Ruffled, she hurried back to the condominium.

After the security guard waved her into the compound, she said a prayer before stepping into the house. Back in her room, she found herself wishing that she had taken down the car's license plate.

Natalia tried to sleep but just lay in bed, dreading the day. The Chans usually woke up at about six thirty a.m. There was no predicting their moods, particularly Mrs. Chan. Ma'am was in her mid-thirties, successful, and wore sleek power jackets. They made quite a bit of money, but their condominium was small. Even so, Mrs. Chan seemed to think it was the size of a mansion and made Natalia clean every room, even the rarely used spare bedroom, every day except Sunday.

When Natalia heard the alarm go off in their room, she got up and started brewing coffee and making scrambled eggs and toast.

From the moment she stepped out of the master bedroom, Mrs. Chan started with her litany of complaints. Were the eggs fresh? Natalia had added too much milk to the coffee. Had she ironed the clothes? Did she manage to bring the clothes inside before it rained yesterday?

Natalia tried not to shrug and simply nodded, knowing that Mrs. Chan hated her talking back. She apologized often, saying she would try better. When Mr. Chan emerged, he already had his company lanyard on even though he was still in his light blue pajamas. Natalia wondered if he had slept with it on. He propped his feet up on the coffee table and ate his toast, flipping between channels and letting his wife continue her nagging.

Moving over to the balcony to do his morning stretches, he suddenly remarked, "Look. The police again." The block in front of their apartment gave them only a partial view of the reservoir, but still, when Mrs. Chan and Natalia joined him in peering over the railing, they could see a crowd milling about by the water.

"Another drowning?" Mrs. Chan surmised, craning her long neck for a better glimpse.

"Looks like," he said. "Suicides attract, like magnets. We should sell this place. So many deaths."

"Can't get a good price now," Mrs. Chan replied before turning back to Natalia and giving her a look that sent her scurrying back to work. "We're leaving for Madrid tonight. I know you're happy we'll be gone. I want you to send me a photo every evening of the rooms."

Natalia nodded. Even though she was glad, she kept her face blank. What did it matter whether the rooms were clean when they were away? All they wanted was to get something out of her salary, even if they weren't here to see it.

"How long away, ma'am?"

"Ten days. I'll get my mother to come check on things some days. I should send you there to work for her but she doesn't enjoy . . . never mind." If Mrs. Chan was awful, her mother was a tyrant. Natalia knew enough Cantonese to know that her mother's insults were racist and vulgar. A missed spot warranted a reprimand or even a slap. Mrs. Chan talked about how her mother had once scalded a maid for burning some chicken.

Still, ten days was a boon. Even if Mrs. Chan's mother turned up, she never stayed long. She hated the smallness of the place and nagged her daughter for buying it. It occurred to Natalia that her prayers had worked.

Mrs. Chan was now chattering to her husband in Mandarin as they tried to gauge what was happening at the reservoir. Natalia waited until they left to change into their work clothes before cleaning up, making sure to pick up bits of toast from the couch.

Once Natalia saw the Chans' car leave, she headed to the reservoir, getting as close as she could to the heart of the crowd. There were a few policemen standing around, not far from where she had been earlier that morning. The locals were taking photos on their phones and posting them. The ambulance arrived a few minutes later; as they placed the body on a stretcher, she could see it was a Chinese woman in a red dress. Her hair was loose, her nails were pale pink, and her wrist had a red string looped around it. One of the medics threw a white towel over the woman's face.

Natalia knew the stories about how those seeking to be reborn as vengeful ghosts would drown themselves wearing red. She thought about the man in the cap that morning and the splash. Did he have something to do with the woman? What had he been carrying? It had been too dark to tell. No, she knew nothing. There was a house to clean, she told herself, hurrying away.

Trying not to think about the dead woman, she focused on the list of chores Mrs. Chan had left. She packed their luggage, pretending that it was her going on a trip, started cooking dinner at six, and let the food simmer.

The Chans came home late that night, spending just ten minutes in the apartment—enough time for Mrs. Chan to scold Natalia for cooking dinner and wasting food. Even as Mrs. Chan was dragging her luggage out the door, she was shouting instructions for more chores and insults in the same breath. Her husband, amused by the tirade, said nothing to stop her. His work lanyard was still on, until his wife turned her scolding on him for a moment, reminding him he did not have to use it at Immigration.

Mrs. Chan only quieted down when the elevator doors finally closed. (Though Natalia then received two text messages from Mrs. Chan telling her to air out the mattress and wash the curtains.)

Once their absence set in, Natalia sat on the couch, relieved but drained. That night, she slept with the door to her small room wide open. She had vivid dreams of water seeping all over the floor; the woman in red appeared next to her bed.

When the newspapers arrived the next morning, she looked for a report. The article occupied half a page.

The woman at the reservoir was named XueLing, a twenty-year-old Chinese girl who had arrived in Singapore two years earlier. She worked at a restaurant and had been missing for three days. There were few details about her—the press had not been able to find out the significance of her red dress, who she wanted revenge on. The rest of the article mentioned the other reservoir suicides, including one where only half the man's body was found. Natalia had heard about the drownings before and the friends that she met on her day off enjoyed joking about it.

But this one struck home; the girl had come here with hope. Like Natalia, she wanted a better life. It was true that sometimes Natalia also considered suicide, but she knew she had to press on. If she died, her debts would simply be passed on to her family.

Four days after the Chans left, Natalia was still mired in house-work. Even so, she relished the freedom of knowing that her every move wasn't being watched. The incident at the reservoir was no longer in her mind. The splash was probably just a catfish in the reservoir making a jump. The man was just on an early-morning stroll.

When evening came, she decided to walk to the reservoir. The waters were once again peaceful. Gravel crunched under the feet of joggers. She walked down the slope near the water and sat down with a can of soya bean milk. It was warm, and the sky was thick with crayon-red bands. A crescent moon hung over the world.

Just as she was about to leave, a young man began walking right toward her. He wore a black T-shirt with faded jeans and his slightly tinted glasses partially masked his pockmarked face. She wondered if he was one of the locals who liked to pick up foreign girls.

"Hello," he said, extending his hand even before he reached her. Though surprised, she took it. His handshake was practiced and firm. "Terrible thing that happened here, yah?"

"The drowning? Yah." She was cautious. It was hard to remember when she last had a conversation with a local, instead of just replying to orders.

"So many . . . I think I've seen you here a few times before. Have you noticed anything strange?"

"No. It's very peaceful here. Maybe those people who come here to kill themselves just want some peace as well," she said.

"That's a nice way to look at it. But not if you're wearing red. She wanted revenge."

They talked a bit more—she told him she was a maid and that even though her employers were away for two weeks, she cleaned every inch of the house each day. He introduced himself as Simon, a manager in a logistics company.

"I see. Hey, since you're a maid, are you open to jobs outside of your place? How about you come clean my house for me? I had a cleaner but she hasn't turned up and I'm bad with household tools. I destroyed a painting with a vacuum cleaner."

Natalia didn't find the joke funny, but she sensed an opportunity and laughed.

"I'll pay well; maybe $500 for a day's work? It's embarrassingly dirty now. Those bloody midges on the windowsill . . . wipe them off once and they always come back."

Five hundred was a lot of money; more than a month's pay. With that kind of cash, Natalia could pay her agent back and still have money left to send home. She remembered what a friend once said: in Singapore you have to find what other people need, and grab every opportunity that comes along.

"Is the place big?"

"No. It's a condo—you know how they are. So small. Two bedrooms."

He sounded sincere so she agreed. She passed him her phone and he typed in his number and wrote his home address on the back of a business card.

"It's good fortune that we met," he said, waving goodbye before disappearing down the trail.

The next morning, Natalia packed up some rags and detergent. Simon's condo was only about five stops away—on the bus, she kept a careful count of every stop.

His condominium building turned out to be flesh pink with green ionic pillars, reminding Natalia of a birthday cake melting in the sun. The Indian security guard eyed her suspiciously and told her to sign in, then didn't let her up until Simon came to fetch her from the guard post.

This time, Simon looked businesslike, wearing a yellow long-sleeved shirt with black pants. Natalia showed him the detergent she brought and asked if it smelled okay. He said it was fine but that he had his own supplies. "I'm not that incompetent, you know."

The apartment was oddly shaped, with triangular rooms. Porcelain statues of Chinese gods were the only decoration. Simon told her not to bother washing the large windows. "Don't want an incident of you falling out," he said, laughing as he brought out a green apron and latex gloves. "Don't want you to get dirty."

Natalia heard a radio blaring in Hokkien from one of the rooms.

"My father is inside," Simon said, waving her over for a

peek. An old man sat on a wheelchair facing the wall; heavy brown curtains covered two windows. "Don't worry about him. He had a stroke so he doesn't talk much. Don't bother washing his room." He closed the door, leaving it slightly ajar.

Simon handed her $250 in neatly folded bills and told her he would give her the rest that evening. As he left for work, he asked her to call him if she had any problems. She carefully stuffed the money in her small handbag the moment he left.

Natalia got to work right away, sweeping the floor. She thought she heard the old man grunt several times and rattle his wheelchair. Because his room door was ajar, she couldn't help but feel as if she was being watched. This made her quicken her pace—perhaps his father was there to make sure she did a good job and didn't run off with something valuable? She wanted the remaining $250 and wasn't going to chance it. And so she scrubbed at the mold in the bathroom until her arms ached. When the lemony detergent started to make her gag, she tied a kerchief over her face. She heard the drone of Hokkien radio in the background wherever she went.

Simon messaged her at two, asking how it was going. When she replied that all was fine, he told her to stay for dinner. She hesitated a little, wondering if this was odd. But then she thought that perhaps she could suggest cleaning for him one Sunday a month; it seemed like he needed it and was generous. More money was always helpful.

By five she had finished with the master bedroom and kitchen. Outside, a storm had descended. It made the radio echo worse, and Natalia felt as if she were in a cave. She was taking a sip from the kitchen tap when she heard grunting from the old man's room. She approached, gently knocking on the door. Simon's father lifted his head to stare and grunt, then turned back to the radio.

She had not touched his room. But now she wondered if she should clean it. Maybe that would persuade Simon to ask her back.

So she put on her gloves and worked around him as best she could, opening the window slightly to air out the room's staleness and the smell of urine coming from the bedsheets. Looking for fresh sheets in a drawer, she came across a crumpled green dress. She left it where it was; maybe Simon had a sister.

On the dresser, there was a black-and-white photo of a family; a couple with a boy who could only be Simon right in front of them. From the way they each held one of his shoulders, she could tell he had been the main focus of the parents. So much hope placed in him—did he manage to satisfy them?

Finally, she found a plain gray sheet and set to work on the bed. The old man's wheelchair squeaked and his breathing became more pronounced.

The room was relatively clean but she decided to sweep and mop anyway. The old man was more mobile than she thought; he moved the wheelchair away when she needed to mop beneath him. There was an odd expression in his eyes as she got close—though she did not dare look directly at him.

When Simon returned, he was surprised she had cleaned his father's room. "I thought I told you to leave him alone."

"It's okay, sir. I had time."

She thought she detected a flash of anger in his face but his smile quickly returned. Why would he be angry? She regretted cleaning the room now. She thought he would be grateful, not mad.

Simon set out Styrofoam cartons of food on the table and opened them, showing her the duck rice he'd bought. Then he ran his thumb along the table's wooden surface and examined it.

"Clean. Very clean," he said. "I'll give you the $250 after dinner."

She had been hoping to leave quickly and felt uneasy, but said nothing. The smell of hot salty duck was making her hungry—the old man as well, as she heard him coming out of his room for dinner, his wheelchair sounding like metal spoons rubbing against each other.

Simon started to dish out the rice on plates that she had just washed. She took out spoons and forks and placed them on the table. She offered to help but he told her to sit down; there was an edge in his voice. He sat close to her and they faced his father, as if they were having a meeting.

"Why are you here, Natalia?" Simon asked.

"Here? In Singapore? To earn money," she said, surprised at his question. She took a bite of the duck; the meat was soft and tender.

"How long have you been in Singapore? Does your employer treat you well?"

"Two years. They're all right." She didn't want to say too much about them. She wanted to finish her food, get her $250, and leave. The rain was still coming down; it looked as if someone was pouring glue on the windows.

"You are happy here?" he asked. He had not touched his food.

"Yes," she said.

"You need to know what you want in Singapore, Natalia. If you don't, how will you know when you have it?" He turned to his father. "Right, Pa?" Then he looked back at her. "You like the reservoir?"

"It is peaceful," she said.

"Were you there five days ago, in the morning?"

She didn't know where this questioning was going. "I can't remember," she said, starting to feel frightened.

He turned toward his father.

"Pa, what do you think of her? Do you like her? I'm going to marry her."

The old man stopped eating and looked up. "Would she please you better than Mei?"

"She's already pregnant." There was a rising rage in Simon's voice. "There's nothing you can do this time."

"Sir, what are you—" Natalia started.

"Shut up!" Simon snapped. "I'm going to marry her and there's nothing you can do about it, Pa."

The old man shot out of his wheelchair and his right hand curled around her neck. Her plate of rice fell to the floor, shattering. The man's hands felt like sandpaper on her throat. Simon did not raise a hand to help.

"You're going to kill her too?" Simon's hands then locked around his father's right wrist. "Is that what you want?"

Her fingers searched the table. She found a fork and quickly stabbed Simon's father on the head. He did not let go, even as blood streamed down his gnarled face. She struck again with all the strength she could muster.

This time, the force made him let go and Natalia jumped away. Simon shouted at his father in Hokkien. The old man crumpled to the floor, bleeding. Natalia dashed to the door and bolted out, ignoring Simon's shouts.

The security guard downstairs was reading a newspaper and didn't even look up when she came out. She ran home in the rain. Then she dialed 999.

It was odd to read about the case in the newspaper, with Natalia as the star.

The paper said that XueLing and Simon had been seeing each other. The old man, incensed over his son's relationship with a "Chinese dog" and his desire to marry her, leaped out of his wheelchair and wrapped his hands around her throat. Unlike Natalia, she lost the struggle.

Out of filial duty, Simon hadn't reported his father. Instead, he hatched a plan. Dressing XueLing in red, he painted her nails and slipped her into the reservoir. He hoped she would return as a spirit and avenge her death.

Natalia spotting him that morning had been his undoing. And so he'd hatched another clumsy plan, one that would silence her. But both father and son ended up in prison—both were expected to spend their remaining days there.

That evening, Natalia headed to the reservoir, escaping her small room once again. The Chans would be back shortly, a distraction she now welcomed. In the last peaceful moments before they returned, however, she wended her way over to the water. Placing her hands together, she prayed—for XueLing, for her spirit, for the power of her red vengeance.

# MURDER ON ORCHARD ROAD

BY NURY VITTACHI

*Orchard Road*

His New Year's resolution was to give up murders. Murders were horrible, messy, smelly, difficult, heart-rending things. And not nearly as profitable as they used to be.

"Red or white?" the waiter asked.

"Tea," C.F. Wong responded.

The feng shui master sat at a table at the ballroom of the Raffles Hotel, thinking about the trajectory of his career. For many years, he'd been a geomancer specializing in scenes of crime. He had masterfully cornered the niche, aided by the fact that no one else wanted it. Which was not surprising. His competitors had conditioned themselves for years to recoil from anything that could even metaphorically be associated with death, from kitchen knives to broken bowls.

So crime was Wong's patch alone. Tenant murdered? The landlord would pay Wong to "do his feng shui thing," to cleanse the place so it could be rented out again. Gang wars in your district? Wong would fix the bad vibes so that all the negative energy would move out of the area.

But lately, his job had started to depress him. He began to realize what his young assistant meant when she said that murders were "real downers." The dead body and the room in which it was found were often in a highly unpleasant condition. You spent your time in dark corners, breathing foul air, dealing with unhappy people, one of whom might be an actual killer.

The money had compensated for that, but even this delight was seeping away. Property prices had risen so high in Singapore that people no longer shied away from renting places where horrible things had happened. Some tenants even sought them out for the discount from the market price. Thus, Wong's share of the pie was shrinking daily.

His rivals in geomancy preferred to work for stupid rich people, who would pay them vast sums for visiting their luxury homes. They worked in mansions, sipping silver tip tea and sitting on designer sofas as they spouted random platitudes about chi and the flying star school and the flow of good luck. And these days, they usually got paid more than he did.

So Wong had decided to taste the easy life. Step one had been to muscle his way into the "designer" feng shui business, offering his services to event organizers.

After weeks of pitching, he had been hired to oversee the geomantic side of the arrangements at a major car racing event. This wasn't Singapore's famous Formula One race. This was a grudge-match-as-spectacle showdown between Emerson Brahms and Andreletti Nelson, who were among the world's greatest racing champions. The men had long been archrivals, although it was hard to tell whether they really hated each other or were just media-savvy enough to know that finger-wagging and fist-thrusting attracted TV cameras.

Wong had checked the feng shui of all the venues, including this gorgeously decorated pink-walled room at the luxurious hotel on Beach Road—an avenue at the heart of the urban district, many kilometers from the nearest beach. The only major negative he had found was a grotesque clash between the event date and the birthday of the main sponsor, a businessman named Lim Cheong Li. But that had been solved easily enough.

Arrangements had been made for the official opening of the event to be led by a Buddhist abbot named Sin Sar. This man had the perfect birthday in terms of earth roots and heavenly pillars. His presence would ensure the event would not just go well, but be an unforgettable triumph.

Wong had promised the abbot a big lunch and a small fee, and gave him strict instructions: "Don't say anything. Don't do anything. Just sit there. Pretend you don't know English. When they give you a bell, just ring it. Then sit down and shut up. Shut up all the time. Got it?"

The man had nodded, but not without an audible sigh. "I'm not stupid," he said, in his oddly high singsong voice.

Wong had responded with a fake smile. The man was not stupid. But he was an idiot, all the same.

The event opened smoothly. Wong sat at the staff table at the back and watched the VIPs take their places at the top table. Abbot Sin Sar sat down and smiled stupidly at everyone. He accepted a big glass of red wine and grinned.

Wong started mentally counting his money. He had given them a big invoice and had inserted a 20 percent "contingency fee" for unexpected events. Now all he needed to do was to create some plausible difficulty which would enable him to write in the 20 percent surcharge. No way was he letting that get away from him. This was going to be a good day. He sat back in his chair and reached for his tea.

Which was when someone tapped his shoulder.

"C.F., gotta talk to you," said a voice he knew meant trouble.

"Go away," he spat, without turning.

"This is important."

"Go away. THIS is important."

"Alberto's dad is freaking out," said Joyce McQuinnie, his assistant, who was suddenly standing next to him. She was talking in a stage whisper, much too loud, catching the attention of others at the table. "He's totally lost it. I dunno what to do."

Wong paused for a moment. Alberto Siu Keung, a small fat young man obsessed with food, was always in and out of trouble—but his dad was the wealthy recluse Sigmund Siu Keung, a client who paid every bill, however absurdly inflated, without ever examining any of them. "I call him back later."

"It's urgent. He says Alberto's been arrested for killing two people. He said that if you don't handle this now, he'll go off and find some lawyer to take his money instead."

Wong rose to his feet.

Ten minutes later, the two of them were in the luxurious Marina Bay home of Sigmund Siu Keung, known as the hilltop hermit because he almost never left his home, and had once lived on a hilltop.

"My son has been arrested. You find him," Keung said, sitting so far away from his guests that the conversation almost had to be shouted.

"Where is he?"

"In a place with a palm tree on the pavement," said the nervous old man, thin but solid as he sat on a distant oversized armchair in his pajamas and dressing gown.

This sounded like the beginning of a longer utterance, but turned out not to be.

"Like, can you give us more details?" Joyce asked. "Like what street, what district, what area, what building, et cetera?"

Keung looked annoyed. "How can I know that? I am agoraphobic. You can't expect me to know these things. I don't know anywhere."

"Can you call him? We need the address. He must have a mobile?"

The old man seemed exasperated now. "If I could call him, I would. Whoever detained him turned off his phone. I saw the man snatch the phone out of his hand."

Wong was confused. "You saw him?"

"He sends me Facetimes."

The feng shui master looked blank.

"It's an app," Joyce said. "No, wait. Never mind. You won't know what that is." She tried to think of the right way to describe it. "It's like a video-phone thing? Like on *Dick Tracy*? You see someone's face and they see yours? On the screen?"

The geomancer said nothing.

Keung explained: "Alberto was going to a job. He's a food taster. Perfect job for him. I called him. He put me on Facetime, that's a video-phone thing like this girl says. Says he has a job and can't talk now. I don't know anything else until an hour later, when he calls me again. This time he is frantic, worried. Before, the first time, he was outside, near a palm tree. Now he's inside a building, all dark. *Dad,* he says, *I'm being arrested. Get help. They say I poisoned two people.* And then someone grabs his phone and it goes dead. So I called your office."

Wong nodded slowly. "So where is he? Where is he working? His job."

"I told you," said Keung. "In a place with pavement out front and some palm trees."

"But that could be anywhere in Singapore."

"You are detectives. You find it."

Joyce leaned forward and gave the old tycoon her most winning smile. "Mr. Keung, we'd love to help. When Alberto was talking to you the first time, could you see where he was?

Can you give us any details about the pavement, the trees, the buildings? What color were they, for example?"

Keung thought for a moment. "The pavement was pavement-colored, sort of light-grayish, what else could it be? There was a building which was sort of darkish-brownish, or maybe gray. And the trees, well, they were tree-colored, of course—green leaves, gray trunk—what other color can trees be?"

Wong stood up. "I have a very busy day today. We need to get this finished. We need a taxi. Find this place. You look around, tell us when we get there."

Keung was horrified. "No way. I have agoraphobia! You know that. I never leave this house. Nothing you say will make me go out that door."

The sun was hidden by clouds as they drove through the central business district of Singapore. Sigmund Siu Keung lay down in the back of the car curled up in a fetal position, his hands over his face, still in pajamas and dressing gown. He swore under his breath.

Wong sat next to the driver, his lips a tight line. The sports event seemed to be going okay. Maybe he didn't need to be there. If he could help Keung with his son's problem, he might be able to get an extra fee today. This could be good. Yet he didn't feel celebratory. There were still too many variables.

He turned around to stare at the old man huddled up on the backseat. Joyce, squashed against the door, was absently patting the shoulder of the hermit tycoon, as if he was some kind of large dog.

"Mr. Keung?" she said. "Every time we get to a palm tree in front of a brownish building we'll stop, and you sit up and take a look, okay?"

Keung howled: "I am not going to open my eyes until you take me home again, you horrible bullies. I could sue you for kidnapping, do you realize that?"

Finding the right spot turned out to be tricky, they discovered over the next twelve minutes. The problem was that Singapore appeared to consist entirely of palm trees, and every one of them had a brownish building in the near vicinity. The only helpful factor was that occasionally the pavement was pink, so those streets could be ignored.

After several stops produced negative responses, Joyce tried to fish out more information. "Mr. Keung, can you remember anything else at all? Like sounds, were there any noises in the background?"

"No," the old man said. "Of course not. If there were I would have told you before." Then his eyes shot open and he glanced at her. "Wait. Maybe." He closed his eyes again. "There was a *shhhhh* sound. Like a tap, or water. Alberto raised his voice to speak over it. Probably a fountain behind him, or next to him."

"Good boy," said Joyce, patting his head. "Okay, that gives us more to work with—a brownish building with palm trees and maybe a fountain in front."

The hermit rearranged himself so that his head was now on Joyce's lap. She absentmindedly played with his hair.

They traveled slowly down Orchard Road. They passed several places that seemed promising. And then Joyce jerked to attention and pointed out the window to her right. "There. Look," she said. "That could be it."

Singapore's overbright sun chose that moment to peek out from behind the clouds and shoot a laser death-ray into the car—and right through Keung's eyelids. He groaned and curled himself up more tightly. "I want to go home," he whined, cupping both hands over his face. "I'm an agoraphobic. I could have a heart attack. Then you two would be locked up for murder."

"Like your son," growled Wong.

"There, there," said Joyce, patting the old man's head again. "If this is the right place, we won't have to drive around anymore. Just open your eyes and have a look. It'll only take a second." She spoke in the tone of a kindergarten teacher coaxing a recalcitrant child to do something. "I'll say, *Three, two, one,* and then you jump up and take a look. Then you can put your head down again. Three. Two. One. Up you go!"

She grabbed his shoulders and heaved him upward.

They had stopped in front of Ngee Ann City, a shopping mall on Orchard Road. It had dark brown walls. There was a wide expense of gray pavement in front of it, a small fountain, and several palm trees. Joyce wound the window down so they could hear the fountain.

"Yes, that's it. Go inside and find him. Can I go home now?" Keung closed his eyes and lowered his head back into Joyce's lap.

Wong told the driver to move ahead slightly, where some construction was underway. The line of trees and stone buttresses preventing drivers from parking on the pavement was interrupted by a pile of pipes. The car edged onto the pavement just behind a road work sign.

The geomancer scanned the scene. "Wait here," he told the others. "I go see."

It didn't take long to find the right place. Two police officers were hurrying into the building. Recognizing one of them, Wong followed.

The case was open-and-shut, said Detective Inspector Jonathan Shek, who was given to using ancient clichés from crime movies. As they moved up the escalator, the officer explained that it was a special day for the victims: "Today is Lap-ki and Hester Wu's annual dinner. I think we all knew it was only a matter of time before that little tradition turned dark."

Wong nodded.

The Wus were a "colorful" couple often described as "known to the police." Lap-ki Wu had moved to Singapore from Southern China forty years ago as an industrious young man. There, he met a pretty actress called Hester Lum. They had married and enjoyed an astonishing run of luck on the shadier side of the business world. They moved five times in their first two years, upgrading each time. By their second decade together, he was an influential property developer, his land bank boasting holdings in several prime areas.

But their relationship had been increasingly fiery, and they eventually learned to hate each other. Divorce was the obvious option—until they got the idea, probably planted by one of Wong's colleagues in the feng shui industry, that doing so would ruin their luck. The pair was led to believe that their legendary good fortune would instantly vanish. So they separated, but did not divorce—and agreed to meet once a year for a token dinner, which they had been advised was the least they could do to keep the luck alive.

As the years had gone by, each became convinced that if they died, the other would have somehow "won." So they started to fear poisoning. Thus, they agreed to take turns organizing the food at the annual dinner, and an independent consultant provided a taster: this year, it was the young gourmand Alberto Siu Keung, who had actually taken a course in this unusual skill.

As the two men marched toward the restaurant, Shek said:

"I've had a full report from my men at the scene. Alberto Siu Keung tasted all the food, pronounced it clean, and watched it be taken into the room where Mr. and Mrs. Wu were having their annual dinner. The couple ate it, and seemed to be getting along reasonably well—in that they were stabbing their steaks, not each other. But after about ten or twelve minutes of eating, or so Alberto says, something went wrong. Lap-ki Wu started groaning and rubbing his stomach. Then whatever it was hit Hester Wu, and she started moaning too. The husband fell forward into his meal, spilling the drinks and smashing a glass. Mrs. Wu dropped her cutlery and her glass and slumped off the chair onto the floor. My man arrived just before the ambulance. He thought one or both of them had already stopped breathing. Extremely powerful poison."

Wong put his hand on the police officer's upper arm. "Wait. So each one expects the other to be the killer. But both get killed at once?"

"Yes. And the obvious candidate is the food taster, who we understand has been in and out of trouble all his life."

"Except he didn't do it."

"How could you know that?"

"He's my client's son. And besides, if he's like his father, he's too stupid."

Shek turned and gave Wong a wry smile. "Perhaps he rose to the occasion."

The geomancer's mobile phone rang.

"Wong? Where are you? Have you left the hotel?" It was the voice of Lim Cheong Li at the race's gala lunch. He sounded irate.

"No, I'm here," Wong lied. "Er, in the bathroom."

The businessman spoke in a screech: "I need you back in

the ballroom immediately. Your monk friend has messed the whole thing up."

Wong's heart sank. "Sin Sar? What he say?"

"He was supposed to open the event by clanging his holy bell, right?"

"Yes. He forgot the bell?"

"No, he didn't forget the bell. He had the blasted bell. But he forgot that he was supposed to keep his mouth shut and jangle the thing. Instead, he made a little speechette and *then* jangled the bell."

"Oh. He said something bad?"

"Yes. He said something very bad indeed."

Wong sighed. "He's a monk. You have to expect people like that to talk all sorts of rubbish."

Lim said: "Sin Sar told us the race should be spiritual. It should be a race of the heart. It should be a competition about who can crave less than his neighbor." The man spoke in a whiny, mocking tone. "It should be a race about giving money and glory away to others, not grabbing money and glory for yourself. He said it was wrong to worship money."

"Clearly rubbish, but no harm done," Wong offered.

"Well get this. He said that many scriptures, including the Buddhist and the Christian ones, dictate that the first shall be last, and the last shall be first. So he declared that good fortune would only continue to prevail if the title and the money and the trophy went to whoever came in LAST, instead of whoever came in first."

There was silence. "Er, interesting," said Wong, wondering how he could put a positive light on this. "Makes your race very unique and unusual and historical. You are very lucky."

"Lucky?" said Lim, sounding close to apoplexy. "It's a disaster. The last person wins the money and the glory. The idiot monk has turned it into a slow race, like those bicycle races where you have to go as slowly as you can. The winner is who-ever is last, and the loser is whoever is first. Do you understand what this means, Wong?"

"I think so. Maybe small small problem."

"It means that Emerson Brahms and Andreletti Nelson are going to drive as slowly as they can. That's the only way they can get the title and the money. They might not finish until next Tuesday. They might *never* finish. It means there is going to be no race. It means there will be nothing for the millions of TV cameras and viewers and sponsors to look at. It means the whole event will be a multimillion-dollar disaster."

"Ah. I see. Can't you just ignore what Sin Sar said?"

"He said it in front of the whole crowd and the TV cameras and everything. It was so unexpected that everybody laughed and cheered, not realizing what it really meant. Even the driv-ers were amused at first. It was only when he sat down that we realized the race would be destroyed."

"Too bad."

"Yes, it is too bad. Especially for you, since YOU are going to pay for it."

"Huh?"

"You brought the blasted abbot into this process. If the whole thing goes belly-up, you're paying for it."

"Oh. Maybe I talk to Sin Sar," the feng shui master offered.

"You'd better. They're serving the last few courses of the Chinese banquet now. That means you have about ten or fif-teen minutes."

Wong pressed the red button to end the call.

The abbot's birthday meant he had practically been born for this event. How could he have been a bad choice? This made no sense. And what would happen? Was Wong's huge payoff going to turn into a massive bill? Should he leave the country immediately? What else could go wrong?

Detective Inspector Shek marched up to him, turning off his own phone. "Just got word from the hospital. Lap-ki Wu was declared dead on arrival. The wife is expected to follow shortly. We're now talking about murders."

Shek spun around on his heels and headed to the restaurant kitchen where Alberto Siu Keung was waiting.

Wong, not knowing what else to do, stood at the door and eavesdropped.

"Really, I don't know what happened," the young man said. "I did my job properly. I tasted every dish. It was all fine. The poison didn't come from the kitchen. I swear. I'll bet my life."

"You are betting your life," the detective said. "How does it work? Do you actually eat a bit of everyone's steak right off their plate?"

"No. There's a system that food tasters use."

"There is?"

"Yes, we're professionals. You think we're like mothers with toddlers, tasting the food and feeding them? It's not like that."

Wong could hear Alberto sigh. Even when he breathed you could hear a vibrato tremor. The young man was trying not to cry. He sniffed twice, and then continued.

"I'll tell you my system. Each dish is served from the cooking service onto an intermediary platter, preheated to keep it warm. I select a piece at random from each dish and give it a smell test. Sometimes I do a chemical test too. But if it smells fine, usually I just take a small bite. Then I wait to see if there's any reaction. After a short wait—I can usually tell immediately if something's wrong, but I usually wait two minutes, to see if anything develops—I take another bite. Most strong poisons you can detect surprisingly easily. There are a few which are tasteless, but most of them have a slight smell. It's not a foolproof system, but it works. Once all the items have been tasted, it's our job to look after the chain of custody, just like a police officer monitoring his evidence. We watch to make sure the items we've cleared are served onto the diners' plates and handed to them."

"So you did all that?"

"Of course. In this type of situation, where individuals are genuinely scared of being poisoned, I take a lot of care. I tasted everything. All the meat, every vegetable."

"Drinks?"

"Even the drinks. I pour a little out of each into a separate cup, and smell it and taste it. I don't let it out of my sight until it reaches the diners." The young man started to weep. "Please believe me, wherever the poison came from, it wasn't from anything they ate or drank."

Wong found Alberto's story believable. He turned and sniffed the air. Could some sort of gas be the culprit? Or a poisoned umbrella tip? Or a radioactive teapot? He'd done the reading. He knew how creative villains were these days.

His mobile phone rang. It was Joyce outside in the car.

"He's freaking me out."

"He's freaking out?"

"No, he's freaking *me* out. He says he wants to spend the rest of his life with his head in my lap. He's creepy. I think he's smelling my crotch. I'm standing outside the car. I said I was going to go and get drinks for the two of us. I got no money on me. Where are you?"

Wong told her which restaurant they were in. A minute later she appeared, and asked the bartender for two cold drinks.

The feng shui master sat down to make plans to escape from the slow-motion disaster that was unraveling at the hotel around the corner. Option one: go straight to the airport and leave Singapore forever. Option two: contact Sin Sar and get him to rescind his decree immediately. Better try that first.

He called the monastery and got the staff to give him the abbot's phone number. He dialed it with growing anger, stabbing at his phone.

"Sin Sar, this is Wong. I am not in the room. I had to go out. Urgent business. But I heard about your decree. Last one gets the prize. You have to get up, tell them you were joking."

"I wasn't joking," the monk said in his high, singsong voice, giddy with delight. "People here love the idea. You should have heard the laughter."

"But that's because they didn't realize that you were spoiling the race. These guys famous for driving cars fast. Slow race no good. Makes bad TV. Sponsors very angry. Race organizer very angry."

"It's still a race. But the loser gets the prize. That's the Buddhist way."

"That's not the Buddhist way."

"Well, it's the Abbot Sin Sar way."

"Change it. I order you. Otherwise they will make me pay for everything. It cost millions of dollars. I can't pay."

"Look, Wong, I have to go. The next course has arrived. The food here is *so good*. Thanks for inviting me, by the way."

"You are my friend. Why are you doing this to me?"

"I am not doing anything to you. I am doing something good for the people here. They are competitive in the worst way. They always want to win win win. Everything has to be bigger, stronger, faster. I am teaching them something good."

"They are not bad people. You don't have to spoil their race."

"They have competitiveness in their hearts. That's bad. They have a craving for money and glory. Those are poisons that will seep out and destroy their lives. I am doing them a favor."

"Don't talk to me about poison," Wong growled.

The abbot hung up.

At that moment, Joyce stomped back into the restaurant, irritation on her face. She placed one of the drinks on the counter. "He won't drink it."

"Why not?"

"It's a boiling hot day but he wants it with no ice. He's crazy."

She waited until the barman made another gin and tonic, and then headed back out. She stopped in the doorway and turned around. "Oh, and by the way, we got a parking ticket. The driver says you have to pay it."

Wong winced. She disappeared.

The barman looked over at him. "And that's three drinks your lady friend ordered. You'll have to pay for them too."

"Aiyeeah," cursed Wong. "Why do the gods hate me so much?"

The barman gazed down at the ice-filled drink that Keung had refused to accept. "You want to drink this? You look like you need it." He slid the drink over.

Wong glared at it, as if it was responsible for all his troubles.

And then his eyes widened.

The clouds were clearing as C.F. Wong, Joyce McQuinnie, and Sigmund Siu Keung sat in the car, inching through the traffic on their way back to the Raffles Hotel.

"Driver, take me home FIRST," said the tycoon, his head on Joyce's thigh. "Marina Bay."

"Later," Wong said. "First, Raffles." The feng shui master pulled out his phone and called the police detective. "Shek. I just want to ask you one question. Mr. Wu is dead, right? But Mrs. Wu is okay, recovering in hospital? Is it right?"

"C.F.? Yes, that seems to be the case."

"What were they drinking at the meal?"

There was silence for a few seconds. "Not sure. Scotch, I think. Lap-ki Wu is from a Cantonese background. Probably cognac."

Wong nodded. "I think I know what happened. Mrs. Wu puts poison inside ice cubes. When Alberto taste the drinks, they are fine. Poison locked inside the ice cubes. But after five minutes, ice cube melts. Mr. Wu drinks poison. He dies. Old system. Seen it before. Common."

"But Mrs. Wu is also sick. Why would she poison herself?"

"You forget. Mrs. Wu is an actress."

"*Was* an actress."

"*Is* an actress. They never forget. Like bicycles, elephants."

As the car pulled up outside the Raffles, Wong leaped from the passenger seat and sprinted through the lobby and into the ballroom.

He arrived puffing to find the room full of raised voices. It was clear that people had now realized that Abbot Sin Sar's stricture meant the race would be unlikely to go ahead at all.

Lim Cheong Li was onstage, trying to maintain order.

The feng shui master marched up the tiny stage staircase and took the microphone from him. "So sorry, Mr. Lim," he said. "Must just fix this small small problem for you." C.F. Wong tapped the microphone hard, twice. Then he started speaking: "Excuse me, rich people, sponsors, businessmen, and et ceteras, I want to say something."

He continued to tap the microphone and call for attention. The crowd's attention was eventually caught by the skeletal man on stage with the thick Chinese accent. Conversations died down.

"Ancient Chinese legend says exactly what Abbot Sin Sar said," Wong explained. "The first shall be last and the last shall be first. I know this is also in the Bible. But Bible originally was Chinese, as everyone knows. As Sin Sar says, whichever car crosses the line first will be declared the loser. Whichever car crosses the line last will be declared the winner. But Sin Sar forgot to say one important thing: Chinese legend says that racing-horse riders should ride each other's horses. This is the traditional way."

He glanced down at an event program before continuing. "So Mr. Emerson Brahms will drive the car belonging to Mr. Andreletti Nelson. And the vice will be versa. Mr. Andreletti Nelson will drive the car belonging to Mr. Emerson Brahms. The car which crosses the line last will be the winning car. This is the Buddhist way. This is the Singapore way. This is the best way. Thank you. Goodbye and good night."

There was silence. People took a few seconds to ponder the implications of the change he had outlined. Slowly, the room broke into laughter and applause.

As Wong carefully climbed down the steps from the stage, he wondered how long it would take for the drivers themselves to realize what his proposal meant. If Brahms and Nelson were driving each other's cars, each would do his damndest to try to get that car into the most UNdesirable position: first place. Each would drive with as much speed and skill as he could muster. And there was a certain Zen quality about the paradox that would give the race a truly Asian flavor.

The heavens had been right when they guided Wong to select Sin Sar.

Lim saw immediately that it would work. He followed Wong offstage. "Nice going, feng shui master. Let me buy you a drink."

"I like iced tea," Wong said. "But no ice cubes."

# ABOUT THE CONTRIBUTORS

**MONICA BHIDE's** work has appeared in *Food & Wine,* the *New York Times, Parents, Bon Appetit, Saveur,* and many other publications. Her food essays have been included in the *Best Food Writing* anthologies (2005, 2009, and 2010). She has published three cookbooks, the latest being *Modern Spice: Inspired Indian Flavors for the Contemporary Kitchen.* In 2012, the *Chicago Tribune* picked her as one of seven noteworthy food writers to watch.

**COLIN CHEONG** was born in Singapore in 1965 and graduated from the National University of Singapore in 1988. His debut novel, *The Stolen Child,* was awarded the Highly Commended Fiction in English Award by the National Book Development Council of Singapore in 1990. His novella *Tangerine* was awarded the Singapore Literature Prize in 1996, and he also won the Merit Award in that competition for his novella *The Man in the Cupboard* in 1998.

**DAMON CHUA** is a playwright, poet, and film producer. His plays are published by Samuel French and Smith & Kraus, and his poetry by Ethos Books. A recipient of grants from UNESCO, Durfee Foundation, and the Singapore Film Commission, Chua is a lover of film noir and is delighted to be a part of this collection. His grandfather once operated a pig farm in Mandai village, a stone's throw from Woodlands.

**DAVE CHUA's** first novel, *Gone Case,* received a Singapore Literature Prize Commendation Award in 1996. *Gone Case: A Graphic Novel, Book 1* and *Book 2*—with the artist Koh Hong Teng—were recently published. Chua's latest book, *The Beating and Other Stories,* was longlisted for the 2012 Frank O'Connor International Short Story Award.

**COLIN GOH** writes and illustrates Dim Sum Warriors, the multiplatform children's graphic novel series that *Fast Company* named one of the Top 10 Coolest Original Digital Comics of 2012. He also wrote and directed *Singapore Dreaming,* a feature film that won the Montblanc Screenwriters Award at the San Sebastian International Film Festival, and Best Asian Film at the Tokyo International Film Festival.

**PHILIP JEYARETNAM** is a novelist and short story writer, whose first book, *First Loves*, topped Singapore's *Sunday Times* best-seller list for eighteen months. His novel *Abraham's Promise* was described by the *New York Times* as a "novel of regret for actions not taken and words unspoken, eloquent in the spareness of its prose and the gradual unveiling of the narrator's self-deception." Jeyaretnam has chaired the Singapore Writers' Festival since 2007.

*Claire Newman-Williams*

**JOHANN S. LEE** is the London-based author of a triptych of novels (*Peculiar Chris, To Know Where I'm Coming From, Quiet Time*) depicting the experiences of gay men in Singapore, where homosexual acts remain criminal under the country's penal code. "Current Escape" is his second short story.

*Russel Wong*

**SUCHEN CHRISTINE LIM's** latest novel is *The River's Song*. The winner of the Southeast Asia Write Award 2012, her other novels include *Rice Bowl, A Bit of Earth*, and *Fistful of Colours*, which won the inaugural Singapore Literature Prize. Other published works are *The Lies That Build a Marriage, Hua Song: Stories of the Chinese Diaspora*, and fourteen children's books. Awarded a Fulbright fellowship, she was an international writing fellow and writer in residence at the University of Iowa.

**LAWRENCE OSBORNE** is the author most recently of *The Wet and the Dry* and the novel *The Forgiven*, both published by Hogarth in New York. His short story "Volcano" was selected for *Best American Short Stories 2012*. Born in England, he lives in Bangkok.

*Ashley Gilbertson*

**S.J. ROZAN** is the Edgar Award–winning author of fourteen novels and three dozen short stories. She's also half of the thriller-writing team of Sam Cabot. She lives in New York City but travels widely and her goal is to write at least one story set in each place she's touched down. She loves Singapore, especially for its food.

Jesse Pesta

**CHERYL LU-LIEN TAN** is the New York–based author of *A Tiger in the Kitchen: A Memoir of Food and Family*. A native of Singapore, she is working on her second book, a novel. A former staff writer at the *Wall Street Journal*, her work has also appeared in the *New York Times* and the *Washington Post*, among other publications. She has been an artist in residence at Yaddo and the Djerassi Resident Artists Program.

**DONALD TEE QUEE HO** (a.k.a. **SIMON TAY**) is a writer who occupies roles in politics and academia. He has published five books of creative writing. His novel *City of Small Blessings* won the Singapore Literature Prize in 2010; *Stand Alone* (1991) was shortlisted for the Commonwealth Writers' Prize. He has been an International Writing Fellow at University of Iowa. One international magazine called him "Singapore's answer to Haruki Murakami."

**NURY VITTACHI** is the author of more than three dozen books, spent part of his childhood in Singapore, and visits regularly from his current home in Hong Kong. He is the founding editor of the region's top literary journal, the *Asia Literary Review*, and chairman of Asia Pacific Writers, the region's largest author association. His works have been released by major publishers in Asia, the US, the UK, Europe, and Australia.

Kar-Wai Wesley

**OVIDIA YU** has written over thirty plays, novels, and short stories. Her latest book is *Aunty Lee's Delights*, a mystery set in Singapore where she lives with two dogs, two turtles, a tank full of fish, and too many plants. She is a Fulbright alumnus of the International Writing Program at the University of Iowa, recipient of the Young Artist Award for Literature, the Singapore Youth Award, and an Edinburgh Fringe First Award.

---

## EDITOR'S ACKNOWLEDGMENTS

Deepest gratitude to the terrific authors who contributed to this anthology as well as the National Arts Council of Singapore. Thanks, too, to the Studios of Key West, which provided a haven for editing at a crucial time, Johnny Temple and his lovely team at Akashic, S.J. Rozan for getting this ball rolling, Mike Hale, Jonathan Santlofer, Gordon Dahlquist, Jesse Pesta, and my agent, the inimitable Jin Auh with the Wylie Agency.